The Reincarnation of Tom

Aden Simpson

Copyright

Copyright © Aden Simpson 2020

ISBN: 9780995352391

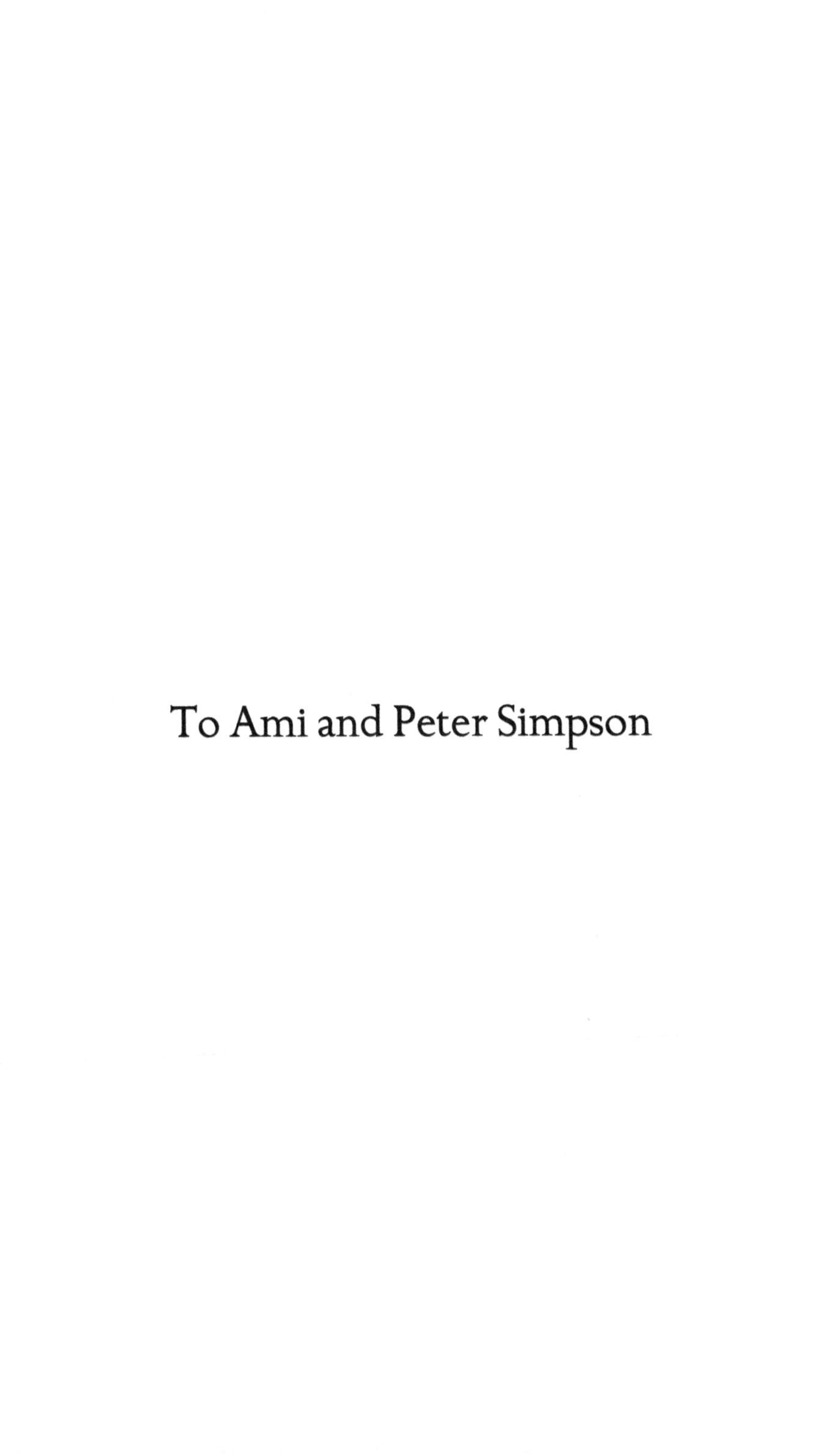

To Ami and Peter Simpson

"If at any stage you find the story making little sense, imagine
all the characters are naked and scared. This should reduce
confusion."
— God

Tom

"I'm Blue daba dee daba daa..."

These were the last words of Tom Robinson.

Not the most heroic of declarations, or remotely coherent. Funny what the mind deems important at the moment of death. What it scrambles together as the lights go out.

Funny, and oddly pathetic.

For his last few dwindling breaths, Tom Robinson's brain treated him to the customary final walk down memory lane, a curious intermingling of the trivial and the profound.

He remembered falling off his chair at Thanksgiving dinner and rolling around the carpet in hysterics at his uncle's impression of a turkey begging to be cooked just right.

He remembered dancing in his room to the Beatles the first time he heard "Come Together" and thinking one day he'd understand it all.

He remembered Lily White, his co-worker and, unbeknownst to her, the love of his unremarkable life.

But most strange and lucid of these memories was a recent incident in a mystical new age head shop Tom had wandered into once on his lunchbreak. Because he passed it every day on his short walk from the subway to work, Tom's mild curiosity eventually got the better of him and, despite the usual anxiety of stepping outside his comfort zone, he entered the dimly-lit bodega and its haze of new age incense. It was his hope that he could find a novelty gift for his office crush's upcoming birthday.

The shopkeeper, bearing a zen aura that was either natural or a requirement of the job, waved Tom over from the dreamcatcher rack with hushed excitement. Without any prompting, he revealed a supposedly ancient chant as the secret to remembering one's past lives. The chant was to be uttered in the moments preceding death, he explained, as if this was something one could easily predict.

Apparently, it went something like this:
"I'm blue daba dee daba daa,
Daba dee, daba daa,
Daba dee daba daa…"

Tom instantly recognised the chant for its uncanny similarity to the chorus of a late '90s Europop dance anthem by Italian music group Eiffel 65, about a man living in both a metaphorical and literal blue world, although it seemed this had escaped the earnest shopkeeper. Well, if it had to be anything…

Unwilling to offend and fearful of a confrontation, Tom decided not to bring this to the attention of the wild-haired man, who continued with his mystical pronouncement:

"Chant this tune in the last moments of your life and you will retain your memories when you roll into the next. Be warned, though, reincarnation remembering is not for the faint of heart. That'll be $20 for the dreamcatcher."

In his 31 years of existence, Tom's spirituality had progressed about as far as a lazy sloth on a hot summer's day. The shopkeeper was clearly a lunatic and the dreamcatcher incredibly overpriced. Tom left the bodega empty handed and inhaled a big breath of fresh air to reclaim his sanity.

At the time, he thought the experience could make for an intriguing conversation starter with Lily. Unfortunately, he never found the right time to bring it up and two months later, he was hit by the M101 bus.

Lying there, dying, watching all those big and little memories fall short of a life truly lived, Tom's fading brain felt the chorus of a silly Europop song offering him an impossible second chance.

Really, what did he have to lose?

Chicken

Cheep cheep.

Cheep-cheep. Cheep.

These were Tom's first words as a chicken.

But he wasn't a chicken. He was Tom. Wasn't he? Not that he came to this conclusion straight away. Confusion rose in him as feelings became memories and slowly unravelled like a spool of yarn. But before then, as a chick with wet feathers and a cute little beak, Tom bathed in the warmth of the straw and cotton wool that surrounded him and his brothers and sisters, below a grey sky covered in dust.

Cheep cheep.

It was only when he began to notice and comprehend the glass walls, the fetid, artificial warmth and the huddle of little yellow bodies all around him, that he started to remember being Tom…

That wasn't the sky. It was the metal lid of an incubator.

Cheep cheep.

Suddenly, things weren't so chipper.

As Tom grew, and so did his compatriots, they were moved to a larger pen; this enclosure part of a mammoth indoor barn bustling with hundreds of beaks, feathers, and confused pairs of eyes.

Bawke, bawke.

Time passed, as time tends to do. He was still a chicken and there appeared little he could do to alter the fact. His feathers moulted and he grew depressed. Chaos reigned. He could understand the others, but they couldn't understand him—all they knew was squawking and clucking and endlessly pecking at seed, with the occasional flutter of wings. Conversation was limited to one topic: the all-important pecking order, and how unremittingly good it felt to be at the top. Tom considered this significance when he studied the order of the stacked cages in which they roosted at night—the strongest, most aggressive and most handsomely dappled birds did seem to wind up at the top. Tom was not one of them, and even then, the real top was far from what they knew.

Day in, day out, it was much of the same, until a man in gumboots and a grimy, red-chequered shirt came to separate the chickens according to what was to be their life's work: laying eggs, being a rooster, or becoming Sunday dinner. Tom was surprised when he was taken to the hen shed where he would be expected to lay eggs for the rest of his life. There were no mirrors in the barn, but he had just sort of assumed he would wind up a rooster. He had never been a female before, at least not that he could remember, and wondered with a brief flurry of panic whether laying eggs would be painful. He was forced into a cage—metal, straw, wire mesh for walls—and seated himself as comfortably as he could. The comparative solitude was not unwelcome, though he could have done with a bit more wing room.

As it so happened, the excreting of eggs was not painful, but after a few weeks it certainly grew dull and monotonous. A constant feeling of fullness about the belly, a pressure that grew ever more insistent, then a push and a throb and the act was barely finished before the next in line began to form. Looking around, still adjusting to his rudimentary and somewhat cramped confines, he noted another hen down the way in the row of cages opposite. This old-timer had greying feathers and didn't squawk like the rest. Most tellingly, it seemed like she deliberately avoided looking in Tom's direction. Around the time of his hundredth egg, a milestone unnoticed, Tom confronted this old mother hen.

"Do I know you?" he shouted over the squawking of the other hens.

The old-timer did her best to ignore him.

"You just seem so...familiar."

The old-timer dipped her head like she was attempting to bury her face in the Sunday newspaper, and the familiarity of this action set off a light switch in Tom's bird brain. "You were a human! You remember too!"

The old-timer finally acknowledged him and gave a sigh. When she spoke, Tom heard it less as a shrill, caged mother hen and more like a grizzled, impatient Queens businessman. "Yeah, OK, you got me! Jesus, I just wanted a chicken phase in peace this time," the old hen chided, flapping her wings in frustration.

"Sorry to bother," Tom yelled over the din of clucking. "Just thought it would be nice to have a conversation with someone while I'm stuck expelling foodstuffs from my asshole in a cramped prison. It might be business-as-usual for you, but this is my first time being a chicken. Or anything other than a human, for that matter."

The former businessman from Queens flapped her wings again. "Fine, OK, so you're new to the merry-go-round. Congratulations. What do you want? You want me to bake you a cake?"

No need to be so cruel, thought Tom. "I'm terribly sorry to bother," he persisted, "it's just I have so many questions—like how long will I be in here? And what happens after this?"

"Well, after about another two years and a few forced moultings, when you can't lay eggs no more, they'll cut your head off and I imagine you'll end up on somebody's plate."

Tom gulped. "So what happens when I die? Do I just sing the song again?"

"What song? You mean the chant? Sure, if you *want* to remember."

"You mean some people don't?"

"How should I know?"

"But you just said... All right, forget it. Can you at least tell me, how I can become human again?"

"Jesus, kid. Figure it out. You're at the bottom of the pecking order. You gotta ride the karma train up to the top." The old-timer raised a wing towards the ceiling.

"How long does that usually take?"

"Depends."

"Depends on what?"

"Depends on how much you annoy me."

"Doesn't being a jerk set you back?"

The old-timer shrugged. "Not always. Sometimes it's worth the risk." He glared, as though to emphasise his point.

The old-timer's unwarranted animosity particularly offended Tom. He thought he might cry and blamed it on the hormones they had undoubtedly been putting in his seed. Such abrasiveness was uncalled for, yet Tom tried to rationalise it; maybe the older timer was just tired of being a chicken and ready to move on. Tom was already miserable, and it hadn't even been a year (as far as he could guess).

"So you got any advice, or not?"

The old-timer calmed down. "Look, just be patient and try to enjoy it. Take something from each experience and if you can use it in the next life, good for you. Remember, you don't always have to think like a human. Sometimes it helps, sometimes it doesn't. Also, don't try to overthrow humanity, at least if you can help it."

Tom bobbed his head, things both a little clearer and a little more confusing. Especially the part about overthrowing humanity. "Is there any way to control the process? Say I wanted to be an eagle..."

Once again, the old-timer simply ignored him. "And if you *are* human, don't kill Hitler, or anything like that."

"Do you mean like a 'future Hitler' or 'Hitler-Hitler'?"

The old-timer glared at him as if he was an idiot. "Both."

"Right, of course, because of the butterfly effect?" asked Tom.

"Yeah," said the old-timer, "Incidentally, try not to become a butterfly—tough dating scene. They look all pretty and delicate, but really they're a bunch of little sluts."

Tom was uncertain whether this was the most helpful information. After further unanswered queries, the old-timer drew their conversation to a close by pretending to be asleep. Tom resolved to try again at a more convenient time for his new mentor. He felt he was owed a comprehensive explanation. Christians had the Ten Commandments, Muslims the Quran and Jews the Torah; so where was his Buddhist handbook? You couldn't just tell someone the secret to remembering their past lives and then leave them to it, unsupervised. It was irresponsible and indicative of systemic problems in upper management. Answers were owed. Unfortunately for Tom, the old-timer was carted off to his/her death shortly thereafter. As they took her, she hummed, "I'm blue daba dee daba daa..." in preparation.

Left alone in a crowded frenzy of feathers, Tom had little to do but ponder and plot his next move. He decided to be a better person the next time around, if only to avoid the horrors of being a chicken again. He also wondered what time period he would incarnate into next. He'd presumed, on the basis of never having given it much thought, that reincarnation was linear. But the old-timer's specific mentioning of Hitler suggested it was equally possible he could be storming the beaches of Normandy during WWII, or flung far into the future, with the ravages of climate change having scorched the land, and humans popping over to Mars for the weekend. With the unhelpful old-timer gone and the aforementioned Buddhist handbook nowhere to be seen, all bets were off.

Tom waited out the clock on his chicken life the same way he waited for 5.30pm each day at his insurance firm: with long, transcendental daydreaming. It was a nice distraction from feeling his skin crawling more or less constantly with parasites. Tom hoped to be something cool in his next life, like an American eagle, astronaut or rockstar, and wondered if a higher power was paying attention to these wishes, like how when Oprah or countless motivational speakers spoke about the power of manifesting one's dreams and visualising success. This transformed into paranoia when he realised someone may also be casting judgement on his frequent, uncontrollable lusting of Lily White, a finance analyst at the insurance firm he worked for. Or used to work for. Of all the mistakes he'd ever made as Tom Robinson, not asking Lily out on a date before his abrupt meeting with the M101 bus was his greatest regret. Never mind the fact it was a million to one shot she'd say yes. He was hopeless with women but he'd never been as hopeless with anyone more than he was hopeless with her. She was more than her amazing body, perfect natural brunette locks, retrousse nose and soft ocean green eyes—she was smart, passionate and witty (from what he overheard and saw online) and over everything else he wanted to be the kind of person she wanted to be with. This chant was his ticket to being just that: worldly and wise; full of exotic experiences. And if it was possible to reach her again, he'd tell her the secret to reincarnation remembering and she'd be so damn grateful she'd say something like, "Tom, we've barely spoken in person except for that one Christmas party where you were slurring a bit but now that you've done this for me we can finally be soulmates forever and go on lots of adventures as many different creatures and rich lovers who laugh together on their yacht."

If he could confirm it was possible, this would be his ultimate purpose. He promised to himself he'd do anything—he would even overthrow humanity or change the course of history if it meant rigging his chances to win her heart. Tom didn't make many promises, but those few he made he kept, and he was quite proud of this little known fact.

Tom tried to take stock the rest of his time as a chicken, tried to appreciate the many burdens chickens were made to endure on behalf of the stomachs of mankind. He'd been guilty of overindulging in his past life as a single, self-loathing schlub; gorging on chicken nuggets, chicken tenders, BBQ chicken, buffalo wings and buckets of the Colonel's original recipe, his fingers greased in the fat of poor souls like the ones to the countless left, right, above and below him. So the next time he was a human he'd be a vegetarian. Several months spent as a chicken had exposed too many of the horrors of the poultry industry. Also, Lily was vegetarian, so if this gift ever gave him another shot at life as Tom, his being one could only improve his chances.

Knowing the greatness that life offered outside of these cages slowly eroded Tom's optimism, and just like back in the insurance firm, Tom got stressed and his work suffered. His egg production slowed and after a steady decline in his monthly numbers, Farmer John's Cruelty-Free quality assurance team decided to "retire" him.

They took Tom over to the processing bay. A worker in thick gloves picked up a big, shiny knife, and held it over his head. Suppressing a squawk of terror, Tom recited, "I'm blue daba dee daba daa," as loudly as he could for as long as he could.

He'd read once that a chicken could live for several minutes without its head. Thankfully, he only had to chant for 40 seconds or so.

Cow

Tom preferred being a cow to being a chicken. His new colleagues felt the same way and had only bad things to say about the fowls of their acquaintance, especially that bloody rooster, always waking everyone up and prattling on and on about their stupid damn pecking order.

"Tell me about it," said Tom, glad to be rid of that pecking order nonsense. Nor did he miss the incessant preening, the endless ordering and reordering of feathers, or the previously mentioned parasites itching him all over. It was undeniable; being a cow was definitely a step in the right direction.

Not that Bovine University wasn't without its own set of challenges. He was already an adult by the time his memories came flooding back to him and he had to adjust effortlessly to the art of moving on all fours, lest he be laughed at by his friends for forgetting how to plod with grace. Then there was the other sole expectation thrust upon a dairy cow. Tom was milked every morning. It was somewhat painful, and Tom didn't enjoy the constant cycle of pregnancy, lactation and the cold, thin metallic insemination rod that kicked each cycle off. He wished he were instead a bull, maybe one of those ones in Pamplona who got to do all that running. That looked like fun. Back when he had been human, The Running of the Bulls had been high on Tom's bucket list, perhaps only to make him appear more exciting than he actually was, because he knew he'd never make it to Pamplona. It was just one of those things you say, his version of swimming with dolphins. He wondered if being vegetarian meant he couldn't do the Bull Run. How would he be able to justify that? Surely Lily would say it was cruel. She once scolded Renshaw from Sales in the lunchroom for wanting to ride elephants in Bali. So maybe Pamplona was out the question. Oh well. It wasn't like he actually would have done it anyway.

Afternoons were spent in the meadow, basking in sunshine and fresh air. Hanging out in the meadow after milking was pure bliss. It reminded Tom of that ubiquitous Windows desktop background from the early 2000s, the one that came preinstalled and showed the rolling green hills of pristine English pastureland. Tom deduced he was in England based on the accents of the other cows, and, judging by the Freddie Mercury moustache on the farmer and his children carrying on in ragged Live Aid shirts, it appeared he had ended up sometime in the 1980s. The fact that a herd of cows spoke with English accents didn't make a great deal of sense, admittedly, but Tom accepted it all the same, because it confirmed that he could reincarnate backward in time, and, hopefully by that logic, potentially reincarnate into his old self for another chance with Lily.

He breathed in deeply, revelling in the country air, before giving a contented moo. *Moo*, said one of the other cows by way of acknowledgement. That old chicken/Queens businessman was right—you had to make the most of it, look on the bright side. At least he wasn't a veal calf.

Times were simple, and all was well. He was even getting used to his daily milking. One day, however, Beatrice started mooing uncontrollably, complaining about her brain being itchy. All the other cows tried to scratch Beatrice's head, but there seemed to be no abating the sensation. Beatrice kept complaining and complaining until the others herded her over to an adjacent meadow and told her to cool off, but poor Beattie never recovered her wits. It was only a couple days later that she violently bumped Nancy into the fence and had to be taken away by the farmer.

The mood around the farm turned sour, and when Nancy told the herd she now felt her brain was feeling a little itchy too, Tom's docile bovine eyes widened in fear. England. 1980s. Mad cow disease. Oh dear.

When he realised the unfortunate truth and informed all those within earshot, the others failed to grasp his explanation. What the heck was the 1980s? they asked.

"Never mind that, that's not the point. The point is that we're being fed the remains of other cows!"

"What, like Beatrice?" They hadn't seen Beatrice in two days and rumours on the paddock spread faster than the rooster's morning call.

Tom shrugged, as best as a cow could shrug. "Maybe."

The other cows did not take this information well. A chorus of distressed mooing commenced and several of them vomited on the spot. The wild sight of rampant sickness and spooked eyes gave the otherwise kindly farmer no choice but to put down the entire herd. When Tom was prodded to the slaughterhouse he began wailing, "I'm blue daba dee daba daa..." and the other cows shook their heads in dismay. "Poor sod, I guess he got the 1980s."

Pig

Tom was growing tired of being a farm animal. He'd seen the film *Babe*, but as it turned out there was little accurate representation of daily farm life in that film. Kept in a pen with eight other pigs, his only respite was wallowing in the mud to keep his skin nice and moist, and, frankly, because there wasn't a whole lot else to do. Discouraged by the rapid deterioration of proceedings as a cow, Tom maintained a low profile this time around. Because of this, the other pigs thought him rather snobbish, and it took some time for Tom to open up. After a month spent mostly in silence, Tom remembered that pigs were known by humans to be very smart. He expressed this fact to another pig, who replied, "Why, of course, we've always thought this—in fact, we were also considering that perhaps a change in leadership on this farm might serve us well..."

Tom struggled to recall where he'd heard such rhetoric from a pig before, but by the time he realised this stumpy little runt held similar notions to Napoleon from *Animal Farm*, the would-be emperor had moved on, suggesting to Tom they go for a roll in the mud before the humans filled the trough for supper. Tom squealed at the notion, the overthrowing of the capitalist machine averted for the time being.

Oink oink. It was a particularly enjoyable wallow.

Being a pig turned out better than expected. Tom used his time once more to daydream about Lily White, with her soft pink lipsticked lips blowing him kisses in between ripping Renshaw from Sales with some particularly withering burns because he'd gotten flirty again. God, he hated that guy. Tom busied himself making mud angels, gazing down at his handiwork and seeing nothing but Lily; remembering how at the end of every day, no matter how tiresome it may have been, she would still beam with this bright, unexpected energy and say goodbye to everyone on her way out. Often it was the best part of his sad little day. And with these memories came a yearning to feel this gooey nourishment within his soul again; to return to the world of humans and the presence of Lily, to be brave unlike before and converse with her freely; dive deep into her passion for wildlife conservation and major league soccer without his mind overboiling at a whiff of her alluring scent...

This unshakeable yearning settled it. Tom promised to himself he would become a vegetarian starting from this point onward, the first step toward a new, enlightened Tom, no sense waiting until he was human again. Surely such good intentions would help him skip a few rungs on his way back to humanhood, and maybe even help him trade up from his original doughy shell into the body of a major league soccer star? A fair reward for his noble lifestyle.

This foolproof upward trajectory was abruptly skewered by lunchtime. It turned out that whatever was in the trough was all that was on offer, and though it was undoubtedly some mighty fine slop, its omnivorous texture meant putting his vegetarian plans on hold, at least for this lifetime.

***

Ever mindful of the old-timer chicken's brief warning, Tom attempted to keep his new friend in check on the days when Napoleon swore that violent upheaval was the only viable means of progression. "Look how nice the mud is today," Tom would say, wallowing with extra gusto. By the time Napoleon decided that the moment to strike was ripe, it was exceptionally apparent that nothing could be done; like Tom, he'd grown old and fat, the love of the trough conditioning his body for rashers, not revolution. "I left my run too late. They always win in the end. Damn those humans."

"It wasn't so bad," Tom comforted, feeling guilty, "the humans *did* provide us the trough, with more or less all the slop we could eat. And the mud, don't forget the mud."

"Whose side are you on?" Napoleon snapped.

Tom didn't answer right away. He had that nagging feeling that neither of them were long for the chopping block, and he didn't want to spoil what might be one of their final moments together. He also realised that it would be a shame to waste such a fine brain in a pig—even with the associated risk of overthrowing humanity.

"My own side. At least, I was..." he finally responded. "I know this sounds silly, but before we're taken to the house the others never return from, I think you should chant these words... 'I'm blue daba dee daba daa...'"

"That's ridiculous."

"Just trust me," said Tom. "You never know, it might help."

Tom and Napoleon were sent to the slaughterhouse not long thereafter, Napoleon's political dreams finally gone pork-belly up. Daba dee daba daa.

Vegetarian progress: Difficult to distinguish the exact ingredients of slop. Vegetarianism off to a shaky start.

Tiger

Tyger, Tyger,
Burning bright,
In the forest of the night...

Tom awoke and came to the almost immediate realisation that he was a tiger. A motherfucking tiger! This was more like it. As a child, the first animals he'd wanted to see on any trip to the zoo were the Bengal tigers in the Big Cats exhibit. Tigers were so much cooler than lions, with their slick stripes, solitary nature and undercurrent of graceful ferocity.

His eyes widened, his night vision perfect for hunting. He rose, ready to move and hunt for flesh, vegetarian agenda be damned! He wasn't even hungry, but gosh darn it, he was too bloody excited to sit still and learn the ropes slowly. He took in the cold night air, expecting to inhale all the scents of the jungle, only to find it rather lifeless and inert. Odd, but he shook this off. It was time to hunt.

He snaked through the trees, each paw enjoying the feel of the dirt and leaves underfoot, and then he saw the wall of cement; the confines of his enclosure. *Goddammit.*

***

Feeding time took place once a day in the early afternoon, usually in front of a slew of clicking Kodak cameras and stupefied, slack-jawed, gawking humans of all ages. Tom slept most of the time, though never deeply—he couldn't get used to the feeling of all those eyes being constantly on him. A few days into his new life, he swore the next time he was human, he'd break into the nearest zoo and free all the animals.

Freedom. That's all he wanted. He was born in this zoo (as it turned out), yet felt the call of the wild instinctively in his bones. And he planned on answering that call by escaping, first chance he got. What was the point in remembering his past lives if he didn't put the knowledge to good use? And wasn't trying to make his life better something that fell under the category of "good use"? It wasn't like he was going to overthrow humanity—NO! He was merely going to use the concise communication skills he'd exaggerated so lavishly in most of his job applications as Tom Robinson to secure his freedom. Seemed fair enough.

***

Shirley was his main zookeeper. If Tom were to describe Shirley using his New York sensibilities, his fair-haired feeder was the lovey-dovey hippy type, of the sort who was not above describing herself as a "child of nature" and getting as close as possible to the dangerous animals during feeding time. Frankly, Tom was unsure how she hadn't been eaten or fired for gross violations of the zoo's stringent safety code.

"I have a special connection with the animals," she'd often remark to her co-workers, presumably sending eyeballs rolling. Tom didn't want to stroke Shirley's ego any further, but if there was anyone foolish enough to help him escape, it was Shirley Constance. The first step in his outlandish exodus plan was to clear space in the dirt for his "whiteboard". He then began separating the straw of his bedding into strands and pawing each over, one by one. This was more challenging than merely scratching a message in the dirt, but he felt this would make his presentation really pop. He waited until it was Shirley's turn to feed him. There was only a small window in the morning where he could spell out his concise message. It was painstaking work, and Tom completed his introduction with only seconds to spare.

Shirley opened the door and dragged the meat to Tom's bowl. It was a miserable autumn day, so luckily there were no spectators or prying cameras. He had chosen his moment well.

"Raj, we've got a wonderful meal here for you, come get it!"

But Tom stayed still on the other side of the exhibit, the message laid out in front of him. He lowered his head to indicate its existence and then stared at her. *Take the hint.* Shirley took a single step forward, but then stopped. She was foolish, but not that foolish. Tom retreated slightly, and then, maintaining eye contact, bobbed his head in what he hoped was a knowing, human-like manner, as best he could muster. Shirley, not the tallest, lifted up on her toes and squinted. A look of confusion creased her face. She closed the door, but Tom remained hopeful, and the door reopened again a few moments later, this time Shirley holding a stepladder and some small binoculars. She put the step-ladder inside the door and raised her binoculars with one hand while holding the door ajar with the other. She almost fell to the ground in shock when she finally read Tom's message.

"CAN U KEEP A SECRET?"

***

Communication was slow and frustrating, but it was also the only passably interesting thing he had going on in this prison of his: it turned out that in captivity, a solitary nature quickly devolved into unbridled isolation. Passing notes brought Tom back to his school years. Shirley would talk to Tom from the door whenever it was her turn to feed him, and Tom would try to answer Yes or No with a bob or shake of the head.

One day, probably to assuage her fear that she was losing her mind, Shirley brought in a set of acrylic alphabet cards like one might find scattered over the floor in a kindergarten. She had to reach for a wall to steady herself when Tom used the letters to spell out a response to her first question and thus confirm her new pen pal was a 400-pound Bengal.

"What is the secret?"

"HELP ME ESCAPE."

They had time for a question and response only once every few days, during Shirley's times on the feeding and cleaning roster. They had to be careful not to be seen. Talking to Shirley was one thing, but the world at large probably wasn't ready to accept a talking tiger. "Where did you learn to write?" she asked.

"U HELP ME I TELL U."

"...Is this a prank?"

That last line crushed Tom. It was in her eyes. Despite her upbeat view of a rainbow world, she'd clearly been hurt many times before. Tom started to consider the ramifications of a potential escape on Shirley's career. Setting a tiger free in some national city? PETA would cheer, but the law would surely make an example of her.

"I WAS HUMAN."

"Was your name Raj?"

"TOM."

Stuck in his enclosure, waiting for days on end for Shirley's plans and painstaking communications, Tom grew restless. He'd growl and snarl at the audience, bare his teeth, and put on ferocious shows during public feeding time. He wanted out. He didn't want to perform for these jerks, but he had to expend his anxiety somehow. Every time Shirley came to feed him, she looked a little more desperate, a little more unsure of what was real.

"Soon," she said one day, on the verge of tears. "I've been talking with a group. They love helping animals. They're going to come and take you away in the night and make sure you're placed back into the wild. You'll be free, Tom."

Tom's gut lurched. It was not hunger. This would cost Shirley everything she knew. Tom wondered if there was another way. Maybe, if he could somehow get her to tell the other zookeepers, he could show them all his special talents and escape would be easier. Or maybe that would just bring scientists and researchers and a media frenzy of blinding lights, more gratuitously invasive than any feeding show Tom had endured. No, he had to escape. He deserved freedom. And he'd tell Shirley the chant of reincarnation, so it wouldn't all be in vain for her. She would be able to consciously remember her past lives, whereas everyone else would simply forget. Surely that was fair recompense.

***

One starless night, under cover of darkness, the rescue team arrived. The door of his enclosure slowly swung open. Shirley appeared, trailed by others, all wearing black. Shirley shuffled forward with unsteady legs, while the others stayed by the door.

"Tom?"

Tom emerged from the foliage and Shirley froze. As he neared her, she shuffled back in trepidation. It turned out being approached by a tiger in the dead of night was an unsettling experience even if the tiger in question retained a human consciousness and you were actually quite good friends. "Tom, it's me, Shirley."

He was only a foot away from her now. She shuffled back even further and the voices behind her told her to move out of the way. Tom went that extra bit further, as calmly as his sleek tiger frame would allow, and then he licked Shirley on the hand.

Shirley dropped and hugged Tom with the greatest relief.

"He's mauling her!" one of the other voices panicked.

And then Tom felt a puncture in his side, and the world went black...

Blue daba—

***

Tom woke as the van swerved hard across an intersection. The first words he heard were, "Crazy bitch has doomed us all."

Tom saw Shirley's face, right up close for the very first time. He wasn't listening to her protestations, or the accusations of the others about the out-of-control situation at hand. Instead, he was stunned by the earnest beauty in her eyes and the purity of the soul that flickered beneath their surface, leaping out at him more intoxicatingly than any pheromone. He'd screwed up in enlisting Shirley in his rescue efforts, and he knew that some way, somehow, he would have to make it up to her, either in this life or the next. (Or the one after that one.) He didn't know what year it was, though it seemed like he was back in the 1980s, judging by the jazzy neon windbreakers and big volume hairstyles. He didn't even know which zoo they kept him in either (though he judged from Shirley and the other zookeepers' accents that it was somewhere in Canada).

He couldn't bear to look at her worried face anymore. The guilt overwhelmed him. That was when he first noticed the other man sitting in the back of the van. The man was bald, tall and bony with a wispy moustache, dressed in office attire and wearing thin-rimmed glasses. His stare was one of parental disappointment. He was not a part of the rescue team, nor did the others in the van appear to acknowledge him. Tom recognised him, just like he had "recognised" the old-timer chicken, and assumed he had to be another reincarnation rememberer. (Side note: he'd have to come up with a better name for that later.)

You're making a real mess of this. He was right about you, the tall man with ghostly skin shook his head, his thoughts as critical as they were telepathic. From out of nowhere a clipboard appeared in his hands and his pen became very busy.

Who are you? What are you writing? And who was right about me? Is it God? asked Tom, also telepathically.

You're being very selfish with this whole escape plot. Your friends are all looking at hefty jail time, if they don't die in a horrific crash, the way this baboon is driving.

I'm sorry, thought Tom, *is a baboon really driving?*

The man huffed at this and pressed down harder against his clipboard. *Figure of speech. Point is, this selfishness will affect your karma in a major way.*

Tom instinctively tried to swipe a paw at the man, but found his limbs strapped down. Shirley jolted back. "Tom, what's going on? What do you see?"

I'm sorry, Tom continued at the man with the clipboard before another swerve sent them all scrambling for a hold, Shirley falling heavily onto Tom's side. The man remained curiously unaffected by the pandemonium inside the van, the pen still firing away on the clipboard.

I'm sorry, Tom pleaded, *I know I stuffed up and I've already decided I will make it up to Shirley as soon as I get the chance. It's a Tom Robinson promise—I'm good at keeping those!*

The man with the clipboard shook his head and tsk-tsked with derision. *We prefer to judge on actions and outcomes rather than thoughts and intentions. We're not mind-readers, you know.*

But you're reading my mind right now! Tom growled, and all hands in the van moved to keep him restrained.

Figure of speech, again! the Auditor chided.

The vehicle swerved hard on a hairpin bend and the driver screamed, "More cops!"

What are you going to do to me? Please, I'm new to this, don't take this away from me!

The tall man stood with preternatural balance, ducking his head and sliding his clipboard gracefully under one arm. *We don't take away a creature's chance to learn. We simply make professional recommendations to maximise the learning. I hope you do make it up to Shirley, if you earn the chance. She's a caring soul.*

Wait! shouted Tom. The tall man paused expectantly.

Please. I need to know. Is it possible to return to your original life?

The tall man tsk-tsked again. *You are pathetic.*

And then the van swerved wildly once more, sweeping everyone in the back off their feet. They rolled and rolled and on the third roll Tom started to think that maybe life in the zoo hadn't been so bad after all. When they finally came to a crashing halt, Tom groggily stumbled upright, his straps broken. He found Shirley and tried to nudge her awake, but a deep red wound had opened up on her forehead, running in a horrid bloody slant from the top of her head down to the bridge of her nose. She remained still. No amount of pawing was going to wake her, and he hadn't even taught her the chant yet. Tom said sorry and swore he'd somehow make it up to her before swivelling his head to look around for the tall, otherworldly Auditor, but the man had vanished. Tom slowly hobbled out of the back of the van and was met by a blinding wall of blue and red lights flashing in the night. They had evidently reached the city's outskirts, and Tom beheld the dark, open expanse of forest at the road's edge inviting his escape, but he was too sad and too injured to consider making a run for it. Another two police cruisers arrived from the other direction and joined the party.

Surrounded, Tom meekly decided the jig was up. He whispered softly, "I'm blue daba dee daba daa," as the animal control ranger decided tranquillisers would not be sufficient in this case...

Vegetarian progress: hampered by manslaughter.

Ant

The best parts about being an ant were the steady stream of chemical odours that bubbled his brain into a frenzy, the constant work, and an inherent sense of belonging. Here in the colony, Tom had a well-defined purpose, and unlike his insurance claims job where he droned along intermittently between bouts of fantasising about Lily, there was no room for error, no isolated patches of boredom. This proved especially fitting given his most recent past life. He wasn't ready to think about Shirley, lying still, that gaping wound disfiguring her once-exuberant face. Her life forever ruined—if she'd survived.

Tom wanted to work and forget, at least for the time being. He certainly got his wish. He had been surprised to learn that ants don't sleep. Ever. The thought occurred to him one day as he was hoisting a leaf the equivalent of a small car onto his back, and he realised he'd been working for thousands of hours continuously without even the merest hint of fatigue.

He was yet to experience life as a bee, but his mind was made up: the busiest bee had nothing on the work ethic of the ant. No matter how miniscule he knew himself to be, he felt far from insignificant, and the sense of purpose was more fulfilling than anything he'd encountered before. Every movement was exerted with electric focus and this made him feel larger and stronger than he'd ever been. It was truly inspiring to think he could transfer this kind of work ethic to any future human lives, and he'd already formulated the title of the self-help business book he would pen in the event: *Upping the ANTe*. A self-help business guru, not a bad investment for a future life. Not a bad pun for an ant either, especially considering the lack of sleep.

This was the first life he felt OK not applying his human understanding to everything. Maybe that's what the Auditor with the clipboard and the old-timer chicken were getting at.

***

The least enjoyable part of being an ant was that one time when he was gruesomely dismembered. The chemical trail was like a warm soup on a cold winter's day. Tom was one year, ten months and three days into his frenetic ant existence. He'd just finished delivering a deliciously fungus-laden leaf back to the colony and, as always, he dutifully returned to the trail to begin another run. Scurrying along, his compatriots Quartz in front and Tenazz on his tail, he found himself at great ease in his MUST FEED THE QUEEN AND COLONY marching pace. This was living. The sense of purpose and teamwork, of being a small yet integral cog in a very large machine, was almost as intoxicating as the constant chemical scents informing his every waking hour (which was all of them). Tom had never felt so energised, so alive.

This was their fifth run along this particular trail. The trail had been longer than usual, winding around the great big tree and down through the pebble valley. They were somewhere between the two landmarks, when from the sky a large droplet of water crashed down onto the ant in front of Quartz with the velocity of an asteroid.

"Srekkes!" Quartz screeched in his chemical scent. (This roughly translated to "sky water", a term Tom had initially tried to change to "rain" without success. Ants, as it happened, were sticklers for their own vocabulary.)

The ant in front of Quartz attempted to pick himself up and, pushed along by Quartz, was eventually able to scramble back into line despite his abdomen dragging. Then another unfortunate drop of srekkes made a deep impact on the unlucky ant and finished the job.

"Srekkes-srekkes!" the rest cried.

Quartz, Tom and Tenazz all screeched in unison and the mad dash of the trail kicked up a gear as faint sky water transitioned into monsoonal bedlam.

They tried making for the pebble valley but the all-important scent was being washed away. Ants going the other way with leaves and other foodstuffs in tow found the sky water knocking their payloads to the ground. The ants scurried to rescue the precious cargo, but not even their awesome weightlifting prowess (something Quartz and Tenazz bro'd on about all the time) could enable them to lift the sodden and soggy food. All the ants panicked, a slew of frantic chemical signals pulling them this way and that. In the confusion, the trio of Tom, Quartz and Tenazz became separated from the others. They eventually made it to the pebbles, though they weren't sure if these were even the right ones, the trail's scent having completely washed away. They sought shelter beneath one of the larger pebbles, their antennae working overtime to locate the rest of their nation.

"Jebuk, where'd that come from?"

"The sky, idiot."

"I know that, I was just surprised, is all."

"Did you see Rollokz trying to lift his payload?"

"Yeah he was struggling—bet I could've lifted it."

"You? No way. I could've though."

"Both of you are wrong," snapped Tom.

"How you figure?"

"That was at least sixty times your body weight with the sky water on top. You know Rollokz lifts way harder than both of you, no offence."

This shut both of them up.

"We need to focus anyway," Tom continued, "WE MUST FEED THE QUEEN AND COLONY."

"WE MUST FEED THE QUEEN AND COLONY," they responded like ants.

"Hey, is that ant from our colony?" asked Tenazz.

All their antennae aimed squarely at the ant stranded underneath another pebble across the way. From the other side of the pebble came three more ants. The three ants appeared to converse with the first ant, and soon all four were staring back at Tom, Quartz and Tenazz.

"Is that Rewaz?"

"Don't know, can't smell them from this far away."

"Maybe they know where the rest of the colony is?"

Tom studied them through the pouring rain of no-ant's land that separated them. They sure as Jebuk didn't look friendly. He nudged Tenazz. "They look like they want to disassemble us with their mandibles. I think we should skip the meet-and-greet and look for the trail in the other direction."

Tenazz heard only the first part of Tom's warning and took this as a challenge. "There's no way they could tear us apart. They look like they can barely lift a leaf."

"Yeah," agreed Quartz, flexing his mandibles, "we're not scared of them, I don't care how big their mandibles are. We can take them, and we will, unless they're from our colony."

"We could still take them anyway, if we wanted to," clarified Tenazz. Tom slapped his antennae over his eyes, a very human thing to do that the others always found peculiar. "They outnumber us five to three. I'm positive the trail is the other direction anyway..." He threw in a "WE MUST FEED THE QUEEN AND COLONY," to sway them.

"WE MUST FEED THE QUEEN AND COLONY," they responded.

"...But what about protecting the colony if they're from another colony?" probed Tenazz.

"We gotta protect the Queen, Tom," added Quartz.

Tom sighed, the eagerness in their mandibles and pungent aroma of attack pheromones past the point of dissuasion. And if Tom left them for the trail they were certain to stand even less of a chance.

"Fine," he sighed. "But if they turn out to be hostile and we have to fight to the death, instead of our usual war cry of 'FIGHT FOR QUEEN AND COLONY', I'd like you to instead chant this: 'I'm blue daba dee daba daa...'"

Quartz and Tenazz both stared at him, confused and disappointed. "I'll never get you, Tom, with your funny name and the way you're always trying to change the word for 'srekkes' to 'rain', which just sounds stupid. This war cry though... Now that really is a whole other tunnel system."

The sky water stopped. All antennae were sprung forward in readiness. "It's gonna be fine," Quartz reassured.

But it wasn't, because they weren't from the same colony, and Quartz and Tenazz were predictably not as strong as they thought they were. And that's how Tom got dismembered, leg by leg, antenna by antenna. Daba dee daba daa.

Vegetarian progress: Fungus is morally sound to eat, right?

Salmon

Of all the trillions of fish, in all the rivers, streams, lakes and oceans, this little fishy was Tom, the salmon.

He was swimming upstream, already at the end of his life as a salmon. It had been an immense journey and for the first time in his reincarnation odyssey Tom felt slightly cheated that these moments out on the high seas were just memories for him. He'd crossed oceans, escaped the nets of humans, evaded the teeth of sharks and was now back in fresh water. He was going home. Home to the river where he was born and where he was destined to die. Almost an entire lifetime lived vicariously through the memories of a fish.

Tom had seen the salmon run before on television, where some outdoorsy presenter in waders spun folksy tales of plucking hard-won salmon from the river before the local bears got them. Tom remembered snickering at the TV, safe and warm in his living room. This was different. Tom was now terrified. He couldn't help but imagine the eagles, black bears, brown bears, wolves, and innumerable fishermen joining in the hunt. A whole litany of monsters ready to snatch him out of the air or swipe him from the shallows.

He was a mere five leaps away from the same bed of gravel where he'd spawned, all those years ago. It had been a happy fryhood and Tom couldn't help but grow nostalgic, despite the adrenaline and underlying sense of doom.

His cohort, whom he'd stuck with for his entire life, was a school of fifty-four fish. He made his first leap with Marli, Trevor, Rita and Ramone. They burst out of the water, flapping away, feeling the refreshing air on their glistening scales and all the threats that wanted to tear them fin from fin. The splash into safety was exquisite.

In the next stream they saw the big black shadow looming and knew better than to approach. "What an idiot," said Rita. "Doesn't he realise we can see him?"

The school waited until the big black shadow disappeared. The coast clear once more, they flew into the air with gravity-defying grace, except for Rita, who was swiped by a white-coated spirit bear. A moving eulogy was conducted as they swam further up the current. The next leap went fine, if one counts a massacre as fine. It claimed Evelyn, Trevor, Corey, Red and Trudy (who reminded Tom of Lily in the way she used to talk about the vastness of the ocean. Lily had done that once too, within earshot of Tom). The bears would carry them off to devour, trailing their fish-guts across the forest, the nutrients supporting the brutal circle of life. An impressive system, yet Tom made it a point to avoid becoming fertiliser if at all possible.

There were only two leaps to go now, but these were spaced far apart, and in between, more and more of the friends Tom had swum with since spawning were picked off by the large talons of swooping eagles.

For the final two leaps, Tom swam as hard as his tired body and fins allowed, closing his eyes each time he flung himself into the air at the complete mercy of Mother Nature. Both times he thought he was done for—that he'd soar in the air like a bird, and just keep soaring, because the bird that caught him preferred takeaway. But no talons sank into his scales, no fish net swept him aside, and slowly it dawned on him, through the magnetic forces and familiar smells overwhelming his spent little brain, that he had reached the riverbed of his fryhood. He was home. Sweet relief. As he lay down and began his final life purpose of fertilising the spawn bed Vera had dropped her eggs in, Tom thought what a wonderful novelty that at least in this life he hadn't been brutally killed, and decided that despite awakening into consciousness only at the end, being a salmon had been the most complete life he'd lived thus far.

He then died, as all salmon do after spawning their offspring.

Salmon II

It appeared Tom's earlier wish of truly experiencing life out on the ocean, and not just as a memory, had come true. He was at first confused, a little bit hesitant, but then had to laugh about it; he hadn't seen the Auditor swimming around with the clipboard at the time of his wish, though it was nice to know the universe was listening. That there was some reward to not being devoured.

While he wasn't exactly ready to be a salmon again just yet, he realised this meant that if he became human again, assuming he ever did, then maybe he could double up with back-to-back human lives?

This time around, Tom began as spawn, and he pondered if he had indeed given birth to himself. An intriguing thought, though it counted for little when Tom was eaten by a dolphin only a few days after making it to the ocean he was so excited about swimming in. Luckily, he had time to sing the magic words to himself as the dolphin swallowed and regurgitated him over and over until he went down the right way.

Human

Tom first came to know he was Hubert Muller, a respected Austrian art teacher, mid-sentence during an emotional lecture on the merits of Anselm Feuerbach. He stopped abruptly and his audience was left on the edge of their seats, buoyed by last week's wildly entertaining critique of Rembrandt and the

Dutch golden age, eager for him to do the same to Feuerbach and all the other conservative forces holding them back from enlightenment in the new world at the turn of the 20th century.

As Hubert, Tom remembered the two most pressing things: he had a wife and two children, and the Imperial roll he'd brought to work in his bag was most likely soggy and would need to be thrown out after this lecture. Why had he not remembered to wrap the tomato in wax paper?

Everyone in the lecture hall leaned forward, dumbstruck by his silence, and Hubert, or Tom, as he now thought of himself, promptly suggested they all go outside and consider the art of nature, as he was feeling unwell. The students, having never experienced such a strange request from their teacher, slowly stood and made their way outside under much apprehension.

The first thing Tom, err, Hubert Muller, did was leave the prestigious university on his bicycle, homeward bound, the memory of his path returning with increasing clarity at every prevailing turn. It was less Hubert remembering he was Tom and more Tom remembering he was Hubert. He was suddenly a husband and father, an entire life of Muller's memories and accomplishments now his own to try to piece through. Unlike his animal lives, this time he felt he was stealing an identity, overpowering the consciousness of poor Hubert and bringing along an encyclopedia of baggage to throw into the mix. He was momentarily struck by the crazy notion that by removing all of his clothes he could somehow rid himself of the guilt. He thought of his wife, all the intimate moments they had spent together, and knew he'd violated something in the universe, some sacred principle. Invading the privacy of a stranger, rather than his own life. It didn't feel right. Never mind that he'd done it to several animal species—this was a whole other kettle of fish.

Helena Muller was surprised to find her husband home early for the day. What surprised Tom was the frisky feeling that accompanied the jarring notion of meeting your wife for the first time. What was he to do? They were man and wife, with a full 18 years of shared emotional history, despite the fact that to Tom she may as well have been a stranger. He couldn't just fall upon her in the heat of passion then and there, could he?

After they'd made love, and Tom had experienced the singular sensation of ejaculating from a penis that was not spiritually his own, there were sentiments of quiet appreciation muttered from a decidedly flushed-looking Helena, and this reminded Tom, err, Hubert, that he was also a father.

"Where are the children, Helena?"

"School, of course. What's got into you, *mein* Hubbie? You're home early, then there was this *surprise...*" She gestured at the room of sweat and passion.

"I..." Tom began, wondering how he could express this feeling of stolen identity, but despite a large vocabulary amassed through seven years of study at the same university where he now taught, all expression seemed hopeless, meaningless and trivial when weighed against telling the plain crazy truth of his multiple past lives, which he was most certainly not going to share. Helena stared expectantly at him as they lay entwined in embrace.

"I'm just...tired," he finally said, to both their relief. Maybe it was nothing more serious than that.

Helena went to pick up the children from school while Tom remained in bed and tried to piece together more of his life by scanning the memories of Muller. It emerged he'd had a short-lived affair with a student, a male student in fact, and this marked the first time he had experimented with being gay, or at least bisexual. Back in his younger years as Tom, he'd had a passing curiosity, but never pursued this path further. Now that he'd experienced this affair with Tobias Waltz as a vicarious memory, he found it somewhat liberating; and was open to mixing it up again if the opportunity arose in one of his many future lives before he settled down with Lily for infinity.

Naked, he slipped out of bed and wandered quietly around his quaint and cosy home, taking in all the artefacts but never touching them, his restraint like that of a polite houseguest. The Mullers were well-off for the times, and their narrow, two-storey house was comfortably appointed. Tom's greatest shock, however, occurred when he arrived at the kitchen. My oh my. The sudden explosion of panic was tremendous. They had no refrigerator, but of course they didn't. The year was 1896. That would explain Helena's lace bodice and tightly-bound corset, the latter of which had taken him several minutes to unclasp, not to mention his own stiffly starched collar and what was, in hindsight, a welcome absence of cars on the road. No, instead of a fridge they had something called a root cellar, with an icebox kept outside for when they could afford the ice, which was evidently something of a luxury. Trying to keep it together while the memories of 21st century comforts reverberated around in his brain (he particularly mourned the absence of a microwave), Tom checked the Mullers' root cellar but discovered only some lumpy potatoes and a bottle of milk. He carefully opened the bottle and whispered a heartfelt thanks to the cow it came from. He tried a sip and found it bearable, flashes of being milked swirling in his mind, before carefully returning it to the shelf. Like Tom, Herr Muller was thoroughly useless in the kitchen. He probably could've whipped up some chips, but there was no electric fryer. Had electricity been invented yet? All he knew was that before, whenever he flicked the switch, it was there, ready to power his appliances. Contemplating another swig of milk, he decided he would wait for Helena to come to the rescue.

***

The pitter-patter of smallish feet at the front door arose him from his re-reading of an art book with fresh eyes. He arrived at the door and realised he'd forgotten to commit the names of his children to memory. The door swung open with great gusto and in burst the boy, his hair a sunny blond in a bowl of ruffled youth.

"Papa!" cried the boy as he ran up to hug his father.

"My son...err...Hans!" Tom recalled at last; an entire childhood cramming into his already overloaded brain while he squeezed the fruit of his, or rather Hubert's, loins.

"How was school?"

"Dreadful! Can I go kick the ball with Lukas at the square?"

"No," said Helena, but Tom had already nodded his approval and Hans dashed out the door on this merest of technicalities.

"Be back for dinner!" Tom shouted in what he hoped was a suitably authoritative tone, before turning his attention to Anna, his eleven-year-old daughter, who seemed mopey. "Whatever is wrong, Anna?"

Helena answered for her. "One of her classmates told her that girls can't attend university and now she doesn't want to finish school."

"What's the point?" Anna sulked. "Why do the boys get to but I can't? Hans is an idiot," she said, referring to her younger brother, "and even he'll be able to go if he wants to? It's not fair!"

Tom recalled Anna was his favourite and thought he was helping when he let slip that girls couldn't go to university *yet*. Anna perked up at this before Tom realised he had no idea when society allowed girls to attend university, especially in Austria, and with his 21st century sensibilities still melding with his new-found Austrian cultural knowledge courtesy of Hubert, Anna's future certainly seemed grim. "Never mind that—if you want to be a doctor, you can start as a nurse and we'll figure something out from there…"

Anna beamed and this made Tom's heart melt. She hugged her father. "Thank you, Papa."

Helena lifted from her basket a parcel of butcher's meat and waved it at Tom. "You were in such a good mood, I thought we'd have your favourite!"

Veal. Hubert Muller's favourite meal was four sizzling strips of veal. Helena was taken aback by his sudden apprehension. "What's wrong?" she enquired in a slightly scolding tone.

Both mother and daughter eyed Tom with confusion.

"I…" Tom panicked, unsure if he should just concede the one meal and work something out later regarding his pursuit of vegetarianism, but he had a sense it had to be now or never; he'd made excuse after excuse as other species…

"I…" He tried to muster some sincerity. "I have decided to become a vegetarian."

***

Hans ate the strips of veal in front of Tom, slurping them up with messy affection, much to Tom's salivating dismay. Helena remained in shock and stared accordingly. "Since when did you become vegetarian? Marie from church was telling me about them, and they sound to me like a cult."

"Since today. It's a new thing. A health thing, for me. We'll save money. Money we can spend on the kids—on *you*."

Anna perked up once more, the prospect of getting the education she dreamed of still fresh in her mind.

Helena was unconvinced. "A health thing? Save money? Are you going to quit drinking too?"

Tom did not appreciate her tone, but on closer introspection it appeared he was in fact somewhat of an alcoholic (helped his creative flair and coping with 19th century life). He then realised he hadn't poured himself a wine and that dinner had become unbearable.

"Yes..." Tom declared, his voice choking and his chest tightening. "Yes. I won't be drinking anymore."

The children were in disbelief. Hubert rarely hit them in his drunken state, but the unpredictable yelling was often psychologically scarring, psychology having been invented the preceding decade.

Once again though, and unlike the rather expensive veal, Helena wasn't buying it. That night, as Tom tried to combat Helena's pronounced distance in bed, he couldn't help but suffer in silence as she pondered this stranger in her bed.

***

The next day, Tom rose early and shuffled about the house awkwardly, hesitantly preparing his papers and lunch before he set off for work. He couldn't afford a repeat performance of his previous lecture. It was all very daunting, and Helena quietly observed his anxious pacing before setting off on her own errands. As per his usual routine, Tom took the children to school, making a hash of which neighbours to greet warmly and which could be safely ignored. Hans would regularly leave his grasp and bolt ahead, running and bounding about the cob-blestoned street with youthful abandon. Anna kept by his side and when she sensed he was lost she tugged at his hand and asked him if he was OK. He blushed, here was a child that neither he nor Hubert deserved.

"Yes, Anna, I'm fine... How much further is it?"

From little school to big school he went, and when he got to the beautiful grounds of the architecturally-astounding Vienna Academy of Fine Arts, he felt very small indeed. Displacement grew with every step toward her hallowed halls.

He taught drawing classes and art theory (where he exhibited some of his best ranting). First up was drawing, and as soon as he walked through the door and saw the expectant faces of his students, he gave an audible sigh of relief. He remembered. The butterflies fluttering inside his guts stopped their flapping and settled comfortably.

Briefly eschewing the old-timer chicken's rule of not interfering with history, he decided to fuse his past life as Tom with the artistic talents of Hubert by drawing aeroplanes and spaceships that he knew would blow his students' minds.

"What is that?" they asked.

"It's a mechanical bird," he offered casually, and their jaws dropped. "I have a feeling that people will use this someday to travel across the lands and oceans, for holidays and business."

"Like air trains—or air boats!"

Seeing the wonder in their eyes, Tom thought he could share this with Helena and perhaps restore the spark that had faltered when he'd hijacked her husband's life.

Art Theory was held in the afternoon, and Tom did not address his abrupt abdication of yesterday's class. Eager to move on, Tom knew the students wanted a rant, and this time Monet was in the firing line. The lecture went off without a hitch.

School finished for the day, Tom returned home where he told his wife all about the mechanical birds he'd drawn and had his starry-eyed students emulate. Helena was still a little hesitant—a bold move on Tom's part to go weirder in trying to restore normality—but Hubert's charisma and insistence that everything was normal won through for the time being. There was no meat eaten at dinner that night, nor the next or the night after that, and after a month Tom had settled into his routine and was on his way to becoming more comfortable as Hubert, though Helena had yet to fully let go of his previous strange behaviour and remained guarded in her conversations with him. He worked six days a week at the art academy, organising schedules on the Saturday, with church on Sunday. His other lives grew distant in light of his busy routine, and in this he found peace, though he took from them what he could: the work ethic of the ant, the persistence of the salmon... Well, in truth the only helpful life had been the ant and the least helpful, most painful, being Raj the Tiger.

***

Two months later, on a warm spring Sunday, there was a knock on their door. It was Jakob Drexler, a childhood friend of Hubert's who had recently returned to Vienna. Helena answered the door and laughed when Jakob announced he was going fishing and wondered if Hubert would like to join.

"You'll be surprised to hear that Hubert is a changed man. He doesn't fish anymore. He doesn't eat meat anymore."

Jakob took personal offence to this. "Is this true?" were the first words he'd said to Tom in years, after Tom descended from the stairs, completely unaware.

"Jakob! Good to see you! Is what true?"

"You don't eat meat anymore?"

Tom blushed a deep red, thrown off by this surprise inquisition of character. Helena smirked, clearly enjoying herself.

"Uh, no, I don't..."

"But why?"

"I just don't care for the taste anymore—I... I think I may be allergic."

Helena raised her eyebrows. Hubert had mentioned nothing of the sort.

Jakob scratched his head. "Well, I was going to suggest we go fishing at the river while we reminisce about the old days, but apparently you don't fish anymore either?"

Tom shuffled his feet uncomfortably as Helena and Jakob awaited his response.

"It's a great day to be outside," he nervously declared. "Let's go fishing!"

Helena stiffened, disappointed Tom had so weakly pandered to a friend, telling outright lies about allergies, when he was more assertive and forthright with her. She stormed off, the growing distance between them now open for public viewing.

The river was six kilometres from Hubert's house. Tom dusted off his rod and suffered flashbacks of his time as a salmon, ever fearful of the dreaded hook. He found himself caressing his lips, smacking them together to ensure they were free of holes, that there was no painful hook stabbing into them, ready to yank him up into the sky.

Jakob was already regretting his invitation. Hubert had under-gone some kind of character lobotomy and Jakob didn't care for it one bit. "You don't even drink anymore? I don't believe it. You used to say it helped you with your painting, among other things."

Tom shrugged. "I was losing control."

They reminisced at some length about the good old days of their childhood, though it came with great sadness when they talked about those they knew who had passed away in the small-pox epidemic over a decade ago. Jakob's reluctance dissipated with the warm spring weather and when they finally made it to the river, there were lilacs and blue lilies—almost as if Monet himself had sat along the bank and painted his most famous work (which Hubert loved to critique as insipid and wishy-washy). They set up and cast out, though Tom hoped that neither he nor Jakob would catch anything. The sun glistened off the river as they rolled cigarettes and basked in the idle calm.

"I was a salmon once," remarked Tom.

Jakob didn't bat an eyelid at this, the day so beautiful and in-vigorating that he was now willing to entertain Hubert's offbeat company. "Oh really," he said, "What was that like?"

"A lot of swimming," said Tom, dryly.

A smile broke on Jakob's face and they cracked into laughter that echoed their younger selves. They talked again with great-er connection, Tom describing the waves of new art he thought would come in the following years and Jakob listening intently.

Things were going swimmingly until there was a tug on Jakob's line. They both froze and with a bolt of furious energy, Jakob splashed into the water, breaking the still calm of the river. There was a whoosh as the grayling flapped out of the water and with all its might dived back in. Tom wasn't a fan of graylings, in fact they could be downright pompous pricks, but even they didn't deserve the searing pain and sudden shock of the hook.

The grayling gave a dogged fight but was soon hoisted from

the water for the last time. Jakob swung it onto shore, and when it thrashed he brought his gutting knife down upon its head. The look on the wide-eyed grayling was horrendous. Tom froze as flashbacks of the massacre leap in his salmon youth played over and over in his mind.

Jakob turned to Tom with a beaming grin, only to grow sheepish when he saw the shock in Tom's eyes and the stiffness in his manner. There was an awkward silence as Jakob stood, the dead grayling at his feet.

"Friend of yours?" he finally said, attempting levity.

"Not exactly..." replied Tom, looking away.

The mood seemingly unsalvageable, they decided to call it a day. Walking back, Jakob defended himself. "I mean...we *did* go fishing. That's kind of what happens when you go fishing. You catch fish."

"I guess you're right," Tom said, knowing he was being unreasonable by any ordinary human standard, before matters grew even worse when he spotted Tobias Waltz, student and former lover, emerging from the reeds with a classmate, Jasper Fuchs. The pair looked decidedly flushed, and Jasper was still buttoning his shirt. The jealousy Tom felt was immediate and went straight to the gut, like when he'd overheard Lily talking with Vicky in the lunchroom about a date that had gone particularly well. Tobias froze when he saw Tom. In fact, his mortified features reminded Jakob of Tom when the fish had been stabbed with the knife.

"Tobias." Tom acknowledged the young man curtly as he kept walking past, stiff and forced. "Hubert," Tobias gave a small, surprised nod as he did likewise.

After gaining some distance, Jakob finally asked. "Student of yours?"

"Something like that..."

***

He stood outside his home; Helena, Hans and dear sweet Anna somewhere inside. *Go inside and brush it off*, he thought at first, *let whatever gossip Jakob spreads about town play out as it may*. Perhaps Jakob hadn't noticed how flustered he had been when he saw his former lover with another. How his heart violently ripped in two. Perhaps Jakob thought nothing of it and Tom was merely being paranoid. Perhaps...

But he couldn't let it go, couldn't return and act as if everything were normal. His head was reeling, and he knew from Hubert, the old Hubert, just what to do with a feeling like this. Each step to the Old Habsburg beer hall was a step towards the relief of oblivion.

Why had he screwed his life over so? Who was to blame, was it him or Hubert? It wasn't fair that he had inherited this pain without experiencing the joy of childhood again, or the chance to make better choices along the way if he'd remembered who he was earlier. Was him remembering later on in life some kind of punishment for discretions in his past life—or lives?

"Where have you been?" asked Gertie, the bar wench.

"Being foolish."

She poured him a drink. "This will fix that."

The beer hall was mostly empty. He drank alone at a table in the darkest corner, staring only at his drink, finishing it, and straight-lining it back to the bar for another. He did this many times before the sun set and he began to sway; he almost lost his footing near a raucous party of six downing beer and being the loudest in the hall. They laughed at him and he was about to explode at them when a new entrant to the beer hall caught his eye. The young man had slick, gelled-back hair and piercing black eyes, with an assuredness in his gait. If Tom weren't so morose, he'd have tried to hit on him.

"Sorry for bothering," Tom said to the obnoxious party, before turning to leave. As he reached the door, there was a tap on his shoulder. It was the man with the slicked-back hair.

"You're one of us, aren't you?"

They sat down and the man ordered two drinks. *Is there a language you prefer?* The man communicated telepathically.

German, said Tom.

German it is, agreed the man.

The man was lucky. He'd been blessed with superior DNA and his sharp clothes indicated considerable wealth. This was the first thing Tom remarked to the man when they sat down in the beer hall for this fateful drink.

"I'm not lucky, I earned it. Sincerely."

When he was a man, he was Sal. When he was a woman, he was Sal too. "I've been a human over eleven times—that I can remember—and ten of those times, where possible, I've become a detective. I even caught Jack the Ripper once."

"What happened the one time you weren't a detective?"

Sal was taken aback by the lack of acknowledgment for his crowning Jack the Ripper achievement. His face drew grim and he took a drink before answering Tom's question. "I was a twelve-year-old girl who died in the showers of a prison camp in a devastating war half a century from now."

Tom's eyes lit up. *Oh my.* How had he missed this? "Just like Anne Frank," he muttered.

"Who?" Sal questioned, brushing away Tom's response as he took another sip of his drink. "And while you could say my being here is lucky, I stand by the belief that it was earned, because I suffered *greatly*." He leaned in. "The person who started this war—he is here in Austria, on the other side of the country. He's only a boy at the moment and I will make sure he'll only ever be that. Tomorrow I'll get on a train and kill that boy before he becomes a true monster."

Tom was rattled. The old-timer chicken's words still rung true in his brain: *"Don't try to overthrow humanity... And if you are human, don't kill Hitler, or anything like that."*

Sal downed the rest of his drink. "What's the furthest you've been in human history?"

"Huh?" said Tom, blinking. He was, after all, quite drunk.

"When you were a human, what year of human history did you reach?"

"2019," Tom muttered hesitantly, knowing full well the verbal lashing that was to follow.

"2019! Incredible! Wait. So you knew about Hitler? And you haven't killed him yet?"

"It slipped my mind." Tom threw his hands up in embarrassment.

"How do you *forget* the Second World War? And while we're at it, what did you intend to do about the first one?"

"I've been busy! It's only my second time being a human," Tom stuttered, scrambling to think of any credible excuse for this gigantic oversight. He clicked his fingers. "There's more of us, I'm not the only one, and yet nobody else has killed Hitler yet... so it probably can't be done, right? I don't know how it all works, what actions stick and stuff..."

"But you've got to at least try, for God's sake!"

An uncomfortable silence followed. Sal was clearly disappointed, adding to the number of people Tom let down today.

Sal shook his head, determined to redeem Tom's failure. "Okay, you haven't killed him yet, but there's still a chance. I'm taking the train to Linz tomorrow morning. Hitler's in Fischlham, that's only a couple of towns over from Linz. It's a rural village where Hitler is attending school. Join me, and together we will make sure *it sticks.*"

***

That night Tom returned to his house reeking of liquor and regret. When Helena caught a whiff, she smirked and said, "Look who's back."

Tom did not take kindly to her tone. He screamed at her to shut up, waking the children. Fear filled her eyes and Tom withdrew his rage, brought back from the brink. His head was hurting, not just from the impending hangover, but from the defining moment Sal had offered him: a chance to watch Hitler die. Or the other side of the coin: help murder a young child who, at this stage, lacked any discernable facial hair. He wrestled with both sides of the argument for some time, before he eventually passed out on the hardwood floor of his bedroom.

In the morning the house was empty, Helena having taken the children to school in lieu of their messed-up father. Nursing a hangover of monumental proportions, Tom attempted to compose himself and checked the time. Sal's train had left half an hour ago. But there was still time, there were other trains, and Tom couldn't shake the words of that old-timer chicken: *"Don't kill Hitler, or anything like that."*

If there was no World War II, there'd be no technological progress the way it went, with advances in telecommunications and the rise of cubicles and large-scale insurance firms. Maybe Al Gore doesn't end up inventing the internet, and suddenly there would be no Facebook for Tom to learn more about Lily. Maybe Lily wouldn't even exist? Or Tom for that matter!

Tom hastily packed a set of clothes and a kitchen knife into his art bag. Holding back tears, he scribbled a rambling goodbye letter to his wife and children. Money was promised and everything hastily explained; the chant offered in hope of reconciliation. Maybe he'd return, maybe he wouldn't. He was still deeply unsure.

***

Fischlham was a rural backwater of forest and farmland northwest of Vienna. No train ran direct to Fischlham, so Tom had to catch a train to Linz and then make his way by other means south-west to Fischlham. He arrived at Linz in darkness, just after eight, and paid for a single night at an inn, where he battled his thoughts over what exactly he was going to do. He used his small knife to whittle a sharp end from his favourite paint brush as a backup weapon. This was mostly to settle his nerves.

He had prepared two speeches in case he found Sal before the deed was done. The first one stated his support for killing Hitler. This was a short speech, its positives clear and self-evident. The second speech offered an alternative to killing the boy: teaching him the moral failings of his future self—Hubert was a respected teacher at the art school that would eventually reject Hitler, now that Tom finally recalled—surely something could be changed that way? This would at least delay Tom's conundrum and give him more time to settle on a final solution. But behind both options came the inescapable fear that by disobeying the words of the wise, albeit gruff, old-timer chicken, Tom would somehow ruin his slim, not yet confirmed possible, chance to end up with Lily. That damn, slutty butterfly flapping away without a care for the consequences.

Was this a selfish reason to abort the assassination? Absolutely. Would he really not do it? Maybe.

Did it make sense? Sort of.

Sal was four hours ahead of Tom. Tom scoured all the hotels, bars and inns, but came up empty. He considered going to the police to locate Sal, but decided against this, fearing it would only complicate matters. During his search he learned that Fischlham was over six hours away by horseback. Neither Tom nor Hubert could ride a horse, so he would have to hire a cart in the morning.

But after returning to the inn and lying in his single bed, tossing and turning, unable to sleep, Tom decided instead to walk towards Fischlham in the night and try to beat Sal there.

The road was dark and Tom had little confidence in the hastily-sketched map the innkeeper had given him. Instinctively, he reached into his pocket for an iPhone that didn't exist yet, and swore quietly. After about three hours with only the moonlight to guide him, he concluded that he was totally lost and would have to wait for daylight before he reorientated himself. He lay down under a tree by the side of the road and covered himself in his spare clothes for warmth. He shivered in the cold, very much regretting the decision-making process that had led him to be in this situation. He dreamt of Lily for warmth and eventually slept until sunrise.

***

Tom awoke, covered in dew, and was relieved to find that he had not been robbed by human or animal; a possibility he had only just come to consider at that very moment. Riding this luck, he set off for Fischlham, or at least in its general direction, as best as he could extrapolate from the map.

The early morning roads were quiet. Gradually, the swathes of trees peeled away and the serene landscape transformed into farmland. Sometimes a horse-drawn cart would pass in the other direction, off to Linz, and Tom would narrow his eyes to see if it were Sal in the cart or carriage.

After a few hours of slogging along, Tom retreated to the side of the road to check his bag for rations. He had an apple, some nuts...and at the bottom of his bag a mouldy Imperial roll, which gave him second thoughts about the safety of the apple and nuts. He tossed away the mouldy bread and took a tentative bite of the apple. A rider approached from the direction of Linz, his slick hair unmistakable even from afar.

Sal slowed to a trot when he recognised Tom. He offered a smile by way of greeting, but did not dismount. "Have you come to help?"

"Of course!" said Tom, deeply unsure how convincing he sounded.

Sal brightened at this news and patted his horse. "Tom, this is Rudiger. Rudiger, Tom."

Hello, the horse communicated telepathically, as only a reincarnation rememberer could.

"Hello," said Tom. "Victim of Hitler too?"

I was both a World War One horse and carrier pigeon. I don't want to go through that again in another war.

"Have you been a horse often?"

Yes, a few times now. I like it. I seem to be rather good at it. Just like Sal is good at being a detective, catching bad guys... Rudiger's eyes narrowed in on Tom and our hero tried not to seize up in fear. Sal paid it no mind, however, unsaddling from Rudiger to greet Tom. "It's good you've decided to help make it stick!"

They walked the rest of the way, Rudiger laden with their bags and satchels. Sal spoke of their plan of attack, but Tom found it hard to keep up.

"We have many options. We locate the school, find our boy, and then pose as his long-lost relatives who have come to pick him up and return him to his father in Hafeld. I've already written the letter of consent."

Tom nodded without enthusiasm.

"Or, we wait until the bastard is skipping home from school, kidnap him and then take him to a field where we will charge him for his future crimes, beat him, and then kill him."

Tom's face paled at this. Nevertheless, he nodded again, mumbled a few words of assent, and wondered whether now would be the right time for that second speech of his. Growing more nervous in the quiet that followed, Tom asked Rudiger what it was like to fly as a carrier pigeon, or any bird for that matter (except for a caged chicken). Truth be told, apart from getting another chance with Lily, Tom wanted most of all to be a bird, preferably an American eagle, clichés be damned.

It's a terrific joy, when you're not at war.

That was all he said.

***

Fischlham "school" was a single schoolroom of tiny dimensions that would only ever house one notable person of history. The rest of the village comprised a small church, a postal house, a tavern and a bakery. They pulled up two hundred metres from the village entrance.

Sal saddled up on Rudiger and told Tom to stay put, as the sight of two male strangers travelling together might arouse suspicion. Tom agreed—only to then sneakily flank Sal once he'd set off, edging along the outskirts of town to keep a closer eye on proceedings. After briefly losing sight of the pair behind the church, Tom spotted Rudiger trotting up alone to the school and its children, who appeared to be out playing for lunch. The female teacher was alarmed and tried to shoo the unmanned horse away, with Sal appearing in the nick of time to apologise for not hitching his horse properly. Thrown off by his piercing eyes, the teacher quickly forgave him. The children were encouraged to pat the horse, and as they did, Sal scanned each face for the eyes of a monster. He found him smiling at Rudiger from afar, waiting his turn. When the boy finally reached Rudiger, Sal casually asked the boy his name. The boy sought approval from his teacher, who urged him to speak to the handsome stranger.

"Adolf," said the boy.

"Adolf Hitler?"

The boy was shocked. The teacher answered for him. "Yes, his name is Adolf Hitler. How did you know?"

"I'm a friend of his father, Alois. I'm on my way to visit him. Is school nearly over? I could take Adolf home if he wants?"

The teacher was reluctant, citing it wouldn't be fair to deprive him of his education—and that his sister would take him home in any event, but Sal's charm won her over.

"It's only one day, what could possibly be the harm?"

Little Hitler was hesitant to join Sal, what with the man twitching every time he locked eyes on the child, but the teacher eventually came around to Sal's side and told young Hitler to run along and get his things. They both saddled up on Rudiger, the boy clinging onto Sal from behind in clear discomfort as Sal bid the rest of the happy school children goodbye.

Tom watched all this from afar and realised they were already making their way towards the boy's family home in Hafeld without doubling back for him. It was at this point Tom's awe of Sal turned to fear. How the hell was he going to stop this, if he was to at all? He jolted into a sprint and intercepted them just as they were leaving town.

Rudiger almost bucked with surprise, and Sal apologised profusely to the boy for nearly falling off. "Adolf, this is a friend of mine and your father's; his name is Tom."

Tom greeted the boy and, to little Hitler's credit, he seemed to know something was amiss, his shifty eyes darting between the growing number of strangers taking an interest in him. Once they'd trotted far enough down the road to be certain no one was watching, Sal looked out to the expanse on their right, a beautiful hilly meadow similar to the one Tom had enjoyed in a simpler time as a cow, and Sal remarked to Tom that this field seemed as good a place as any.

"That's not the way to Hafeld..." said little Hitler.

Sal replied with a stiff back elbow to his face, breaking the boy's nose. Little Hitler's subsequent bawling startled Rudiger and sent him galloping off into the field, Sal yelling at Tom to catch up. They were soon over the crest of a hill and Tom tumbled over in pursuit.

When he finally made it over the hill, he was greeted by Rudiger, standing guard while Sal prepared to destroy the child that would one day grow up to be a maniac.

He was already tying the boy's hands. The boy's mouth was stuffed with a handkerchief, and his broken nose had caused blood to drip down to his mouth, recreating in blood the moustache he would later become synonymous with. Tom approached with his kitchen knife drawn, shaking.

When Sal saw Tom's unimpressive weapon, he laughed. "Don't worry, I brought my own," he said, pulling out a large hunting knife from a sheath on his leg. Tom's legs grew weak.

Once little Hitler's feet were also tied he was told to sit down, and Sal stood back to begin his rehearsed speech.

"We stand here today in the good graces of the universe, to deliver justice against the greatest monster-to-be in human history. Adolf Hitler, in the future you will cause the deaths of millions in a crusade of hate. For this, you will be slowly sliced for each million that your twisted vision caused. Tom, how many millions of people died in the Second World War?"

Tom wasn't quite sure. "Uh, maybe sixty?"

"Sixty? Christ, that's worse than I thought."

Little Hitler was now squirming in protest. He was unable to speak, but his eyes said, *It couldn't be me, I'd never do that!*

"Well, keeping him alive for sixty slices—that will be difficult—but it *is* the right thing to do..."

"WAIT!" shouted Tom, finally locating some semblance of courage.

"It wasn't sixty?"

"No—Sal, we can't do this. He's just a kid."

"Who eventually orchestrates a genocide!" spat Sal.

What's going on back there? Rudiger neighed.

"Listen," hissed Tom, "I'm an art teacher at the fine arts academy he gets rejected by. I can overturn that! He can be an artist and not hurt anyone!"

Sal's gaze drifted into the air as he considered this proposition, for all of three seconds. "No. This will be a lot simpler."

Sal turned to little Hitler and brought the knife to his trembling forearm, making a precise cut. "That's one." Hitler gave a muffled scream into the handkerchief. Sal went to the other wrist for slice number two but was tackled to the ground by Tom, who had kept his knife in his hands. When Sal easily rolled Tom over and came out on top of him, Sal realised he was bleeding. He looked down at his stomach and saw the blood pooling from his shirt, Tom's unimpressive knife lodged in there. His hands soon wrapped around Tom's throat. "You stabbed me!"

"I'm sorry!" blurted Tom, his face going red as Sal choked him, while he garbled out an explanation.

"What did you say?" shouted Sal, his grip loosening as Tom heaved in lost air.

"...There was a chicken."

"A chicken?"

"Yes. A wise, old chicken. He told me not to do anything that could mess with history—like, for example, killing Hitler. In fact, he mentioned that specifically."

"A chicken!"

"And a girl—I did it for a girl! From the future!"

"What about all the girls *he* killed?" The millions?"

"Uh, well, yes, but the chicken—"

"A chicken!"

Sal was not too impressed with the old timer's advice. He expressed his disappointment by pulling out the knife lodged in his stomach and proceed to forcefully return this knife to Tom, all while little Hitler tried to roll his way to the river and freedom.

Tom had both hands on Sal's wrist as he struggled to repel the knife that edged closer toward his heart. He considered giving up and saying his usual chant, but another part of him felt he had to see out his mission, however delirious it seemed, to its end. Neither Tom nor Hubert had been a fighter, Hubert's lanky arms trained only for refined artistic assault on a primed canvas, but Tom dug deep and remembered a move he'd learned from Tenazz and Quartz during his days as ant: the chemical kamikaze attack technique. He closed his eyes, and with the feel of six legs coursing through his thin art-teacher frame, he harnessed all his remaining strength and executed his convoluted ant attack. Six indeterminable limb movements and one "chemical" spit in the eye later and Sal was now on bottom and Tom on top, the knife once again lodged deep in Sal's ribs.

"What the hell was that?" Sal exclaimed in shock.

"FIGHT FOR QUEEN AND COLONY!" Tom blurted instinctively, before rolling off Sal. They paused their scrap to see little Hitler now almost by the river, still trying frantically to loosen his ties. Rudiger was galloping after him.

Sal spat up blood and Tom apologised once more.

"You will pay for this," Sal rasped, "I'm going to come after you in every single life from here on out. I'll get others to help, and they'll hunt you too. You'll wish you were never reborn."

"I was told we weren't supposed to mess with history!"

"A chicken!" Sal exclaimed, though this expended a lot of energy and he clutched at his fatal wounds.

"I'm truly sorry," Tom pleaded. "You were right. I'll go kill Hitler now."

"You're worse than Hitler," Sal muttered before he closed his eyes and reluctantly began repeating the chant.

Tom heard yelling from the road. It was a big lumbering man. Tom turned back to the situation with Rudiger and little Hitler. The boy was drifting down the river, screaming his lungs out, with Rudiger following him from the shore. Tom turned back to the big lumbering man, who was now hurtling towards him. Tom's eyes widened and his whole body awoke into action, setting him running for the safety of forest half a kilometre away.

***

Seventeen days and one-hundred-and-fifty-three kilometres later, Tom arrived back at his home, emaciated and clad in rags. There, he was to find a counter-goodbye letter from Helena, informing she'd left with the children to go to her parents' house on the upper side of Vienna.

Tom was OK with this, though he regretted destroying Hubert's life. He particularly wished his daughter Anna well, and hoped that, of all of them, she'd take his advice on the chant seriously—if Helena had let her read his goodbye letter.

He resolved to return to his old life the best he could and try to stay at the art academy long enough to influence Hitler's enrolment—assuming the boy survived Sal and Rudiger's attempted assassination. He realised that stopping Hitler from being a dictator by becoming an artist was probably changing history just as much as killing the boy, but he was so thoroughly depressed and disillusioned with the whole mess he thought to hell with history and the words of the old-timer chicken. Any hope of another shot with Lily White was deservedly long gone, and saving a life was probably more redemptive than killing one.

It didn't take long for this disastrous experiment as Hubert Muller to come to a merciful end. Only a week later, walking through the streets to the bar where he'd first met Sal and now drank his miserable thoughts away, he was set upon and trampled by a renegade horse who shouted in telepathic thought, *This is from Sal!* The black horse was not Rudiger, and this confirmed the terrifying reality that Sal's merciless vendetta had been taken up by others. It appeared Tom was in for a bumpy ride.

Nevertheless, daba dee daba daa...

Vegetarian progress: wished he'd tried equine.

Tree

He couldn't see anything but he could feel everything. The sun on his bark, the wind in his leaves, the subtle writhing of his roots in the dirt. Ants built colonies around him, and each of those million legs tickled, but in a good way. He searched for other trees, out of sheer curiosity, but found none. Perhaps he was a lone tree in a large, empty field. This did not bother him. This life was quiet. This life was merciful.

Tom needed time away from the horrors of life. He welcomed the notion of a hundred-year stint in solitude and he slowly calculated he'd already been around for sixty years before he found himself once more. He recalled the growing of every part of him, his branches spreading out and taking in the world with calm assurance.

In the winter, Tom's leaves shed and he grew dormant. In spring, the leaves bloomed and the sun emboldened Tom like the soft notes of a grand piano. By summer, the notes had reached a crescendo, like the operas he used to attend with Helena in the early days of their courtship. Summers were intoxicating, dizzying: like being day-drunk, and Tom lapped up relief from the summer rain.

Thoughts came slowly, and he knew that with this solitude came the need for reflection, a new game plan. Lily was beautiful and everything he wanted, yes, but the memory of her was fading, and he knew that basing these strange fantastical experiences around getting back to her was mostly ridiculous. An office crush, no matter how deep its throes, was just an office crush. He needed to be a better creature anyway before he was ready for her. He needed to understand life more. And if he did all this, then maybe, just maybe, one could argue (he would argue) he had earned the chance to reconnect with her?

There was a couple that had sat under his shade once. They were the only humans to ever do so. Before that bus hit him, Tom had been in the midst of a long, drawn-out process of summing up the courage to ask Lily on a date. The original plan was just to ask her to join him for coffee, an informal happenstance, cool and casual, but as a tree, Tom had time to envision a much bolder first date: out in a field, lying under a tree much like the majestic giant he was now, just like the couple who had entwined in his shade over fourteen years ago.

Distracting fantasies aside, there was the matter of atoning for his decimation of Hubert's life, to say nothing of Shirley's. It was strange; he felt no guilt for crimes committed as an animal against other animals. This was something that had to be addressed and was done so for the next few years in his quiet contemplation. For animals, the world was black and white, while humans invented the grey. For any interaction in which Tom applied his human understanding to the detriment or even betterment of his fellow animals, there was a sense of impingement, of the complex greys of consciousness and morality and ego invading and muddying the delineated laws of the animal kingdom. The animals did not need to know the grey. It was hard enough already surviving the black and white.

But all this philosophising and daydreaming did was skirt around the elephant in the room. Sal. Tom felt safe and secure here, but he knew he'd made a determined and powerful enemy. Sal had every right to be aggrieved, but Tom was confident that once his punishment was re-examined and sufficient good deeds undertaken to balance the ledger, then surely the matter would be resolved.

<u>Tree</u>

***

He was alone for a long time—years, decades even—and then from the seeds and the wind emerged the first signs of a neighbour. An entire year passed before the other tree came into its own, learning to communicate in the subtlest of ways: a slow intertwining of roots, the faintest of whispers on the breeze, a dawning life force breathing through the trunk as its budding green fingers absorbed the sunlight. Tom beamed at every infinitesimal growth spurt. He tried to feed it his nourishment, but was careful not to completely intertwine and find himself melding with it too much—so eager was he to engage with another!

He wasn't entirely sure how long it would take his neighbour to fully develop and how it would interact with him when it did. He had only hazy recollections of his own development as a tree, this now being over some eighty years ago. Regardless, the excitement was electrifying and he believed next spring would bring his neighbour to full term.

Autumn and winter were their usual selves, with Tom slowing his thoughts and memories to a crawl—just enough to retain the necessary flash points of his past lives. The day the snow cleared was like Christmas to Tom. His neighbour was now almost a third of his size, their branches ready to sprout greenly into life.

As spring approached, Tom's neighbour came alive in those imperceptible ways only Tom could feel. He felt the other tree's memories, and this excited him. The flashes of the past were human; there was movement faces happy, sad and morose. A theme slowly developed. The faces were mostly men, and their guilt shone through in sparse rooms comprising only a chair and a table. These were interrogation rooms, and the faces were those of criminals brought to justice in the past lives of... Sal.

The tree was Sal.

Oh dear. How very unfortunate.

OK, Tom thought slowly, maybe this was a chance to clear the air, bury the hatchet, nip all grievances in the bud. After all, they'd be here together for the next hundred years or so, and once Sal found the peace that being a tree brought to the soul it was unlikely his hatred could continue. All would certainly be forgiven. Almost certainly.

Sal had not fully materialised in mind as of yet and so his thoughts still took the more rudimentary form of tree communications, the usual signs of leaf sprouting coupled with bursts of coherence spreading their way along the trunk to the branches and roots.

Everything had turned upside down. For the first time in his life as a tree, Tom saw plainly that he was not just stationary, but stuck. And then, a mere week later, a most horrid week that crawled by painfully slowly, even by tree standards, there came the first words of his neighbour, their naivety bringing no solace to Tom, for he knew how quickly their tone would change.

The following exchange, which on paper takes the appearance of a simple dialogue, was in fact a drawn-out affair that occurred over the course of almost a fortnight. Even with the ability to understand and communicate with one another telepathically, their tree-ness (an ancient word, rarely used) made communication, telepathic or otherwise, a rather painstaking endeavour.

Hello? Sal offered to the world around him.

Hi...

There was silence and only the wind spoke softly across the field. Tom's branches tightened up, his roots curled inwards like cold toes. Maybe Sal had forgotten. Maybe he'd lived so many lives since then and got over this prior misunderstanding? Please, for the love of God, let it be that!

And so, Tom waited and waited in the resultant silence, until he felt rage seep through the soil and begin to taint his roots. He felt the ceaseless angry vibrations bottling away in the trunk of his neighbour.

YOOUU! The angry thought echoed, rattling Tom's branches.

Hey, Sal... w-w-what are the chances... it's g-g-good to s-s-see you... Tom had never stuttered before. Then again, Tom had also never been terrified of a tree.

I've told everyone I met since our time in Austria about what you did.

Look, Sal, I wanted to apologise for that. I really am very sorry...

Sal's hatred bubbled forth like black tar in the soil. *Sorry won't cut it. Not this time or ever. The mere fact that the universe hasn't stripped you of your gift yet proves I must take matters into my own hands. Each life I live, I spread word of your despicable character, and it is universally agreed that you are, by far, one of the most pathetic excuses for a reincarnation rememberer since the dawn of time. I've spoken to thousands like us about your cowardly act, and all have accepted the call to arms. It is simple. You must be punished. Forever.*

Those are certainly... strong words, Tom gulped, the grim mention of "forever" hanging like a storm cloud over his branches. *Well, what would my punishment entail, if you don't mind my asking?*

Death by the most gruesome means imaginable for the rest of eternity—or until you do the only honourable thing left and call it quits to remembering.

Oh, said Tom.

But—and though I don't agree with this at all—you must always be given the opportunity to recite the chant. That's the only constraint I've been advised I need to abide by. Otherwise, I'm free to hunt you down like a dog, life after life after life. So that's what I intend to do. With the help of an army.

So...is there a process for appealing any of this? Is there anything I can say or do to change your mind? What if perhaps you kill me for the next, say, ten lives, and we'll call it a lesson learnt, punishment served.

Sal's burning hatred continued unabated. *If I could spit at you right now I would. No. You cannot appeal. You cannot bargain your way out of this you worm.*

But isn't killing wrong? Doesn't that bring bad karma? I mean, I know I won't kill again! That's a promise.

Au contraire, in this one particular instance, we've signed a special contract. The universe will reward any soul that helps bring you to justice.

Did God approve this? Tom asked, trembling at the thought of the Supreme Being coldly deciding his soul unsalvageable.

No, it was one of the Auditors, if you must know. Tall, thin fellow, with a wispy moustache. Always carries a clipboard. Nice chap, actually. I told him all about you. And when he witnessed and documented your selfish nature first hand, he was more than willing to do things a little differently to see justice served.

Oh, said Tom. *That's who the Auditor was referring to when he said "he was right about you."* So maybe God wasn't disappointed in him after all!

I'm not entirely sure I agree with how they run this show—take karma's misguided attempt to help me find you in this life—but him giving the green-light for destroying you is at least a step in the right direction.

I was going to kill Hitler after our little altercation, Tom protested feebly. *He just kind of got away from me in all the confusion...*

The confusion YOU caused!

Well, Tom writhed, *did you manage to kill him eventually?*

Sal went quiet. His branches stiffened in the wind. *Yes. We did.*

The brevity of his answer and the great silence that followed perked Tom up. Something must have happened that nullified the benefits of killing Hitler, the butterfly effect being its annoying, fluttery self. This at least proved the claims from the old-timer chicken were somewhat credible.

And?

He died.

Well, what did it change?

A sigh emerged from a small hollow in Sal's trunk. *Some things it changed for the better, some for the worse...*

Tom's relief was palpable. Then he realised he probably shouldn't feel relieved that maybe even more people were dead now. *Was there still a Second World War?*

Yes, Sal hissed, and because Sal wasn't used to the slow burn of tree talking, the following flurry left him exhausted and delayed the full sprouting of his leaves for a good two weeks. *Hitler was replaced with another maniac, Karl Kaiser, but because this new tyrant didn't foolishly try to conquer the Soviets and the Germans somehow had a more technologically advanced air force this time around, the war in Europe dragged on for longer than it should have. They dropped an atomic bomb in Berlin then the Soviets took over parts of Western Europe and maybe fewer Jews died but another said that more died and it was just...complicated nonsense.*

Tom couldn't help but fear that one of his inspired students had given the Luftwaffe a helping hand with their advanced design, but wisely kept this theory to himself. He tried to extend a root out to comfort Sal, but Sal's roots were too short. He probably wouldn't have appreciated the gesture anyway.

I'm sorry it didn't work out.

You're not sorry at all! You and your bloody chicken friend are probably joyous! That chicken's on the CARROT hit list too, by the way.

CARROT hit list?

Coalition Against the Reincarnation Remembering Of Tom.

But doesn't your story about the war being worse mean that I was right? YOU had no idea!

But—

No buts! We're going to go back in time and kill Adolf Hitler AND Karl Kaiser AND the Emperor of Japan while we're at it and we will damn sure make sure that YOU—ESPECIALLY YOU—get your just deserts.

Don't you feel like you're overreacting just a little? squeaked Tom.

The screech of rage in response carried long into the night.

Sal was still upset about being murdered—which was probably fair enough—but it was madness to compare Tom's crime with the crimes of Hitler, this Karl Kaiser fellow and the Emperor of Japan. Deep down Sal was a reasonable guy and Tom retreated into his trunk safe in this knowledge, hopeful that over the next few decades he could win Sal over. Heck, maybe when the time was right, Tom could offer for them to sign a TREETY (treaty). A pun like that could go a long way towards paving broken roads.

But in this case, it did not.

***

There was a slight issue: Sal refused to talk to Tom. Peaceful silence promptly transitioned into unbearable awkwardness and then passive-aggressive soil rattling. When spring gave Sal a leafy strength, he willed his branches and roots to grow at unprecedented rates. When the winds allowed it, he would fling his branches at Tom, losing leaves but scraping Tom's bark and hurting his feelings. Spring was ruined, and by summer, after Tom expressed his desire to start another life, Sal finally broke his silence with a deranged rant. Starting a new life was useless, because they'd find him anyway. They were working with the lanky Auditor with the wispy moustache to develop a device from the future, a Tom Tracker, capable of specifically tracking his soul. And this was only the beginning; once they'd dealt with those reincarnation rememberers who did not deserve to remember, then it was time to address other flaws in the system, overthrow this inefficient Bureau of Auditors that apparently existed and explore ways and means of ensuring karma was more swift and exacting in its delivery.

They're coming soon... Sal howled ominously in the wind, his roots loosening their grip on reality.

Tom's roots curled inward like a fist. Enough was enough. Tom waited for the wind to carry his favour, and when he got the chance five weeks later, he swung his left branch with all his might across Sal's "face".

Why can't you be happy? Why can't you let go of the past and just enjoy being a tree? It was peaceful for eighty-two years before you showed up! I hope when I'm gone, you learn the lessons a quiet tree life teaches you.

The only way I will let it go is when you let it go.

What do you mean?

Do.Not.Sing.The.Chant. Reset. And wipe your soul off the face of existence.

Tom was taken aback to the extent his hardwood allowed. Forget his past lives? Lose all his lessons—his memories?

Lose Lily?

I hope I come back as a tree again, said Tom, *this time in the Amazon or another rainforest, surrounded by nicer neighbours than you.*

You deserve to come back as a weed, if that.

Tom remained quiet the rest of the summer and Sal took this as a victory while he grew and grew.

***

Autumn leaves covered the ground. It was a day of grey skies with only the tease of rain. Tom and Sal had each kept to themselves and settled into a period of quiet reflection, with the odd attempted pilfering of nutrients by` Sal. For once, Tom was looking forward to winter. Both would need to power down and become dormant, and this allowed less effort to ignore the grim presence of Sal.

And then the man came, just like Sal said he would.

In over eight decades only three humans had graced Tom's presence. The first two had come with a blanket and wine, while the third arrived in lumberjack gear, carting an axe and a drum of petrol. Tom could sense the insidious liquid sloshing in the barrel and imagined the sharpened axe head hacking into him over and over, 60 million times in the name of justice.

Tom recalled an old Turkish proverb he'd encountered while trawling the internet on his lunch break. "When the axe came into the woods, many of the trees said, at least the handle is one of us." This did not hold true for Tom. His neighbour hated him and the man with the axe was ready to express a similar senti-ment. There was no one on Tom's side in this universe anymore.

The following conversation took place over the course of a day, a long time for humans but a rapid-fire rally for trees, leaving Sal terribly sapped but still intact, unlike Tom. Sal and the man, known as Deborah, greeted one another like old friends. The burly lumberjack then turned his attention to Tom.

"He's just as awful as you described him," said Deborah. "How long have you had to put up with him?"

An unbearable six months.

Tom then detected the subtle whirring of a computer, the rapid beeping coming from what could have only been a Tom Tracker: the device that found Tom through all the geographic and spatial hurdles existence had to offer.

"Sorry it took so long; the tracker is still being improved—I could only get my hands on an early beta version."

You'd think we could just go further into the future and get a later version—but that's OK—you've found us now. They chit-chatted for a while about their time supervising the construction of the railways as consulate members in British India, but Tom tuned them out as he tried to take stock of his memories like he were studying the night before a test, frantic to retain the ones that kept him warm and the lessons he'd gathered. When he felt he could remember no more, he began chanting.

The burly Deborah marked her spot on Tom's trunk. Tom recoiled, but kept singing Eiffel 65's greatest hit.

"You going to chant the whole time?" asked Deborah, "because this will take a good while."

Tom ignored Deborah.

Let him chant, said Sal. *He wants to be hunted in his next life too, so be it.*

Deborah shrugged. "Your choice."

The first cut tore through the bark and drew sap. The pain wasn't as bad as Tom feared, but it still caused him to stumble in his chanting. Then the next blow came, and the next, and the next one after that, and by now the pain was truly excruciating. Tom shrieked, just like in the stories he'd heard in his youth about trees screaming when they felt pain. Even as a child, the notion of trees experiencing pain had struck him as faintly ridiculous. But not now.

Sal laughed maniacally in the beginning, but soon tired himself out. Trees are not the best laughers.

Hack, hack, hack, and Tom felt his balance slowly give way as an ever-growing triangular section of trunk was cut from him. Deborah stopped for lunch as she and Sal chatted more about their time in British India and their separate experiences as gibbons in Borneo. With the triangular chunk taken out of him, Tom had to hold his breath just to keep upright. He felt the joyous vibrations of Deborah and Sal's nostalgic telepathic riffing tickling his roots and it made him furious. He thought maybe, if the right wind came along, he could fall on top of Deborah and crush her to death. He was tall and big enough, he reasoned, but this hate turned him sad, sent his sap heavy. Really, what was the use of trying to crush Deborah and poke her eyeballs out with his flailing branches? There'd only be more coming to finish the job. No good would come of another death, so he decided to fall without incident. He felt he'd matured with this decision, a sign of growth and a reflection of his many decades as a tree, which is what made it personally disappointing when at the last minute the wind he asked for was offered and he couldn't help but succumb to his inner fury and fall towards Deborah, only for her to sidestep out of the way with ease.

"You sly bastard," Deborah remarked.

You said you weren't going to kill again, said Sal, *I guess we shouldn't be surprised that your promises are meaningless.*

No! I didn't mean to! It was an accident! Tom lied with desperate vigour, but was believed by none.

As Deborah poured petrol on trunk and roots, Sal said to Tom, *You know what, maybe you're right. Maybe I should give this peaceful tree thing a go. Maybe I'll even learn to forgive you. Maybe.* And he chuckled away while Deborah struck the match.

Tom needed to remember, he needed to fix the things he'd done, make up for them somehow. He had to hold on. Daba dee daba daa.

Vegetarian goal: achieved. So that's something.

Human II

Tom came rocketing into consciousness while he shined the shoes of a bulky KGB officer. He was young again. His hands were soft and his spirit rejuvenated. His childhood memories, although somewhat horrific in parts, were at least semi-recent, and not entirely devoid of sunnier moments, of love. And the most important thing: he had legs!

He stopped shining the KGB officer's shoes and drifted further into this new mind. It felt good to be human again. The officer's eyes bulged under his military cap. What was the holdup? He scoffed, the knuckles of one meaty fist connecting hard with Tom, err, Alexei's head, reminding the poor boy where his resolute attention should be.

Tom returned to the shoes, inhaling the polish that made his brain throb at night. By afternoon, his arms worn out, fingers frozen, and brain and nostrils thoroughly spent, his friends Dimitri, Victor and Natalia swung past his corner to walk back with him to the night shelter. They'd grown up together in the local orphanage and each had been kicked out early for troublesome behaviour. Natalia was the only one who'd been adopted by foster parents, but she spent as little time as possible there, and seldom talked about it. Dimitri, Victor and Alexei (Tom) were her real family.

Dimitri and Victor were exactly like Tenazz and Quartz, Tom's old ant buddies. In fact, there was no reason why they couldn't be the reincarnated souls of his six-legged bros, even if they didn't know it.

Tom was the only one whose parents were still potentially alive. They had been taken away in the middle of the night to be re-educated. Re-education usually took five years, but if Alexei's parents were anything like him in the way of stubbornness, then further education was most likely required. That was eight years ago. The only real mother Alexei had known since was Mother Russia.

In Soviet Russia, children of enemies of the state were looked down upon with suspicion, unlike the orphans of the war. "The apple doesn't fall far from the tree" was something Alexei heard whenever officials were informed of his upbringing. It was for this reason alone that Alexei had not secured work in the Ulmesh Arms Factory like the rest of his gang, the possibility of subversion too dangerous. This view was shared by the foreman in charge of the factory, who was personally aware of Alexei's story and he had spread his concerns to all the important ears along the munitions belt.

The arms factory was the key to a better life, and while the working conditions were grim, survival was more or less guaranteed. All Alexei had to do was wait until they removed the foreman from his position for any number of arbitrary reasons, and then a bright future was in sight (bright being a relative term).

The gang skipped and laughed and sang old revolutionary songs through Moscow, past the Kremlin and Saint Basil's colourful bonfire cathedral (one of the few churches spared from Soviet ambitions) to the night shelter on the other side of the city, finally dispersed of its bread lines for the day. Every few corners, Dimitri and Victor took turns huffing Alexei's shoe polish, while Natalia stayed close to Alexei and barely left his side. Alexei was oblivious to this love, but Tom wasn't, and he held her hand when Victor and Dimitri were distracted in a scrappy rumble.

That night at the shelter, as each slept in their hard military-style cot, Tom came to experience Alexei's nightly ritual of suffering for the first time, as the poor boy struggled to remember his parents from the one tattered photograph still in his possession. Alexei's longing sparked something in Tom, a longing he hadn't fully realised nor dealt with since he was hit by the M101 bus. There was no escaping the fact that he'd neglected the memories of his own parents. They were not monsters, they were not saints, they were simply his to lay claim to. Sometimes dull, sometimes engaging, but always there, until they weren't. He felt bad he'd never paused to consider the grief they had doubtless felt over the death of their only (if rather run-of-the-mill) son. Sure, he'd been busy swimming up streams, chewing cud, marking art essays and PROTECTING QUEEN AND COLONY, not to mention conducting photosynthesis through a complex leaf system, but there had been time available between these pursuits, only for him to carefully tread past each, unwilling to consider the fate of Craig and Thora Robinson.

And so, like Alexei for the thousandth time, Tom sobbed and suffered for the first.

***

Life was unforgiving. Bread was scarce, and the winter bitingly cold. Dimitri was maimed in a factory accident and they sent Victor to re-education after he assaulted the foreman for ignoring Dimitri's plight.

Luckily for Tom, a spot was now open along the conveyor belt.

Natalia worked in a different part of the mechanical maze. Tom toiled away producing large tungsten casings for tank shells. Sometimes when the muscles ached and the monotonous work felt never ending he thought of suicide, but concluded that the bad karma this would likely accrue was the last thing he needed. Besides, whatever didn't kill him was sure to be superseded by a long list of Russian extremities that would. There was also the knowledge he'd leave Natalia behind, all by herself.

Each day was the same, ten hours of the purest exhaustion, followed by walking to the night shelter with Natalia, hand in hand. They were always tired and cold and hungry, but at least they did this together.

***

A year passed and there they were, in the same factory at the same place on the conveyor belt, working even longer hours for an imminent war with the Americans. Roubles were still hyperinflated, and they had little to spend them on anyway. At one stage, Tom used his Bachelor of Commerce, majoring in Business Admin, to make improvements in the paperwork for the workers' payroll allocation. This innovation was deemed acceptable by the foreman and quickly appropriated by the State. Tom was then sent back to his station on the belt, where he picked up a persistent cough that he passed onto Natalia. They were young lovers now, and only two years away from being able to marry and live in one of the housing blocks being erected along the Moscow skyline. At sixteen months, Natalia was the longest relationship Tom had experienced first hand; the kind of young love he'd failed to find in his youth as a pimply American teenager. Helena was a distant memory, yet Tom still thought often of Lily, dreamed of her, wondering if his future soulmate was willing to endure places such as this to be with him.

When production numbers increased, they were rewarded. Their factory was invited to a military parade, a show of Stalin's great strength. This propaganda excursion was to be held in the parade grounds outside the Kremlin. Despite Tom's innate

American scepticism, he was relieved at the break from the monotonous industrial box he shuffled into each morning.

It was a nice winter day. A top of five degrees centigrade. They shuffled into rows and made their way onto the Soviet's sturdiest bleachers. They were separated into divisions. Natalia was much further along the bleachers than Tom. Row upon row of soldiers marched past and the crowd cheered with all the energy they could muster for the State and its military machine. After the soldiers came the gigantic missiles on wheels and the tanks Tom helped equip with 14-inch rounds of iron-clad horror. They were too far away to see Stalin on his special podium, but apparently he waved magnanimously. A red-footed falcon circled overhead; Stalin's own bird, and apparently something of a beloved pet, inasmuch as a man responsible for millions upon millions of deaths could be said to love anything. Tom stared in awe at the falcon while the others looked on with glum approval at the various Soviet machines of war. Natalia had been treated to Tom's wild stories of reincarnation before. She believed none of it, of course, though did mention she wanted to be a falcon one day. It'd be nice to fly, to experience weightlessness and freedom in a world that knew far too little of both.

The falcon swooped above the bleachers on the other side of Tom. The workers finally took notice of the bird and cheered it on. Everyone marvelled as the falcon swooped and circled with effortless fluidity. That's when it saw Tom, and dived.

***

The following events were unfortunate, and merely a matter of miscommunication, or lack thereof.

Tommmm!

The falcon's greeting gave Tom such a fright that he toppled over, starting a domino reaction among the other workers. The bleachers, which had seen better days, partially collapsed, swathes of people falling through the tiers and being crushed. Tom rolled through the rickety support beams and scrambling mass of human bodies to find himself directly behind the stand, somehow unscathed.

He gazed in shock at the calamity he'd set off. He tried to help. He dragged survivors to safety and away from the chaos of the wreckage. He looked for Natalia but could not find her. Stalin's falcon circled and came to perch atop the rubble. When it spotted Tom, it called out his name again and said it only wanted to talk, but Tom was having none of it. He turned towards the nearest alleyway and ran. He bolted down the slippery passage, turning left and right wherever it dictated. Breaking from the alleyway and into the open street, he passed a shoe shiner who had been lured by the commotion and snatched the boy's bottle of polish from his hand as he ran past. In one motion he turned and hurled it as hard he as could at the falcon as it glided toward him. Tom had played a few seasons of baseball as a kid, back when he was Tom and not Alexei the impoverished factory hand, and though he hadn't been a strong pitcher as a child, this time he found his mark. He struck the falcon square in the face, sending it cannoning into the nearest wall and its immediate death.

An official who happened to see the whole thing unfold was more than happy to arrest Tom for the cold-blooded murder of Stalin's pet falcon and hand him over to the great Soviet State in shackles.

They transferred him to this location and that, bundled into car after car, until he was finally taken through the gates of the Kremlin and roughly shoved towards a side entrance, down some steps and through a worn iron door. Expecting torture, he put up a fight, the Alexei in him getting a few good blows on the guards tasked with delivering him.

A KGB officer halted their advance. Whispers were exchanged and his thuggish captors abruptly changed tack. Instead of going further down the dark torture maze into a grim final room, they took him upstairs, through the halls of the Kremlin and into the office of Comrade Stalin himself.

Stalin was cleaning a gun. He stopped when he saw Tom.

"Tom, is that you?"

Tom recognised the voice, but couldn't put a soul to it...

"It's good to see you, comrade! It's me—Napoleon!"

***

Napoleon was splendidly surprised to be reunited with his comrade from their days as pigs at Manor Farm. He motioned to the gun in his hand. "I was cleaning this gun *for you*, matter of fact. I haven't personally executed anyone in months." He opened up a box and produced two cigars.

Tom accepted the fat cigar and stood awkwardly as he sucked in the air and choked and coughed and spluttered away. "Are the workers on the bleacher all right? Are my friends OK?" he asked after his coughing fit.

Napoleon shrugged this off. "Oh, don't worry about them, all replaceable. What I was really upset about was my falcon."

"I'm sorry I killed your bird, I didn't mean to, it just scared me," he said between a few more coughs.

Napoleon pursed his lips and looked off to the window. "Her name was Cedna. She was a dear friend of mine... Tell me, was she able to sing the chant in time?"

The stare that followed incinerated Tom's soul. Tom gulped.

Honesty was a terrific virtue to be valued above all others, and Tom noted to himself that this was another virtue, like his vegetarianism, that he needed to continue developing in his future lives. However, in this particular instance, lying to a dictator with a gun in his hand seemed by far the better option. "Yes, she was very accepting of my apology and we sang the chant together. A beautiful voice. Quite a touching moment, actually." He sucked on the cigar again, hands shaking, and launched into another coughing fit.

"So, how have you been?" asked Napoleon.

"I've been working in one of your factories—Ulmesh Arms."

"Ah yes, that's why you were at the parade today! You're doing some wonderful things for the State. It's great stuff. Terrific work. Any lovers on the horizon?"

Tom hesitated and Napoleon waved off this reticence. "Oh, you can tell me, we ate from the same trough for heaven's sake! Don't you remember, comrade?"

"Yes. You're quite right. There is one, in fact, Natalia—we both work at Ulmesh."

Napoleon squinted. Tom seemed young, but the tolls of his labour made him appear grizzled beyond his years. "Are you married? How old are you in this strong body?"

"No. Alexei, the person who I am now, is only fifteen years old."

"Too young to marry then, but maybe we can make an exception..." Napoleon raised an eyebrow candidly.

Sensing a chance at a better life, Tom tested the waters of this change in temperature. "We're on a waiting list for one of the eastern tower blocks..."

"Consider it done." Napoleon clasped his hands together, like he was performing a magic deed, whereby some other unlucky folk were to be scratched from the list and threatened with re-education if they dared to complain. "And what about your other lives, what have you been up to since those capitalist bastards took us to the slaughterhouse?"

"Not much really. This and that. Actually, do you mind if I sit down? I think I'm a little weak from all that has happened today."

"Of course! In fact—are you hungry?"

Napoleon took Tom on a guided tour through the Kremlin, brushing off requests for attention from several ministry heads, and eventually the pair arrived at his private dining quarters. A veritable smorgasbord was offered to Tom on a long table: fish, beef, chicken and goat. Pork was noticeably absent.

Tom hadn't eaten a satisfying meal for at least the last year. The factory mostly provided watery stews and cheap vodka. Tom wished Natalia were here to partake in the feast. His vegetarianism had slackened in light of the harshness of his daily life, and if he'd had the chance, he probably would've eaten Stalin's falcon, feet and all.

Just before his salivation swept him into madness, Tom realised that this may be a test—Hitler was a known vegetarian, Napoleon could be too.

Napoleon noticed his reluctance and grew defensive. "Do you think I'm a monster for offering these foods?"

Tom shook his head profusely, though the fear in his eyes gave away his lie.

"Have you been a fish?"

"Yes, a salmon. Twice."

"A cow?"

"Yes, before I went mad. I was a British cow."

Napoleon strained at the British reference. "Just as bad as the

Americans... Of course you've been a chicken—who hasn't? What about a goat then?"

Tom shook his head.

"Looks like we have a winner," Napoleon clapped his hands together. "Please, try some of the cabernet. It's from Georgia."

Tom ate the goat with guilty pleasure while Napoleon regaled him with the propaganda of the day, how the five-year plan was bringing all Soviets closer to their dream of a socialist utopia. Tom nodded politely at each political point and once he cleaned his plate, thoroughly satiated in body if not mind, Napoleon asked him if the feast had been up to scratch.

"It was delicious, thank you. I'm trying to be a vegetarian, but I don't seem to be doing too well—maybe in the next life... I notice you didn't have any pork on offer."

Napoleon shuddered and Tom immediately regretted his comment. A remark like that might have been enough to send anyone else to the gulags.

"We've banned it in the Kremlin," said Napoleon, exercising considerable restraint. "I tried to ban it elsewhere, but the people were so hungry it might've caused an uprising. Concessions had to be made. We give our hooved brethren the finest slops from the largest troughs, though. They deserve it for their sacrifice."

The servants entered and cleared the table. Napoleon offered a fresh cigar and Tom dutifully accepted it. Napoleon's shoulders stiffened and he leaned in close, the aroma of cigar smoke and wine heavy on his breath.

"Tom, I want the truth. Did you purposefully stop me from rallying our hooved brethren and taking over the farm?"

Tom gulped and Napoleon continued before he could formulate an answer.

"Because if you tell me no, and it comes to pass that I later find out you were lying to me, I will be very disappointed in you, and I will not hesitate in utilising the power of the entire Soviet Army to blow your brains out before you can even think about chanting. Now, tell me, did you shy me away from my revolutionary plans?" He glowered, every bristle in his moustache flaring outward, and Tom felt as though he was about to pass out. He gripped the armrests of his chair for support. He gulped again and cast his eyes straight down at the table.

"An old-timer chicken told me not to overthrow humanity whenever I was an animal. I didn't want to rock the boat."

Napoleon didn't appear to take this confession well and Tom realised this probably also wasn't the best time to practise the virtue of honesty. Napoleon scratched at his famous moustache and banged the table with his fist. He took several manic puffs of his cigar and exhaled a large plume of smoke, and, hopefully for Tom's sake, all his fury.

"Well, it mustn't have been easy admitting that, and I'll always be grateful that you told me the truth, though sometimes such knowledge can be cruel."

"So you're not going to execute me?"

Napoleon laughed. "Of course not! Not unless you betray me again. *I won't stand for it again, comrade.*"

Tom breathed a sigh of the deepest relief, as invigorating as the summer rain reviving his parched roots when he was a tree.

"Tom, there's something else I must share with you. Cedna, my late falcon friend, informed me of your troubles with other, rather forthright, reincarnation rememberers. They've set up some kind of union against you. Have you heard about this?"

Tom's head dropped. "Yes."

"They said that there would be a generous karmic reward for anyone who joined their ranks and killed you, on the condition that you're first given the opportunity to forgo your memories.

"That sounds about right…"

"Well, let's just see them try any of that shit here, comrade." Napoleon grinned. "They want war against a good friend of mine? Let's see how they fare against the might of the Soviet Army! What do you say?"

Tom had tightened up and remained uneasy. Napoleon asked what was wrong, even though deep down he knew the cause. That despite Tom's bitter circumstances as a lowly cog in the Russian war machine, he still knew that accepting the help of a dictator would not be looked upon favourably in a karmic sense.

Napoleon sighed and glugged down more of his Georgian wine. "They see me as a monster, Tom. Maybe I am. But this is the life I was given, and I will see my vision through to the end. History will judge me. And then I'll try a different way in my next life… Maybe I'll be a woman. Have you ever been a woman before?"

Tom scratched his head. "I've been a hen and a cow—"

"No, I mean a human woman."

"Ah. Then no."

"There are some excellent ballet dancers at the Moscow theatre. I watch them whenever I get the chance, and I've completely fallen in love with their grace, their beauty. Sometimes I think it'd be exquisite to exude this kind of energy. A nice change for another life, wouldn't you say?"

"Absolutely."

Napoleon stood and walked over to Tom. He placed a firm hand on Tom's shoulder. "You can relax now. You won't have to worry about a thing. You and your lover will be protected. This tyrannic Sal and his CARROTA will be no match for our superior Soviet weaponry."

As Napoleon escorted Tom through the Kremlin, organising Tom's newly assigned security detail and a suitable apartment to raise a family unit with Natalia, Tom found his shoulders relaxing. Maybe this really was a brand-new beginning.

Outside the Kremlin, he was introduced to his new guards, all heavily armed and fierce to their bones.

Napoleon shook hands with Tom. "We'll find a doctor for that cough and then you and your future wife can accompany me to the ballet. It will be fantastic. I will speak with the dancers myself to make sure it is the most excellent production."

Tom thanked Napoleon and was asked to sit in the back seat of a sleek black ZIL-115 armoured car, the top of the line, where he would be taken back to the factory to heroically complete his shift and then make arrangements for his new life with Natalia.

As Tom and his trailing security detail exited from a rear entrance gate of the Kremlin, the ZIL-115 was T-boned by an armoured truck.

Tom's driver was immediately killed and Tom's ribs were shattered in the crash. Pinned in the car, all he could do was manage a brief sigh as he watched a formidable brown bear, a grey wolf, a Siberian tiger, and a woman he recognised as once being Rudiger the horse, roll out of the back of the armoured truck, baring teeth and carrying Kalashnikovs. Nowhere was beyond Sal's reach, apparently. Natalia had never believed his tales of reincarnation, but he hoped that one day she would.

WAR

Tom was not the first reincarnated soul to have a lives-long vendetta held against him, but this did not make him feel like the attention he received was any less special.

The following thirty-two lives were to be a troublesome time for Tom and his recollections of these lives were sparse. If it wasn't a gruesome death from one of Sal's CARROTA (CARROT agents) or Sal himself, then it was at the brutally efficient hands of Mother Nature. What hurt Tom most was the possibility of a safe future being taken away the moment it presented itself. If he wasn't safe with the support of a despot, where and when could he find reasonable respite from this universal madness?

These live were brief, but this was war, and in war, the briefer the better.

Chicken XII

From now on, unless anything of significance occurred while being a chicken, only the time of death and length of survival will be noted.

Time of death: (12/2/2003) one year, eight days.

Chicken XIII

Oh, for God's sake.

Time of death: (12/1/2043) eleven months, six days.

Tapir

A tapir in the Amazon! While being a tapir was nothing to brag about, the Amazon rainforest was another destination on his original bucket list and Tom was far from disappointed to find himself occupying the forest floor. High in the canopy, howler monkeys screeched and colourful parrots argued with colourful language amid what appeared to be the animal kingdom's version of New York City.

Tom's time in the Amazon was short-lived however, as a large, psychedelic anaconda had the evident pleasure of eating him. The anaconda sang him lullabies as it crushed all his bones and swallowed him whole. The anaconda was not affiliated with the CARROTA, but she seemed happy to help.

Brontosaurus

Cue the swelling orchestral music that first time Dr Alan Grant rises from the jeep to behold the most amazing computer-generated creatures mid-'90s filmmaking could conjure.

Cue the child in Tom squealing with joy at the thought of stomping around on the ground as a thunder lizard, a la *Jurassic Park*.

Cue the mathematical inquisition into how long he had before an asteroid cancelled out the sky.

Cue the jubilation at realising that his species went extinct at the end of the Jurassic and were in no harm of suffering the painful end of the world.

Cue the eating of vegetation, and further joyous stomping of feet at the realisation he was once more a herbivore.

Cue the realisation that the other Brontosauruses were not Tom's kind of dinosaurs, attitude-wise. They simply weren't as thrilled as he was to be a dinosaur, taking it all in their not-inconsiderable stride.

Cue the surprise fatal attack from a pair of Allosauruses; Tenazz and Quartz-like in their arguing over who got what.

Cue Tom's dying wish to be a Tyrannosaurus Rex the next time he found himself kicking around in dinosaur times. Vegetarian or not, at least he was less likely to be gruesomely disembowelled.

Huntsman Spider

What has eight eyes and now lived in an Australian share house?

Tom had always wanted to visit Australia, and this was his first time Down Under. He knew he was in Australia, because for one, it was stinking hot; two, he was bloody large; three, a kookaburra told him so; and four, the accent of his human housemates was unmistakable: "Ah fuck, it's a huntsman. Get ya thong and we'll squash the cunt." Once more, they weren't a part of Sal's CARRO-TA. Just typical Aussies, and the end result the same.

Mosquito

He came to life during a bombing run on a South-East Asian hospital. His squadron dove through a hole in the ward's netting and quickly spread out. The fans were on to combat the oppressive heat, but they kept their squad in formation and quickly identified the least resistant target: an elderly man, lying in bed, sleeping soundly, his neck exposed.

The formation hummed "Ride of the Valkyries" and Tom was impressed that Wagner's composition had permeated mosquito culture. Tom tried to back away at the last minute—he knew he must've been carrying malaria or something equally ghastly, but the allure of sweet blood overcame him once the others had landed and inserted their thirsty proboscises like drinking straws.

He buzzed over and landed on the old man's neck, piercing the skin around where his friend Bzz had been moments before. He dug in and greedily sucked away, the blood like a champion hit of heroin, far better than any orgasm he'd ever had as a human.

The man was awake by this stage, and when Tom noticed the looming shadow of a hand coming down on his position, he thought to himself in post-orgasmic bliss, "Worth it."

Daba dee daba daaaaaa.

Sunflower

He was in a meadow of seemingly constant sunshine. His friends were nice. He felt some lingering shame about his ravenous turn as a mosquito and his friends were supportive, albeit no less confused by his stories of past lives than Natalia had been. This was one quiet week of relief. Then Sal's friend Deborah, as she was becoming rather adept at, came waltzing through the sunflower field with her whirling Tom Tracker and another jerry can of petrol.

"Hiya, Tom."

Hi, Deb. Petrol can a bit much, isn't it? Secateurs would have sufficed.

"Don't tell me how to do my job!"

Ah well, thought Tom, *it was a nice change of pace while it lasted.*

Ibex

An ibex is a type of mountain goat. They are mainly known for climbing the vertical-drop sides of mountains to suck on the precious minerals embedded in the rock. Tom did not know this. What Tom did know was that despite his longstanding dream of being a soaring bird, he was in fact deathly afraid of heights. Tom was also unprepared for the fact that younglings such as himself were afforded only three weeks of play before they were expected to make their first trip down the arid mountain for food.

"No fucking way," said Tom.

"It's fine, our hooves are made for this kind of terrain."

"It's a three-hundred-foot drop to the bottom of the gorge!"

"What does 'three-hundred-foot drop' mean?"

Tom sighed. "Never mind."

Instincts were a key component in making it as an ibex. There could be no room for doubt. Unfortunately, Tom was full of the stuff, and halfway down the gorge, against a stunning backdrop of sunset and aeons-quiet mountains, his doubt got the better of him. One loose rock quickly translated into four loose spindly limbs, flailing like something out of a Looney Tunes cartoon. This was the first time he flew. Hopefully the next time, he'd manage an upward trajectory.

Monkey

He awoke in the ruins of a Buddhist temple. Chaos was the order of the day in this monkey city. He was part of a gang that pilfered food from tourists, and tourists' food from other monkeys, but Tom wanted no part of their, ahem, monkey business. He was beset by a depressive mood carrying over from his past few short lives. He tried to meditate through this situation, much like the Buddhist builders of his present locale had been wont to do, but his search for enlightenment only led to horrific recollections of the past. He would routinely shriek and bite tourists and this was far from an ideal situation for the tour operators who sought to maintain a peaceful venture.

Rather than put him down, they sold him off to another human who walked the streets. This human chained him up, forcibly defanged him with pliers, and prodded him to do tricks for tourists on the beach strip. Strangely, the chains calmed Tom more than his search for enlightenment. Resignation seemed a better remedy for these dark times.

One day, he intervened in his handler's social game of checkers with the man who sold them fruit. Both were gobsmacked to find a mere monkey could so promptly grasp the intricacies of the game. Capitalising on this fortuitous turn of events, the handler wielded Tom's expertise on unsuspecting passers-by, hustling tourists and locals alike until one of Sal's CARROTA poisoned Tom with a strychnine-laced cracker.

"This is from Sal. Say goodbye to your checkers career."

Tom sighed. The chains weren't ideal, but the tropics were nice and dumbfounding hapless humans never lost its satisfying punch.

Human III

A war within a war.

He awoke to mud and remembered his family back in Manchuria. The trench was cold and filled to the brim with grim faces. They were preparing to go over the top and capture the next parallel on the peninsula.

The Americans were on the other side. What it was to be hit with the immense history of his current culture and that of his old culture.

Hours before they were to charge, prayers flying up to the sky, Tom caught the thoughts of his commanding officer, who locked eyes with Tom in recognition. The officer's sneer confirmed there would be no reprieve, even in light of larger conflict. What a special pleasure, facing gunfire from enemies that used to be his countrymen, while his own commanding officer prepared to commit friendly fire from behind.

When the whistle blew, Tom, or little monkey, as his wife used as a pet name, rose from the shallow trench and ran, leaving his gun behind, as fast as he could through the intense hail of gunfire, screaming a peculiar chant the Americans took as a war cry and his commanding officer used as a homing beacon.

Who knows which bullet claimed Tom? Returned him to the slop of the earth. The Americans had a dead communist; the Chinese had a brave attacker, and Tom had a fast exit from his war within a war.

Emperor Penguin

Once again, a bird that couldn't fly.

Being a waddling emperor of Antarctica got old and cold real quick. Nothing but frost and blank whiteness for miles. He preferred Antarctica from the comfort of a couch, with the soothing narration of David Attenborough guiding him through. Given the circumstances, the other penguins were fairly enjoyable company, the gossip engrossing, but over time Tom felt alone with his knowledge of places significantly warmer than here.

Tom was eaten by a polar bear nineteen and a half weeks in, despite the fact that polar bears don't live in Antarctica.

Was there no one closer? Tom asked when his assassin rolled up on a floating chunk of ice. The polar bear nodded his cute black nose. *Oh sure, but I said I had this one. Needed a break from the Arctic.*

Quite a journey, remarked Tom.

Yes, it was, concurred the polar bear, having scared off all the other emperor penguins.

Maybe you want to tell me about your travels? Tom stalled, glancing around for any incline in the ice he could power slide to safety down, staving off the inevitable.

Maybe some other time, said the polar bear, as his jaw lowered to reveal his salivating incisors.

Wolf

A run-in with a *National Geographic* documentary team ended with the photographer capturing an amazing, career-defining shot of Tom facing off against him, the spirit of the Canadian wild epitomised in snowy white fur and a dauntless stare that encapsulated all that was eternal and untameable. The photographer would later go onto win several industry awards for his work, and *The Cold Eyes of Nature's Indifference* went a long way to getting him over the line.

Tom thought if this war against him were to dissipate and he could go back to living without fear, then maybe he'd like to become a nature photographer and take portraits of his friends.

He was killed a week after his "Cold Eyes" spread came to publication. Deborah and Rudiger were a moose and a Canadian pilot in a Canadian fighter jet, respectively.

Rhinoceros

He asked his friend if they were the extinct kind. "Not yet," said his friend. They were somewhere in Africa, in the open plains, hopefully a nature park far removed from the threat of poachers. Tom wondered if there were rangers assigned to protect him. He'd seen them on the internet before, surrounding one of the last northern white rhinos. He checked his skin against the reflection of a depleted watering hole. Despite his poor vision, a passing antelope confirmed it was grey and Tom was pleasantly relieved. (What he didn't realise was that the southern white rhinos had grey skin and were in a similarly dire situation to that of their northern counterparts.)

His rhino friend, who was a female and one of the very few rhinos he'd encountered in the drought-stricken land, was quietly attractive in terms of rump size. They soberly agreed to mate for the survival of their species. The big day finally arrived and the girl got cold feet. She wondered if it was worth bringing a young buck into this cruel world. Tom, horny, disagreed. The world wasn't all that bad, surely, all things considered?

She recited a poem that had been making its way around the watering hole and even caused a lion to weep. It was the tale of one of the last northern white rhinos, who also happened to be a renowned poet:

Here I am

The last of my kind

Speaking at the RN (the UN for rhinos)

But how am I to know if I am the last one?

Where is my census tally?

Rhinoceros

I wander through the Serengeti
I see the baboons and lions
Lions can be real jerks
So I push on

I cross the river
And see buxom bodies
Would you like to mate?
I say in my most eloquent fashion
We are hippos, they say
Fuck off, being their inference.
I wander further
Through the plains
I see long-neck creatures
Eating leaves I cannot reach
Are you possibly rhinos? I ask, this time terribly uncertain.
No. We are giraffes. We eat leaves that you cannot reach.
We also look different to you, idiot.
How was I to know?

They took my mother very early
I barely remember
A long stick went bang
And Mum went quiet
What am I supposed to do, Mum?
But Mum didn't answer
So I ran.
They took her horn
No idea why
Must be for a good reason though, right?

93

<u>Rhinoceros</u>

Maybe I'm alone
Maybe I'm the last one
Maybe I don't have a purpose anymore.
Maybe they'll put me out of my misery.
Maybe...

I see meerkats.
Least I think I do.
They were there a second ago
Heads sticking out of the earth
I approach
But they hide
It's very lonely.

I walk up to the water
And spot my own reflection
When I smile I look good.
But I don't smile often.
A dark and scaly head rises on the surface
How about a bite? asks the crocodile.
I shake my horn. No thanks.
Aww, says the croc, what if I become your friend?
The offer is tempting,
But I eventually decline.

One day the humans return
With the long sticks that go boom
But these humans do not make me go quiet forever
They stand tall and surround me
One of them says he did bad in his life before

But now he wants to be good.
He doesn't seem to want my horn for some kind of medicine
For that I am grateful.

Together we search the land for another rhino to befriend.
But we never find her
Because the damage has already been done.
And so finally I complete my census tally
Where the number stays at one.

Tom's female friend was in tears by the end. Tom was also filled with a crushing despair, for he was not just a rhino but one of the disgraced humans of the poem too. And she was right. Life in Africa was not exotic and exciting. It was cruel. Human and animal alike were always at war. Tom and his potential wife decided not to consummate, to both their quiet relief.

They went their separate ways. Like the poor fellow in the poem, Tom wandered, and made the same amount of friends. Thirsty and alone, it felt almost merciful when he eventually came across a pride of lions and a pack of hyenas. Lions usually had the muscle over hyenas, but the great Sal himself was a hyena this time around.

"I would have thought you'd be a lion," said Tom, "given the 'I'm the infallible king of the land' moral high ground you always take."

"What's that supposed to mean? There's nothing wrong with being a hyena."

"There was in *The Lion King*."

"What's that?"

"A movie."

"When was it made?"

"Sometime in the 1990s."

"Then of course I haven't seen it. Give me a break. I've been busy trying to prevent the Second World War and supersede this incompetent Bureau of Auditors and their gross mismanagement of karma."

"You'd have more time if you stopped bothering with me."

Sal growled. His pack joined in.

"Or is hunting me where you get your kicks? Mr 'High and Mighty' addicted to revenge?"

"It's not revenge—I don't enjoy it! Shut up!"

"You're just a bully. You know who else was a bully: Hitler." Tom said smugly.

"This rhino is ours," the other lions roared, to remind the two bickering parties they were there too.

Sal shook his mangy head. "Nope. This one is ours. I have a score to settle with him."

"The score is at least 30–1 in your favour!" protested Tom, but Sal's hyena pack and the lion pride ignored him as they circled each other with maniacal cackling and guttural roars. A dusty scrap ensued, and Tom used this opportunity to lumber away.

Tom was later killed by Rudiger, who had travelled to Kenya as a safari tourist with a vengeance.

Cobra

He ate rats and lizards and each venomous bite drained a lot out of the tank. He snaked his way through the dirt among the long grass and fallen leaves. He recalled the story of Genesis, how God punished the snake by removing its limbs and forcing it to crawl across the earth in shame.

He was a solitary creature and the simplicity was nice. One day though, the weight of a foot on his tail caught him off-guard. The girl looked no older than ten, a shade under Anna's age, and Tom would never forget her screech or the sudden taste of her cocoa skin.

She dropped to the floor in shock and screamed for her brother. Tom was equally in shock. Where had she come from? The girl shuffled away in agony. Tom didn't know what to do. What snakebite first-aid training had he done in any of his previous lives? Should he try suck the venom out, or would that be misconstrued as a second attempt?

Sighing (or hissing, as it came out) Tom decided that staying with the child was the best course of action—maybe his being there would help them select the correct anti-venom, if there was a clinic close enough that could help the girl in time.

There was rustling through the trees, and to Tom's surprise the tall man with the wispy moustache and the clipboard appeared again, his formal office attire very much out of place in the jungle. The girl did not notice him, and Tom realised once again that the Auditor was invisible to others. The Auditor took one look at the girl and began scribbling away furiously on his clipboard. *She's only a child, for karma's sake!*

"It was an accident," Tom protested, and his unintentional hissing made the girl scream once more in fear.

And yet you used venom. Quite a lot, by the looks of things.

That was instinct! How do I help her? Tom pleaded.

The Auditor didn't even glance up from his clipboard. *Every time I drop in to check on you, you're destroying some poor girl's life. You can't save her. You can't even save yourself. Her brother is too far away. He'll never hear her, or reach her in time.*

"Where is her brother?" Tom hissed again. "Please, tell me!"

The Auditor looked up and regarded the girl, who had stopped crawling away because the neurotoxicity of Tom's venom was paralysing her muscles in preparation for certain death. She was rasping in pain and terror, and Tom felt the vibrations of her stilted heartbeat. He turned once more to the Auditor.

Please, tell me where her brother is!

We Auditors do not interfere. We merely observe.

You made a deal with Sal to let him kill me over and over! He's got carte blanche! How is that not interference?

I simply told him I'd stay out of it.

"What's the point of you?" hissed Tom, burying his hood into the ground in frustration. *No wonder this world is broken, the creatures running it are a bunch of indifferent jerkwads.*

And as he buried his head into the ground, he heard the vibration of faint shouting, a brother looking for his sister in the forest. Thinking quickly, he slithered over to the girl and the sight of him caused her eyes to well up in fear. She couldn't move even if she wanted to. Tom slithered up to her armpit and carefully opened his mouth. The girl squirmed, though little sound escaped her. She was fading. Tom bit down hard and tore off a piece of her T-shirt, then dug his head into the dirt floor and waited for the brother to call out once more. When he did, Tom was off, snaking through the trees and long grass, faster than he'd ever slithered before. The Auditor strolled behind him, quietly taking notes.

When the brother heard the hiss, he turned around and picked up a stick. The boy was barely older than his sister. There were tears and mucus dripping down his face. Tom approached cautiously, the fabric of the girl's shirt still in his mouth, and like a dog with a ball, he dropped the fabric near the boy's feet. The boy recognised it immediately. Tom swivelled his head and bobbed it in the girl's direction. He turned back to find the boy had picked up the fabric with his stick to examine it. Tom swivelled his head back to the direction of the girl and threw his head back and forth violently in her direction. The boy said something that Tom did not understand, so he slowly slithered off in the direction of the girl, turning back and doing his best to beckon (without arms) before the grass grew long. The boy followed, hesitant at first, his stick raised the entire time. He said something else. Tom knew three different human languages, but Bangladeshi wasn't one of them.

Tom sighed. *Here goes nothing.* He slowly slithered into the grass and felt the vibrations of following feet behind him.

The boy leapt over Tom when they finally reached the clearing where his sister lay unconscious. The boy picked her up in his arms, looked back at Tom, uttered a few words of thanks and then bolted off.

Tom's head drooped to the ground, exhausted, but relieved.

The feet of the Auditor came into view. He knelt down next to Tom. *Impressive. I didn't think you had it in you.*

Will you tell Sal to call off his war now? Tom rasped.

The Auditor laughed. *Oh, absolutely not.*

Can I at least be a bird capable of flight next time?

You're not in any position to be making such requests. Do another thousand great deeds and maybe we'll talk—Ah, here come your friends now.

Tom bobbed up. He didn't have any friends in the Bangladeshi jungle. He didn't really have any real friends anywhere, as far as he could remember. *He's over here!* the Auditor yelled (another impartial observation), and through the long grass came a honey badger closely trailed by a swarm of rats. Tom had no venom left.

This is from Sal, said the honey badger.

Tell him I said thanks, Tom muttered.

Daba dee daba daa.

Chicken XIV

862 eggs, a personal record.

2 malnourished, useless legs.

142 consecutive nightmares.

One Sunday dinner.

Daba dee daba daa.

Pigeon

Could it be? Had his wish to be a flying bird come true?

He was on a building ledge. Opposite him, tall and radiant, the Empire State Building. Evaporated air spewed from roof vents, coiling upwards like thick plumes of cigarette smoke. Horns honked, traffic lights blinked, and a cacophony of heavy construction pounded and screeched away below. A never-ending engine of grimy, leaky progress. He was home.

He peeked over the edge. Directly below was a hundred-foot drop to the pedestrian-filled pavement. He extended his wings. He flapped once, twice, until he lost touch of the ledge and was hovering over it. He flapped some more and went a little higher. "I'm flying!" he trilled. "I'm actually doing it!"

"Congratulations," said his sardonic friend, Raquelle, landing on the edge beneath him. "Now what?"

"Let's fly around the city!" he exclaimed, returning to the ledge by Raquelle's side, his wings still fluttering with excitement. "We'll go downtown! We'll fly to the Statue of Liberty! And we'll decorate her as only we pigeons can!"

"Since when did you become such a tourist?" remarked Raquelle. "I visit my cousins in Brooklyn for a couple days and you've lost the plot."

"I'm just—I'm so excited! We have so much to do before they come!"

"Who are *they*? You mean the Pest Service?"

Tom flapped off the question. "Never mind! I've never felt so alive. It's been so long! I'm going on a tour with or without you, Raquelle. Up to you." Tom slouched down against the edge, the adrenaline of his past fear of heights filling him with life, urging him to let go, dive in between buildings and soar through the muggy New York air.

"Can we at least go to the park to get lunch before you go off on your little adventure?"

"Central Park?" asked Tom.

Raquelle squinted her eyes and pecked him on the top of his skull. "Did you sleep in a fume shooter while I was away?"

"No! Let's go to the park—we'll have to fly there!"

Raquelle stepped back. "Who are you, and what have you done to Maurice?"

Tom had never been to Central Park as a pigeon before. The park embodied a peculiar contradiction of being both a lot bigger than he remembered and a lot smaller, given his new means of travel. He flew through the trees, diving and gliding with glee while Raquelle picked at the seed Manuel the retiree fed to her and twenty other pigeons of various colours and gangs. Tom joined her after unloading on home base at one of the baseball fields. "This is awesome!"

"You going to eat something, Maurice?"

"Fine." Tom nibbled on the birdseed. It was as expected. Mere sustenance. This did not bother him. This was a life for flying, not missing a New York slice. Besides, every pizzeria had a bin. "Can we go to the Statue of Liberty now, please?"

The trip over the Hudson was tiring, the distance further than expected. Tom regretted he hadn't eaten more. They spiralled up the green lady and Tom perched on her head. He cooed and pooed with joy and Raquelle nudged him. "Happy now?"

He turned his head for his good eye and bobbed for depth perception, the shimmering horizon of the city skyline drawn into sharp focus, the Twin Towers still standing tall. "Yes," he chirped.

The days were simply good again, as Tom relished his chance to be a high flyer in his home city. He swooped along every avenue and stole meals with Raquelle on every corner he could. He soon learned it was 1987. Hip-hop blared from boom boxes on tenement stoops. People wore tight, flashy attire; high-tops and teased hair tied with scrunchies were in vogue, men were not afraid to wear shoulder pads, and hairspray sales were at an all-time high. The movie *Predator* had just come out, Reagan was still in office, and it appeared Stalin's bellicose posturing hadn't yet sent the cold war hot. New York was more grime than glamour, the sterility of Giuliani's zero tolerance still years away. Lily wasn't even born yet, and his parents were still living in Chicago, though he intended on visiting them sometime. Tom ventured to all his old haunts and Raquelle asked him to explain their significance. This was the supermarket where he used to get his lonely microwave dinners, this was where he got his mediocre haircut that disguised his balding, this was the bar he and his friends Paul and Chris R (the human equivalents of Tenazz and Quartz) used to frequent, unsuccessfully trying to pick up women. This was where he used to work; in a dull office building, wasting his life away on dry claims assessments and menial reports, pining after the girl of his dreams. Raquelle, for her part, was often left wondering what they were doing gazing at a rundown apartment block or dive bar and what exactly in the hell Maurice meant by, "when I was a human…"

Raquelle may not have believed his stories, but for Tom, seeing his past again, even one that hadn't arrived yet, brought back his true sense of self. It reminded him of his hopes and dreams, the dreams he'd let wither as he struggled to keep his head above water and also connected to the rest of his body. He had to get back on some kind of path; he needed a purpose again, and there was one face he remembered as clear as day: that of Lily White. She was the inspiration he needed to be a better person—someone who was brave, selfless; not cowardly and selfish. The sort of person she deserved and that Tom owed it to himself to be. How much was that to ask? He brushed aside any nagging doubts and told himself this was something he needed to work towards.

Sal's war wasn't right. Tom had paid for his mistake and then some. He realised he needed to fight back and argue his case for clemency, even if he wasn't sure yet how exactly he would go about doing that.

***

There was one place Tom had not visited from his past life, despite it being the catalyst to his suffering of indefinitely short second chances. Buildings had risen, businesses had fallen, but the little head shop full of crystals, dreamcatchers and "water pipes" had inexplicably stood the test of time. Of all the places he visited it was practically the only thing left perfectly intact. This only furthered its mystical quality. Tom was alone when he perched atop the rooftop opposite, scanning it for danger as he worked up the courage to enter.

Sometime during the human lunch hour, he recognised a woman who entered the shop. She wore almost the same thing as the tall male Auditor—a light striped white shirt and khakis, with a clipboard ready to be scribbled on. When she exited, Tom checked to see if other humans saw her, but no one seemed to pay her any mind. (To be fair, it was New York, where interactions with strangers were not encouraged unless you were in the mood for letting off steam.)

There was something else about the woman he could not place. He'd always recognised a fellow reincarnation remember-er, even if he'd never met them before, but he got the strange feeling he *had* met this woman. And it was a she, not just outside but in. Who had he encountered in his wanderings that could be said to possess a feminine soul?

He resolved to follow her. Investigating the head shop could wait. He bobbed along the power line overhead as she walked down the street. Every so often, she'd stop and look up at the sky, clear joy in her eyes. A person walked directly through her, and even from afar Tom felt that person receive the goosebumps of a nice warm memory. The young woman, her short hair a light brown, turned the corner outside a diner and Tom swooped across the street, narrowly avoiding a moving truck coming the other way.

Coming to rest on the edge of the nearest rooftop, he peered below to watch her shimmer out of existence, her absence in this world completed with a passing cloud that blocked out the sun. Tom cursed his cowardice—he should've at least asked her who she was. She looked more angel than Auditor. Disappointed, Tom flew off to find Raquelle and binge on some leftovers from his favourite dumpster. The head shop wasn't going anywhere.

***

Tom returned to the bong bodega the next day, after his morning poop on some local statues and a Manhattanite who had treated a taxi driver poorly, Tom not averse to dishing out his own brand of karma when the opportunity arose.

Once more he scoped the place out, did a little waddle past and no one was the wiser. He waited until the store was empty before sneaking into the dimly-lit den. Little had changed since his last fateful experience. The place didn't even look newer. Sticky purple carpet lined the floor with glass shelves holding glass "vases", while dreamcatchers hung from spinning racks either side of the front counter. Pungent incense and its accompanying smoke imbued a dreamy haze throughout. The fact that a den like this hadn't been shut down by police was another layer of mystery in its history.

Tom instantly recognised the blonde, middle-aged lady at the counter. She was the guy who gave him the gift that kept on giving. She was off in a daze, but when Tom cooed she snapped awake.

"Oh hey, man! Coming in to buy something?"

Do you remember me? Tom asked in telepathic thought, hopeful she understood.

"Can't say I do. Were you a French jazz musician 24 years ago, man?"

No, though that does sound like a fun life.

"Ah, sorry, man." She scratched at her head. "Were you that real estate mogul guy?"

I'm from the year 2019, but the more I think about it, which is only now, I wonder if it's in your past or your future? Because it's in my past...but it's also the future from now.

The lady laughed like a pig snorting. Tom had a flash of the trough from his pig days and got hungry. "Oh, that whole time jumble thing! I got confused sometime way back in the future and decided it was best to just go with the flow. I think I've been around long enough to know it's something you don't bother getting worked up about."

Tom flew up onto one of the glass casings, above the smoking instruments labelled "Premium Peace". *How long have you been around for?*

"Oh, about eight hundred earth years or so. Different times in history, of course, but in this century, I always seem to be running this store. It's been nice, having a home like this."

How long have you been in this store?

"About 102 years now, from 1963 until I accidentally destroy it in 2053." That didn't quite add up correctly, Tom realised, but it made sense she was incorrect, her brain probably scrambled from too many years and lives (and maybe one too many hits of the Mary Jane). Tom got quiet for a moment while the lady served a paranoid customer who couldn't stop staring at him.

The meeting was a disappointment. This space cadet was not going to be any help to him. She was just a fellow traveller, content with being content—a simple thing that Tom could never achieve until he resolved this dispute with Sal. Tom sighed, and the lady told him out loud not to worry, which made the teetering customer rethink his purchase and mumble an apology before making a quick and awkward exit.

Sorry, Tom cooed, and the lady shrugged. "Ah, easy come, easy go. You hungry?"

***

Tom was treated to a whole pepperoni pizza slice, without the usual accompanying hint of bin juice and cigarette ash. Instead, it was just beautiful, regular grease. And sure, maybe he should have asked for something vegetarian—he definitely should have—but the first chance to eat his favourite pizza fresh in over a century was too much temptation for him to bear. *Sorry, Napoleon*, he said to himself. *Sorry...* he continued, before realising he'd forgotten the names of his cow friends who may or may not have been infected with mad cow disease.

Each nibble was like a slice of heaven. He hadn't felt satiated like that since he was a mosquito. He pecked away contentedly at the melted cheese and pepperoni he was originally so conflicted about, vowing to bring the rest back to Raquelle and the other pigeons.

"You take as much as you can carry, dude. I can get you more anytime." The shopkeeper grinned.

"Do you know many others like me, living in the city?"

"Why yeah, sure! There's Austin the dog—he comes by whenever his owner takes him for walks. There's Chauncey the cat, a slew of Wall Street types and a few policemen. In fact, there should be even more coming in this weekend—"

What about a girl? Tom interrupted. *She wears khakis and carries a clipboard. I think she's an Auditor. She was here yesterday.*

The lady's eyes lit up. "Oh yeah, her! She's in town checking-in before the big rally this weekend."

Huh? What rally?

"Yeah, like I was saying, some peace-loving, far-out musician dude started spreading the reincarnation chant across America a few years ago. Most think he's bananas, but he's got himself a growing following. Revolutionary with a guitar. And that voice, deeper than the ocean but sends you to heaven—ooh la la! Even managed to close off part of E.14th street. Not a large part, mind you. But I hear there could be a few thousand coming in, that's what William was telling me."

Is William the woman's name?

"Oh, no. William is a postman."

What's the girl's name!? The one with the clipboard! Tom shouted in frustration, not that this fazed the bong shop guardian.

"Oh...um, tell you the truth, I kind of forgot." The lady spoke aloud, and a wandering customer gave her a funny look.

Is she going to be at the rally?

"I'd think so."

Tom's hope surged like an overblown light bulb. This was his chance. *This weekend, you say?*

"Yeah!" She grinned another unwitting grin. If Tom had more time, he would have noted it was an adorable grin, warming and genuine.

Thanks! Tom flapped his wings and took off, bursting out the front door, cutting off another customer coming in.

This weekend, it could all change. He could talk to the Auditor with the clipboard and argue his case, maybe try to figure out another way of fighting Sal—what if the other Auditor was wrong about appeals not being a possibility?

This weekend.

But when was that? What day was today? He stopped mid-flight, feathers flying off, like he was caught by an invisible wire. He was a pigeon, he didn't keep track of days. What day was today?

He dived back into the bodega, and once again cut off the same customer.

The lady grinned. "Forget something?"

Yeah—what day is it?

"Um, oh, well, I guess it's...Saturday? Come to think of it, I'm almost sure it is."

So this weekend is today? The rally is today?

Now she was embarrassed. "You know what, it may have already started..."

***

The western section of E.14th was packed, filled to the brim with people of all nationalities and walks of life, bound by a colourful dress sense and the shared hope of breaking free from the pain of their current life and finding peace in the next. Tom could only snicker at their naïve optimism. He perched atop an apartment block rooftop for a bird's-eye view. The crowd were chanting the familiar phrase, letting it drift and echo onto surrounding streets to draw in all those angry New Yorkers beeping away on the street. *Don't they know they'll carry their anger through to the next life,* the crowd sneered haughtily among themselves before returning to chanting.

The crowd made their way slowly west along E.14th, shepherded by a placid showing of the boys in blue. Bystanders watched on in either confusion or derision. Banners with glitter writing were held aloft above the crowd:

"*My dog was Kennedy! I have proof!*"

"Our animals are our friends; we are our animals!"

"End animal cruelty! We've experienced it before!"

Tom flew from rooftop to rooftop, searching for the female Auditor in the sea of colour and confetti. But he wasn't having much luck. He glided down to an overhanging lamp post for a closer inspection. Maybe she would see him instead. He reasoned she must be on the side, doing her audits along the bystanders. He cast his eyes over to the bystanders across the street and gravitated to a pack of business executives in weekend yuppie wear, sticking out like sore thumbs, pointing and laughing and carrying on among themselves at the crowd. And who should he see in this pack of *American Psychos?* Why, none other than the old-timer chicken himself.

His eyes were the same steely blue as the first time they'd met. He wore white shorts and a pink, popped-collar polo, much more befitting his distinguished Queens inner voice (at least compared to a chicken). He was stocky and bulging around the belly, Tom presumed, from an overindulgence in the American staple of fried chicken, bacon, beef and beer. He was balding with strawberry blonde hair. Take away the douchey dress sense and bags of money and he was essentially the original human version of Tom.

When their eyes met after a prolonged death stare by Tom, the summer street between them boiled.

Don't even think about coming over here, the old-timer's bulging eyes warned. Clearly, he had not wanted to be anywhere near this circus, for fear of this exact thing.

Tom swooped over to a closer light pole and the old-timer's fuming eyes followed. His friends noticed he was no longer sharing in their derision and asked him what his deal was.

"I aint feeling well, can we just get to the bar?" said the old-timer, re-adjusting his polo, and scratching at his balding head. Neither man nor pigeon averted their stare.

The other business executives traced his line of sight over to Tom and began cracking jokes. "Do you know that bird? Is that your Aunt Zelda?"

The old-timer ignored them and Tom narrowed his eyes. *You gave me some real shitty advice a long time ago, and I've been paying for it ever since…*

I heard, said the old-timer, his eyes narrowing. *You made a lot of waves. Faltered a lot of fortunes. Seems you missed the point of my advice—to stay out of the big things, not rock the boat. How hard is that?*

Tom's head bobbed back. How dare he try to turn this around! *No, you gave me the wrong advice! This is your fault!*

Take a little responsibility for yourself Jesus. Have you learned nothing?

The old-timer's silent, angry gesturing weirded out the other executives. They suggested they all carry on with their regular party plans, and as the old-timer broke his stare Tom swooped, aiming straight for those unmistakable blue windows to the soul. As the suits froze, the old-timer turned to catch a swift peck in the eye. He swung wildly and knocked Tom in the direction of the crowd, damaging one of his wings in the process. Wincing in pain, Tom miscalculated his next few flaps and stalled like an aeroplane above the crowd before finally careening into the mass of bodies below. Before he thudded into the back of someone's head at full throttle, he realised this is what it must've been like for Stalin's falcon.

***

There were two voices, one with reverberations and microphone feedback that echoed inside his head. The other was softer, closer, more familiar. Opening one eye, he discovered he was being held in the cupped hands of a middle-aged woman who had a prominent scar running down her forehead. This was not the first time he'd been up close to this woman's face. He blinked, trying to remember. Her eyes were green like the ocean on a sunny day. The scar was deep. Makeup might have hidden it, but she clearly didn't consider it something to be ashamed of. Scars were only temporary, that's what her beaming face said.

The scar was Tom's fault and her name came back to him wrapped in guilt. A present he put off opening. Shirley the kind-hearted zookeeper.

Oh my, too many blasts from the past today.

She was gently stroking his feathers, telling him everything was going to be all right, whispering the chant of resurrection, reincarnation, certain she could somehow transfer this knowledge from human to pigeon. Tom hopped back onto his feet and startled Shirley, bumping into the person behind her. She opened her hands, expecting Tom to fly away (despite the damaged wing) but all he could do was stare and whisper apologies over and over. The longer he stared, bobbing his head, cooing, the more she realised he was unlike any other pigeon she'd ever seen. She became entranced, and the crowd streamed around her like a rock in a river.

It was a shot in the dark, what she said next, the occasion of the day prescribing second chances not as miracles, but standard operating procedure. He saw it building up in her, both the courage to believe and the years she doubted herself, and it was the most crushing thing in the world to watch her make that leap again.

"Tom, is that you?"

What could he do but coo?

Her eyes twitched. "Tom, coo four times for yes. *Please.*"

She turned her head right up to his beak and he cooed four times, slowly. There it was, a miracle.

They should have left immediately. Gone back to her place and allowed her to set up the letters like back in the zoo. Let Tom explain all the things that went wrong. Let him tell her how sorry he was. But Shirley was so swept up in the moment she had to tell everyone. Everyone had to know. The truth, right here in the middle of all the believers.

They were at the back of the crowd, most people having passed them to head closer to the stage, erected where E.14th met Fifth Avenue. The sun shone down on them as they clamoured to listen to their leader. Shirley cupped Tom carefully in her hands as she pushed through the throng, exclaiming she had to get to the front. There were roughly one hundred yards between them and the podium, and Tom was by the amount of shoulders and bodies Shirley bobbed through like a drop of water weaving down a wall. There were a few jeers, to the effect her aggressive energy was not what this parade was all about and that they'd been waiting all day to get close to the Master, and she would push Tom in their faces, like he was a feathered VIP pass.

Tom was a little thrown by her pushy behaviour, but boiled it down to her surprised vindication.

The closer they got to the front of the audience, the crisper the voice blaring from the microphone became. "Salvation is at hand, daba dee daba daa..." The voice was faintly recognisable and Tom concluded this was not a good thing. He couldn't see above the crowd and cursed that he couldn't fly up to one of the surrounding rooftops and scan for danger. He wriggled his wings to signal to Shirley his distress, but Shirley was hell-bent on making it to the stage. "No, Tom, please. It's just one small thing. We have to tell everyone. They have to know."

Another few rows of bodies and the voice got closer.

"I wasn't always a kind man, this I know..."

Tom threw up in Shirley's hand. She finally stopped. She loosened her grip and Tom stayed still. Others in the crowd who had noticed the pigeon were all looking. Tom looked at her and waddled up her right arm towards her shoulder. He then turned to see the man on the podium. They were thirty feet away at most. But the man on the podium, his beard and hair grown out like Jesus or Charles Mason, spotted Tom. He stopped his testimony and grinned. *Tom, comrade!*

Oh shit, thought Tom. A litany of timelines crashing into one another like derailed trains in a derailed station. Too much.

The cult leader and breakout musician known as Napoleon continued his speech. "My people, we have ourselves a very special guest with us in the audience. Brother, if you would, please, fly to me. Show the people the truth we live!"

Shirley realised he was speaking about Tom and she raised her shoulder, urging him to go. She was blushing with pride. Tom turned to face her, unwilling to leave.

"Show them, Tom. I'll be right here!" But he didn't want to leave her, and he certainly didn't want to go to Napoleon.

"Tom—comrade?" Napoleon begged, looking foolish as his credibility waned.

Tom cooed. It was all too much and he was all too little, but apparently not small enough for the crosshairs of a sniper rifle.

Hello, Tom, another voice whispered, far away. Another blast from the past, or to be more precise, the painfully recurring present. *Say your goodbyes once again.*

There was a thunderous echo and a heavy spurt of blood, the bulk of which splattered Tom's face. Shirley dropped to the ground, Tom's feet seized up and he was dragged down with her. Sal had missed and struck Shirley's neck. Someone else had been hit in front of her too. Panic ensued all around them, the peaceful chanting suddenly replaced with screams. Tom's eyes were blinded by Shirley's blood and he attempted to wipe this off with his wings, which were also thickly spattered with arterial spray. Lying on the ground, they gazed at one another, the lustre in her green eyes fading, her throat gurgling with blood as she struggled to breathe. She was still half-conscious, and Tom tried to hum the chant to her, tried to get her to remember the words. Her eyes fluttered and she did her best to follow. "Daba dee daba daa..." And soon, the brave ones in the crowd returned to her, surrounding her in a circle, all defiantly chanting the tune of reincarnation. She closed her eyes and it reminded Tom of the last time he saw her like this, in the van after their crash.

All his fault, again.

He saw an opening in the top of the circle and took off with all his might. He broke free into the air, one of his wings damaged, the other heavily soaked with blood. Another shot was fired from the building opposite and he instinctively began chanting as he rose and dipped over Napoleon, lying on stage, held down by his bodyguards, his shocked eyes staring upward. Napoleon called out to Tom, but his pleas were ignored as Tom banked into Fifth Avenue, dripping blood as he frantically beat his wings.

***

The other pigeons crowded around when Tom appeared in his bloodied state. "What happened?" they all chirped and repeated and bobbed, one after the other.

"There was a shooting. It's not my blood," he said to Raquelle.

"Maurice, your wing…" said Raquelle. "We need to get you to a vet!"

"No, there's no time. He's still after me."

"Who—who did you *shit* on this time?"

"His name is Sal, he's a detective."

"A human detective?" asked one of the other pigeons.

"Yes, a human detective!"

"Why is a human detective after you?"

"That's not important!"

"Universally speaking, most would offer an explanation in cases of human detectives hunting a pigeon," said a pigeon, drawing the agreement of the other pigeons. Raquelle ignored them and put her wing on Tom to steady his shaking. "What can we do to help?"

***

The flock, led by Tom and Raquelle, landed on the rooftop opposite the head shop.

"Wait here," said Tom, and before Raquelle could acknowledge this, Tom was gliding haphazardly into the dark maw of the entrance.

The lady was still at the counter. She was comprehensively stoned. "Get your feathers painted at the rally?"

No, Tom snapped, *it's someone's blood. There was a shooting at the rally.*

"Whoa," said the lady, covering her mouth in shock.

Someone was after me, but they missed. They're still after me, but I need to find that woman with the clipboard before they do. If she comes back here, can you pass on a message for me?

"Um, sure, OK."

She stared at Tom intently, but the chances of her remembering much were slim.

Do you want to write this down?

"Yes, great idea!" She flipped open the yellow legal pad already on the counter and got her black marker out to write.

"OK, go!" she said, but Tom's attention was glued to the page which already had a message for him on it:

Tom, Central Park 3.42 pm, bike racks behind the MET.

Is that for… did the woman with the clipboard leave that for me?

The lady's eyes lit up in embarrassment. "Oh—*you're* Tom!"

The time was 3.36pm. Tom had six minutes to make it over twelve blocks away on a faulty wing. He turned to launch, but his damaged wing skewed his flight path and he collided with a shelf. This was going to be a challenge.

***

Manhattan traffic is surprisingly fine 30 feet above the ground. He told the rest of the flock to get to the bike racks before him and be on the lookout for anyone that looked like a cop or a lady with a clipboard (if they could see her). They obliged him, out of curiosity, and also because it was on the way home.

Raquelle stayed with Tom. "Maurice, what do you think you will find at this bike rack?"

Tom nearly hit a light pole, his broken wing sending him careening all over the avenue. "My name's not Maurice, it's Tom, and I'm either going to find someone who might help me or someone else who will kill me."

"The detective?"

"Yeah."

They made it just on 3.41pm (not that he knew the time, pigeons rarely carrying watches) and joined the row of pigeons perched along a branch overlooking the aforementioned bike racks. The bike rack was mostly empty, except for one yellow shiny bike. A young kid with a hood and a backpack was slowly approaching the rack.

Pssst. Up here. A woman's voice, coming from directly above. He thought it was God at first, speaking from the sky, but then saw the woman with the khakis and clipboard sitting on the branch above him.

"Keep an eye on the bike racks, and don't mind me," Tom whispered to the other pigeons. He flew up to the other branch where the woman was waiting. He studied her, but she did not look at him, her eyes trained on the bike rack and the boy approaching.

"It's me, Father. It's your daughter, Anna."

Tom cooed. *What?*

"From Vienna, 1896, when you were Hubert."

Anna!

"I got your letter, years later. I believed you; despite the pain you caused Mother and Hans. You helped me do some extraordinary things... I've lived some truly amazing lives. That's why I want to help you."

How did you get into this?

"There's not much time—wait a minute." She hushed him as she recorded on the clipboard the boy's decision to not steal the bike.

"He steals the bicycle, it leads him down a dark path. Means more paperwork for me. I'm glad he didn't."

You said there wasn't much time.

"Yes, I know Sal's after you. All the Auditors at the Bureau know about the CARROTA. The Auditor who approved it has been recycled—he's now a microbe in the Mesozoic Era. Not because of your matter—different issue entirely."

So that invalidates everything? Sal can't reward himself and others for killing me anymore?

"I'm afraid he still can, for the time being. The agreement still stands, in large part because of its popularity among key Auditor demographics aged 4–8 centuries and 6–32 millennia. They find Sal and his coalition...entertaining. You'll have to appeal the agreement."

Tom's body seized up. *The other Auditor said I couldn't appeal! The nerve of him!*

"New rules," declared Anna, before clicking her fingers in frustration. "Darn. Time's up. Meet me at West 122nd Street, the Hancock Park Building, Apartment 42B, in fourteen minutes. That's the next closest dilemma I can get to you to co-attend."

And then she vanished. The other pigeons except Raquelle had also left, having long ago lost interest.

Tom sighed, and he and Raquelle wearily made their way to the next location, a rundown apartment. There was a couple sitting on a bed. That's what Tom and Raquelle could see from the window. "Doesn't seem like much going on to me." Raquelle shrugged.

Anna appeared on the inside of the window, sitting on the windowsill, facing the couple. "The woman cheated on the man. I'm seeing whether she's going to confess."

Tom passed this info onto Raquelle, who said, "Ah, OK," without really understanding much of anything that was going on.

Anna spoke to Tom while she took notes on the couple. "As I was saying, you can lodge an appeal and take it to trial. If you give me your approval for this, I can get things in motion."

Yes! Tom chirped. *Absolutely yes, what do I have to do?*

"Excellent," she said, scribbling away with full-body intensity. "I just submitted your request for a trial. You'll need to build up a solid argument, drawing character witnesses, and providing evidence of good deeds and any relevant attempts at atonement."

When will this trial be?

"If it's approved, six lives from now."

A sense of urgency shot through Tom, tingling his mangled wing. Suddenly everything was finite.

What are my chances?

"I'm optimistic—provided Sal doesn't get too much sway behind the scenes. He's made a lot of connections in high places of late—another reason I need you to win. The CARROTA's hit list is a who's who of the worst of the worst. Then there's you. It's clearly personal for Sal, and we need to exploit this one-eyed weakness. Get a win and halt their momentum. Because if his coalition gains power in the Bureau, life will get a whole lot more unforgiving."

And if the appeal fails, it's business as usual for me?

"Oh, no, much worse than that."

What's worse?

Anna's answer was interrupted by a sudden outburst of yelling within the room. The woman had confessed. Tom only caught the last part of Anna's answer: "Let's not even think about it. Oh, darn it, I forgot to mention—clear the window!"

"Maurice!" warned Raquelle.

But it was too late for Tom, as a flower vase smashed through the window and pierced his body with countless shards of glass. As he fell to the ground, he wondered if this counted as his sixth life, and if so, well he thought it wasn't all bad. He really enjoyed being a pigeon, right to the frenetic end. And at least he had something to work towards now.

Daba dee daba daa.

The Five Last Lives of Tom

The five last lives of Tom before his trial, about which he still knew very little, were to be instrumental, soul-changing experiences he would come to cherish for as long as he lived; culminating in an emphatic appeal victory that allowed him to return to his original, simple life as typical office-worker Tom Robinson, married to Lily White.

This is what he hoped would happen—the reality was somewhat different.

Human IV

A woman. Tom had been a female cow, chicken, tapir and ibex (albeit briefly), but he'd never been a human woman. Unfortunately, as he was to find out, this was not a great time in history to be a woman, or a human at all for that matter...

He awoke standing in a field. His clothes were ragged and the grass was wet. The clouds ahead threatened rain across the horizon. A man in rags guided a cow along a dirt track in the distance. Tom's home was a long slog down the same track. He had firewood in his hands. He decided the most logical next step was to return home.

Walking back, his arms aching, he remembered the village, and the muddy streets and the cows and chickens trudging alongside their human owners. He remembered he was French, mostly illiterate like his ailing father, and they lived in a small plot on the edge of his village. They called this quaint little mud heap "Moyenne", and the lord of their land was reasonable, at least by the standards of the time. Tom's name was Joan, but he lacked the grasp of French history to confirm if he was *that* Joan, the one with the Arc and the whole "leading her people to war and burning at the stake" business. If he were indeed her, then he would begrudgingly follow his destiny, simply out of fear of altering history again for the worse and incurring the wrath of a Middle Ages version of Sal, swinging mace in tow.

He arrived in Moyenne as dark descended and candlelight sprung from the other shacks. The lord's manor, a small castle made of stone and built by serfs and villeins alike overlooked the estate from the top of the hill. Joan's father had once been the village blacksmith, and this had elevated them from being serfs and into the marginally higher standing of villeins, but his ill-health had forced her brother Guillaume to take over the trade, one he was not particularly suited to. Neither father nor brother held Joan in high regard; this dating back to her birth, which killed her mother.

It would be selfish of Tom to disregard Joan's plight and instead use the hard life she'd struggled through merely to prepare his case, but what sort of life was this, really? When he could see as far as the 21st century, with all its creature comforts (like sewerage), life in medieval France seemed a primitive and brutish struggle.

As cruel as it was, he reasoned to use this disparate life of Joan's in whatever manner possible to figure out how to approach the trial for his soul.

Father was in bed, as he'd been for most of the past few months. Guillaume was not yet back from his work in the soldering shop. Tom laid the firewood on top of the rest of the pile. Everything ached, and he remembered he was required to milk the lord's cows early the next day as part of their rent, then help maintain their family's own small garden of potatoes and carrots. The mere thought of this life was exhausting, even with a multitude of hard lives under his belt.

Father rolled over and asked Joan to fetch him wine from Patrice, the local wine merchant.

"What about some rye to go with the soup tonight?" Joan asked.

"There's already some left," her father dismissed.

Tom winced as he recalled the mouldy bread his father spoke of. His father had been a good man once, but when only wine and rosary beads could soothe his chronic pain, there wasn't much left to keep his spirit together. Shoulders hunched in resignation, Joan sighed, then took the four denier from her father's skeletal hands. What a life to live, thought Tom, already trying to mentally distance himself from this grim place.

Tom trudged wearily through the mud of the main thoroughfare, his feet soaked and chilling the rest of him. On the way, he passed the smithy where Guillaume was holed up, frantically trying to apply the lessons their father had passed on and somehow reach the rank of Master without the help of another. Guillaume was already of marriageable age, and recalling this, Tom reflected on the miserable future Joan would doubtless be forced to endure. Being 16, she was also of age to marry, but a rumour persisted about a brief tryst with one of the lord's knights. The rumour was true, but Joan's consent to the matter dubious, judging from the fogginess in Tom's recollection. Joan was clearly unwilling to relive the two instances in question and Tom was more than relieved to look the other way too. Besides, what use would it be to dwell on something like that when each day had more than its fill of backbreaking toil?

Things Tom would have to consider as a man experiencing life in a female body for the first time: menstrual cycles each month while toiling away in the field; little say in his own future, which would likely be grim in any event; and the whispers and snide looks of a society that prized female virtue above all else.

He finally arrived at the wine merchant's. Patrice, one of the good ones, asked Joan how her father was holding up. "He'll be better after this." Joan shook the bottle to flatter the merchant. The four denier was paid, and Tom trudged back into the dark, empty street. Walking along in the gloom, Tom pieced together the foundations of his forthcoming defence. First, there would need to be a list of character witnesses, he remembered Anna saying, and then there had to be acts of kindness, and then something else? Memories came and went with Tom, predominantly imbued with a palpable sense of *déjà vu*. It hadn't bothered him until now—when his entire history would soon be put on trial and endlessly scrutinised. Would he even have to prepare? Surely there would be recordings of some kind available to the judge? And if that was the case, then wouldn't his unfair persecution speak for itself?

It was then that Tom remembered the time he killed Napoleon's bird friend. The time he was a diseased mosquito and knowingly gave a man in a hospital bed more pain to add to his troubles. The times he'd pooped on all those people as a pigeon; some who deserved it, others because it was a slow day. The time as a snake when he'd bitten that poor girl and probably killed her. The time he convinced a young woman to help him escape from a zoo, destroying her life in the process. The time he killed Sal and failed to kill Hitler...

Perhaps a prepared defence was a better call. And it would help if he could write it all down. Returning home, he found Guillaume already asleep, most of the soup gone and Father groaning for his wine.

"Father, do we have any paper?"

"Paper?" asked Father. "What is that?"

"Parchment," Tom corrected himself, "to write on."

Father chortled, before succumbing to a coughing fit. "You've suddenly learned how to write?"

Joan revised her answer. "I want to draw."

Father scoffed loudly, stirring Guillaume. Her father motioned to their crumbling shack. "You want to draw, while your father and brother suffer like this? Don't be foolish. Have your supper and go to sleep."

His curtness hit Tom like a slap in the face. His eyes welled up, and Tom remembered teasing his baby cousin once for crying like a girl, even though she was a girl. What an asshole he'd been. He checked the soup. Cold, barely any left. He slurped it up in three gulps and then took the mouldy accompaniment outside to the back of the shack, where he sat dejected in front of their modest little garden plot. Ready to break down and bawl his eyes out, he was stopped momentarily by the shining eyes of an animal staring at him from the field; staring like all the others in the village when the rumours of his debasement at the hands of the knight first began. And so Joan and Tom cried, Tom's first evening in the Middle Ages nothing like those stupid King Arthur tales.

***

The mission was simple: parchment, ink and quill. Unfortunately, due to the feudal system of the day, all exertions were to be made in service to the lord's manor. Each day before dawn, the villagers travelled from their ramshackle homes to the lord's manor, where the cows were milked, seeds planted and crops harvested, all under the watchful eye of the knight who had forcibly deflowered Joan.

Tom's experience of being milked helped Joan refine her loving touch to extract more out of the poor cows, but this rise in productivity only meant she had more time for other work in the field. She got caught up in the daily struggle and a demanding week passed with no trial progress made whatsoever.

The week wasn't entirely wasted, however. Joan made a friend. The lord's cat, the animal of shiny silken eyes Tom spied his first night in this Gallic quagmire, was allowed to roam freely at night and routinely found its way to Joan, who stroked the fearless creature's jet-black fur in much-needed respite. The cat's name was Emmanuel and he was a good boy, as far as Joan could tell. Their visits soon became a nightly occurrence. Emmanuel sometimes brought Joan dead rats as gifts and Joan, in her hunger, debated eating them—not before cooking them thoroughly, of course. It should also be noted here that Tom once again decided this wasn't the life to perfect his vegetarianism, as cutting the occasional treat of meat from the meagre offering of watery stew, cabbage, beets, onions, garlic, carrots, potatoes, cheese, gruel and rye was a hardship too many. (And of that list, it was mostly rye and gruel anyway.)

Guillaume told Joan not to play with Emmanuel, fearing anything bad that happened to the critter would be blamed on Joan and the rest of the family. But it was unthinkable for Joan to give up her only friend, her only source of light in this dark age.

The visits continued for several weeks and Tom soon endured his first period, which he had to address with a piece of coarse fabric and nothing whatsoever to ease the attendant cramps. Emmanuel was very accommodating, providing extra comfort during this painful time. Then one night he didn't show up. Tom scanned the manor the next day while working in the fields, but there was no sign of his feline friend. By the second day, after work was finished, Joan approached the knight overseer, who regarded her from a long way across the field she marched. The other serfs glanced over, wondering why Joan dared to approach the knight. Probably for more tainting of the flesh, they whispered among themselves.

"Yes?" he questioned, when Joan reached him.

"Where's Emmanuel?" asked Joan.

"Do you know who you're speaking with?" The knight crossed

his arms. "Your tone is not one befitting a lady. Nor is it recommended to forget bowing."

"I'm sorry," Joan cleared her throat. "My liege, I was merely enquiring as to the whereabouts of the lord's cat, Emmanuel. I've seen it wandering at night and noticed it hadn't been out these past few evenings."

The knight smirked, "So that's where Emmanuel travels to in his evenings, to provide company to poor wenches of loose morals. I hope he's not learning how to be a tart."

Joan gritted her teeth.

"Not that it's any of your concern," the knight continued. "But Emmanuel is staying inside to accompany the lord's child while he is visiting."

"Will they let him out to play after the lord leaves for another of his estates?"

This question was a mistake. Immediately, she knew she'd stuffed up.

"Ordinarily, yes. But I've suddenly grown quite concerned for the poor cat. Maybe it's too dangerous out here for him. Maybe he should be kept inside, away from untoward influences..."

Joan lowered her head and clenched her fists. How stupid she had been for showing interest in the cat.

"Unless, of course, I can be convinced otherwise..."

Joan stared at him, her eyes welling. She knew what he meant.

The chivalrous knight smirked. "Tell me, you still live at the end of the village?"

***

Emmanuel arrived at the back of Joan's family plot several weeks later after the departure of the lord, but the adventurous feline came home to a broken Joan. What little lustre she and Tom had left from the ruin of each day was gone. She was openly called a tart by the baker's wife in the street. Each weekly sermon seemed to concern in one way or another the sin of trampage. The knight sat comfortably in attendance, sneering openly at Joan, who refused to look directly at him.

Stroking Emmanuel robotically, Joan resolved to return to her defence appeal. This focus was to be her distraction. She would source the parchment, the ink and the quill as a matter of principle in her new purpose. And after that, she swore she would cut that knight's dick off and reduce the entire village to ash.

In the morning, she checked to see if her bed blanket would suffice as a writing pad. It would not. That night, she intercepted her brother on his way home from the workshop and asked him how she could obtain parchment, ink, and quill.

"You can't even read," he dismissed.

"Humour me," she said.

He didn't understand what she meant by that. Further badgering was required.

"Parchment you make from cured animal skin, seeing as how we don't have a parchment maker in town. Quills from goose feathers. Ink, well..."

"Well?"

"I could get you ink, of a sort. From the workshop. It's like ooze runoff from shaping metal. Father helped the priest get it once before, when they were in short supply."

Joan made a mental note that the church may have ink and therefore quills to guide the ink and therefore parchment to write the whole tramp-railing rant down. "I'll keep that in mind."

Her brother didn't understand this phrase either.

When service rolled around the following Sunday, Joan stuck

around after the lengthy sermon lamenting how not paying your dues to the lord (the lord in this instance being the one who owned all the people in the village) was a slight against the Lord (i.e. Jesus), so that she could approach the priest.

"Come for confession?"

"Of a sort, Father. I was wondering if you had any spare parchment available?"

The priest regarded her with suspicion. "To make a pact with the unholy one?" he enquired, his lips pursed like a badger's arsehole.

"I was thinking more about drawing the holy one, actually. I want to bring the Lord into our house so that we are always vigilant and thinking of Him."

The priest was impressed. "No need to draw our Saviour, I believe we can create one for you. Brother Croiss will be more than able to draw you a likeness of the Saviour."

"That's wonderful," Joan said, willing to compromise.

"Of course, it will cost you..." said the priest.

Really, you too?

"Three sous... Though maybe a livre would be more acceptable in the eyes of the Lord, don't you think? Brother Croiss *is* an excellent artist." The priest smiled, as sincerely and shamelessly as any common huckster.

Tom baulked internally. The church would be the first building set alight. "Of course," Joan agreed.

So the parchment from church was too costly, besides the fact that the mere sight of the priest made him want to retch. Tom thought about packing it in, memorising as much as he could and then trying his chances in the next life. Or just writing his answers in faeces on an outer wall of the shack, or making his notes out of small sticks and leaving them somewhere he knew they were unlikely to be disturbed. But he recognised a fire in Joan's character he felt it would be unjust to relinquish. There was something about putting pen to paper that brought an air of formality to proceedings. It felt like something that should be written down, preferably not in human excrement, and he'd be damned if it wasn't going to be done properly. And yes, the end result was Tom memorising his defence into the next life, but writing it down was going to help.

With his one free day, Tom went to the fields, where the lord's cows and sheep grazed, watched over by the shepherd. Tom theorised exactly how he was going to steal a sheep in the middle of the night and apologise to the sheep while he slit its throat, sheared it, stretched its skin and then treated it (he didn't know what with, yet). The shepherd cast his gaze warily at Tom, who stood awkwardly, staring at the sheep. The shepherd firmly planted his staff in the ground. He was a big man and not even Tom's chemical kamikaze attack technique would work on him. Tom turned back to head home. Maybe he could try skinning rats instead?

That night Joan asked her brother if he'd obtained any ink. He shook his head. "I didn't solder today so there was none of that runoff. You got a quill and parchment yet?"

"I'm still working on it. Can I perhaps have some more denier from the smithy's strongbox?"

Guillaume grumbled. "I work day and night to fill that damn strongbox!" This was conveniently overlooking the fact the strongbox never seemed to contain more than the tiniest smattering of silver. "Well, I pay for our land and I take care of Father!" Joan spat back.

"I'll get your stupid ink. You get the rest yourself, tart!" snapped Guillaume, who almost immediately regretted his words and regretted them even moreso after Joan kicked him in the shin and gave him a rude shove.

"I'm sorry," he mumbled. "One denier a week. That's the best I can do."

Joan agreed to this, even though at that rate it would take far too long—over a year, in fact—there being twelve deniers to a sou and twenty sous to a livre. No, there had to be another way. Tom was smart. He knew things. About the future, and the world, and stuff... He would find another way.

Night descended and the lord's shepherd had taken his animals to their stall on the far side of the hill. The hill provided an excellent vantage, with little chance of a wolf or desperate peasant sneaking up on the precious flock.

Tom lay prone in darkness by some shrubs at the foot of the hill, knife in hand. This was madness, but hey, this was the Middle Ages.

The shepherd had been still for over twenty minutes. Tom crawled like a snake towards the sheep, his stomach and breasts cold and gross from the muddy earth. The ground beneath his grimy fingers rose and he felt more and more foolish the closer he got. He stopped ten metres away from the stall. He gripped his knife and considered how he would pounce. A flash of movement burst through the grass and landed in front of him, startling some of the sheep. Tom saw two gleaming eyes staring back at him.

Tom, is that you? asked the cat formerly known as Emmanuel.

The voice was unmistakable.

Hey, Shirley...

What are you doing with that knife?

***

They returned instinctively back to their nightly meeting spot behind Joan's shack. The roles were reversed, Tom now the human and Shirley the cat. Tom used the opportunity to apologise for their previous encounters, at the zoo and the rally in New York, both of which had left Shirley bleeding profusely.

It was tough, Shirley recalled, before correcting herself. *No, it was worse than tough. I was sent to prison for three years for letting you loose. No one believed anything I said about you. I was so alone. But when I got out, I discovered our leader, the great Napoleon, and he was saying all the things were true—and they are!* She purred with happiness and rubbed her face into Tom's hand. *I've been so many wonderful creatures already. I've been a swan, a giraffe—even a koala!* Shirley drew a serious face. *I'm still not sure what happened in New York. Was there a shooting? Is our leader OK?*

Tom sighed. *Yes, he's fine. They weren't after him. They were after me.*

But why? asked Shirley, and Tom pursed his lips, unsure how best to answer that.

Because I thwarted an assassination attempt.

Oh, wow, who were they trying to kill?

Tom braced himself. *Adolf Hitler...*

Shirley drew a blank. *Who's that?*

Tom remembered that Shirley may have had the past retroactively shifted out from under her and then grown up in a world where Hitler had been replaced by someone who was replaced by someone who was replaced by someone else. The head shop lady was right: the timeline business was a jumble of wires he wanted no part in untangling. This was an easy reprieve and he was going to take it. *Just some guy they wanted to kill for...personal reasons.*

Shirley accepted this, and Tom drew a sigh of relief, though he knew this was only temporary. He had to explain who Hitler was at *some* stage, especially if he was to call upon Shirley as a character witness. But cowardice has a neat way of delaying the inevitable.

What's worse is the fact that they keep killing me, over and over, Tom sulked. Shirley comforted him with her paws, wobbling on her hind legs as she hugged Tom like a human.

How do we fix this? she asked, her ears raised attentively.

Tom explained the concept of the trial to Shirley and she jumped at the chance to help. He said he needed to write down the main points of his defence, but lacked the requisite writing implements. Shirley considered this dilemma for only a brief moment before she said there could certainly be all three items available in the manor. Tom picked Shirley up and rested her atop his knees. He rubbed her belly and beamed in the moonlight. *Do you like getting your belly rubbed? I never could tell with cats.*

Shirley's eyes winced as her neck skin folded into her face. *Tell you the truth—it's not as pleasant as I thought it would be...*

***

All the next day, while he laboured in the fields, Tom gazed frequently towards the manor, hoping to see a sign of that black cat from atop the hill. Stealing from the lord was a tremendous risk, and now Tom really wondered how much he *needed* to write it all down. The thought of Shirley getting caught and being drowned as punishment was too much to bear, so much so that Tom's performance in the field that day drew the ire of the knight, who marched across the field and spat with rage at Tom to give the lord's land his undivided attention. This was followed by a smack to the side of the head, which pleased a few of the older, more spiteful serfs. That night, around the usual time, Shirley's eyes flashed at Tom in the darkness and he squealed telepathically with joy when he saw Shirley carrying a roll of parchment in her mouth, like a dog fetching a stick. *Couldn't get the ink or the quill. Must be locked away. Was almost caught getting the parchment. Real close call. That knight is nice, though.*

He's a pig.

I'll pee in his armour then.

The quill had to come from a live goose and then be cleaned and hollowed. Tom signalled he wanted to get the feather for the quill from the baker's wife; the same wife who openly called him a tart in the street. Shirley was more than happy to be petted and stroked with "oohs" and "aahs" by the baker's wife while Tom snuck into the goose pen and plucked himself several suitable-looking feathers, hoping the honks of protest would not arouse undue suspicion. When he gave the signal that they were in the clear, Shirley hissed at the baker's wife with a turn of attitude that caused the wife to slap the cat. *Worth it to see the fright in her eyes,* Shirley later said, as they inventoried their winnings.

A gruelling week later (gruel being the major constituent of every meal), Joan's brother finally delivered the ink. The only time they could write was during the night, but it was too dark by the plot and the use of a candle outside their house risked bringing questions from their father as to exactly what kind of sinister acts his degenerate daughter was up to that required illumination. They settled on a place out in the woods, not far from the village.

Were there witches during the Middle Ages? Tom telepathically whispered in fear as they trudged through the darkness on their first outing, the trees curling their branches downward like prying skeletal fingers. Having been a tree before, Tom knew they meant no harm, but remained shaken by their bone-chilling whispers and creaking in the night.

I think witches were a little later on, but I could be wrong.

Luckily, Shirley knew how to start a fire from her time in the Edmonton girl scouts. She chuckled at Tom's pathetic attempts to light the fire. Twenty minutes later still in darkness and Tom was ready to give up, but then, a spark! They produced a candle, courtesy of the lord and a judicious rolling exodus by Shirley, and soon there was enough light to scribe Tom's defence. Shivering away, he explained to Shirley his list of proposed character witnesses. He was usually an accomplished handwriter, Hubert having been an excellent calligrapher, but Joan's lack of natural experience, poor vision, and novice grasp of using a quill made everything a mess.

"*Merde,*" he muttered, rubbing at his mistake. *Well, I know who that is and I'll remember it.*

Aren't you going to have to remember it all anyway?

Yes—I know—but it's better to write it down, I've decided. There's even an off-chance I could bury it, and then retrieve it in one of the next few lives, assuming I'm reborn in this precise region of France in the exact same timeline and the paper hasn't decomposed or been destroyed or had a car park built over it...

Shirley shrugged. All this trouble didn't bother her, what else was she going to do? She was fighting against her animal instincts to hunt rats and keeping Tom company helped with that. Tom wrote the name of each intended character witness, leaving space for what good things they could say about him. It took over five minutes despite there only being eight names.

What kind of names are Tenazz and Quartz? asked Shirley.

Ants I knew.

Is that Napoleon our leader?

Yeah, Tom sighed.

You don't seem so enthused. I thought he'd be a great character witness.

Before he was your leader, he was Joseph Stalin.

Oh. Wow. Shirley recoiled and raised her body like an upside-down "U". Tom weighed her clear distaste for murderous dictators and realised explaining the whole "saving Hitler" thing would not go down smoothly whenever he finally told her the truth behind this universal vendetta.

Shirley slowly digested this revelation in silence. *So that's why you didn't want to fly to him,* she eventually said.

He can be a bit much sometimes. A little intimidating...

Well, at least he changed for the better, Shirley remarked, and Tom couldn't help but admire her resilient optimism.

They both agreed that only eight names (two of them were his parents and one of them was Shirley) after three centuries of re-incarnation remembering was severely inadequate, despite Tom protesting he could've made a better impression if he weren't being mercilessly murdered for most of those lives. Shirley suggested he should try to make more friends in his last remaining lives. Tom became petulant. "Fine," he relented. It wasn't like he hadn't been trying. They returned home shortly after this resolution, Tom shivering away, already weak from having eaten nothing but gruel the week before.

Tom entered the house, waking his father in the process. Call of nature, he uttered as explanation for his whereabouts, lifting the chamber pot. His father drunkenly accepted this and returned to his snoring. Tom hid the scroll under his bed. If anyone were to read it, they'd see it was in English and he'd be executed for treason, the French seemingly no less perpetually at war with the English than Sal was at war with Tom.

Most nights they didn't scribe anything about the trial, didn't go out to the woods and mess around with quill, ink, fire and parchment. They just sat in their usual spot outside Joan's family plot, reminiscing about the future of their past lives.

Their second outing in the woods, designated as serious trial prep, they discussed Tom's prior accomplishments and potential good deeds he could endeavour to undertake in his remaining lives. Tom was quick to highlight his conversion to vegetarianism as a prior *and* ongoing accomplishment, which Shirley commended but gently hinted was probably not enough to rely on, nor did she seem inspired by his follow up of shitting on jerks and assholes as a justice-dispensing pigeon. With Tom unable for the moment to recollect his other supposed countless acts of benevolence, Shirley suggested they move onto potential acts of altruism they could commit right here and now in Moyenne.

There's no good I can do here, Tom argued. *Not in this lifetime, this time period. Everything's filthy, nothing at all like the movies, though I guess that's to be expected. No quests to pursue, no damsels to be saved. Heck, they don't even want women to do the saving anyhow; we're just baby-makers and playthings for those so-called chivalrous knights. I won't be doing many good deeds in this lifetime, not when I've got to till and toil relentlessly for practically nothing, not when I've got to attend to myself with hardly more than a handful of dirty cotton rags every month.*

Shirley was undeterred. *What about Joan of Arc? She seemed to achieve quite a lot as a woman in this time.*

Well yes, there was her, but that's different. She was called by God to defeat the English. I've only got a housecat on my side. Plus, she didn't have Sal and his CARROTA trying their best to hamper her every move.

Well, what about little deeds you can do for the village? Shirley suggested. *You're from the 21st century, isn't there some kind of technology you could pass on?*

That was when Tom remembered tampons. Bras. And the toothbrush. Unfortunately, he forgot about the black plague, which arrived early the following week.

***

The invisible fleas hitchhiked on some nomadic rats, who were living out their dreams of travelling the French countryside. The rats ventured from village to village, touring all kinds of kitchens, nibbling away at every manner of delicious new food and breeding like, well, rats. Joan was trying to explain the concept of the toothbrush to her brother Guillaume as he returned from his mandatory archery defence training when a ragged, out-of-breath stranger intercepted them in the field. The stranger spoke of a dark force sweeping her town. She broke down as she described seeing friends and family with ghastly swollen lumps bulging in armpits, necks and groins. Guillaume, Joan and the other archers surrounded her. Everyone except Joan was left scratching their heads over the news, or possibly due to fleas.

"Ah *merde*. It's the bloody bubonic plague," said Joan.

All eyes shifted to Joan. Guillaume was the most intrigued.

"Bubonic?"

A town meeting was called to discuss how best to stop the spread of plague. The entire village, except for the serfs and the lord, crammed into the stone church. Not a space was spared. Joan wanted to fetch Shirley for a little more modern take on events and best practice, but Guillaume gruffly grabbed her by the arm and dragged her into the stewing pit of dirty bodies spluttering for answers. The chivalrous knight, the priest and the baker's wife crowded the pulpit. Joan was squeezed in between her brother and the wine merchant at the back. The priest suggested fervent prayer, an increase in alms and begging God for forgiveness. The village doctor agreed. Joan snickered at the ensuing sheepish murmurs of agreement from the crowd. She stopped snickering when the baker's wife spoke.

"It's the lord's pet—that stupid black cat, Emmanuel! He's a dark omen that wilfully brings this plague upon us."

Her husband the baker concurred. "I think another cat burning has been way overdue. We don't know what darkness that monster has conjured, and if he'll keep doing it. He must be stopped!"

The crowd rallied in approval. It *had* been a long time between cat burnings, and this was a no-brainer for boosting morale. They turned to the priest, who was more than happy to give it the all-clear. Lastly, the eyes found their way to the chivalrous knight. He shrugged. "We could just say he ran away?"

The crowd cheered, and Joan screeched in protest. All eyes turned upon her. "Emmanuel is not the reason why the plague will spread to us. The plague is spread by rats. If we kill Emmanuel, that's one less cat to kill the very thing that threatens us. I can help us avoid the plague if we take some precautionary measures to help stem its spread..."

The silence was deafening. What replaced it wasn't great either.

"She's in league with Emmanuel!" the baker's wife cried, venomous joy evident in her eyes.

Before Joan could reply, a pair of hands compressed on her shoulders. To her shock, the firm hands belonged to none other than her own brother. "She goes out at night! She talks to Emmanuel! I've seen it myself!"

Merde.

***

A show trial was hastily arranged. The woods and Joan's house were searched extensively for proof of dealings with Satan. They found the parchment. As expected, the fact that it was written in English did few favours for Joan. "I knew Satan was English!" the patriotic priest exclaimed. The chivalrous knight confiscated the parchment that contained only the names of Tom's character witnesses and a smattering of half-baked invention ideas. All that fuss for practically nothing.

The plague arrived at a leisurely pace as the rats took their time to enjoy the scenery. The villeins on the other side of town were the first to be stricken. Family members tried in vain to ease the suffering of their kin, though some gave up and locked the doors behind them. "Bring out your dead!" became a common refrain, except it was said in French, obviously.

Joan was held in the stockade in the village square by the church. Her feet grew cold in the mud and Tom quietly packed it in, preparing for his fourth last life. Shirley had escaped the lord's manor and Guillaume offered Joan greater leniency if she told them where the feline had fled.

All around, the rats happily scampered. Wild cats were found and either thrown onto makeshift pyres or drowned for their potential allegiance to Emmanuel. With pestilence spreading and fear and panic growing, the baker's wife believed a trial for heresy would take too long in delivering results. The rest of the village, those dwindling few still uninfected, happened to agree. Tom watched in languid despair as they began stockpiling wood.

His punishment was set for that afternoon. He decided he'd play the part of a bone-chilling witch when tied to the stake. *Hey,* he reasoned, *I'm about to be burned alive at the stake here. I'm allowed to have a little fun.* It was a shame he would be unable to avenge Joan's torment at the hands of these superstitious neanderthals, but the thought that the few who remained would likely be dead of the plague before the month was out offered some comfort. The villagers dragged her over to the next phase of the medieval justice system and tied her firmly atop a pile of logs and straw kindling.

Joan cast her eyes out into the weakened crowd. Most were now infected. Joan spotted her usual pair of enemies, the baker's wife and the priest, the latter doing his best to stifle a cough and hide his purple, oozy buboes beneath his holy robes, while the baker's wife scratched ferociously at an invisible bite on her hand. The chivalrous knight was nowhere to be seen, probably having fled like the true coward he was.

The baker held the torch. Tom watched the flame and noted he'd never been burned alive before. Entranced by the flames, he almost forgot to begin rattling off his curses and hexes. Tom started with the priest and his monk friends, telling them their god didn't exist and if He did, He'd be more inclined to laugh at their pompous robes than answer any of their dim-witted prayers. He then told the baker's wife the only reason she wasn't a tart was because nobody but the baker wanted her, and even he was mostly blind. That one managed to rouse a few snickers between coughs. And finally, Joan looked out into the crowd for the brother who had turned her in, only to notice beyond the crowd a furry zip of black lightning bounding up the thorough-fare toward them.

Shirley! Joan's eyes bulged, and the crowd got wind of her distracted attention. They turned to see what she was looking at, but thinking quickly, Joan blurted out more accusations of heresy and ugliness to bring the mob back to her.

Shirley! Tom screamed internally. *Stay away!*

But he was too late.

The chivalrous knight, in full armour, emerged from behind one of the shacks carrying a hissing and yelping fit of fur and claws. Shirley. Tagging behind the knight, wearing a lavish purple and green tunic, came the lord. Tom was screaming inside for

Shirley but was quieted by the lord who waved Tom's parchment of names around. *Sal will very much appreciate this.* The lord beamed.

Joan's bones drooped, Tom's soul withered. All that effort, only for it to end up helping his enemy. Shirley was tied up beside Tom. Eventually she stopped squirming, resignation replacing fear. The baker's wife, still scratching at the bite on her hand, hurriedly asked the lord for approval in getting on with it.

The lord nodded. "Any last words?" he offered, much to the baker's wife's dismay.

Joan and Shirley turned their heads to one another. Tom spoke aloud and in English, baffling the mob, yet still retaining the aura of crazy he was going for. "I'm sorry, Shirley. You didn't deserve to be dragged into this, I don't deserve a friend like you."

You saved me, back in the zoo. You showed me the secret. We're going to fight Sal, we're going to figure it out together!

"I lied about what I did, Shirley. The person I stopped Sal from killing—Hitler—he was a complete monster. And I did it all for a stupid reason. I did it for the chance of chasing a girl in the future."

Stunned, Shirley's ears went flat and she forced her face away, the silence pre-emptively burning Tom's heart to a crisp.

The mob exchanged glances at one another, unsure what to make of the witch's one-sided conversation in a foreign language to a cat while both were tied to a stake. The baker's wife, unable to contain herself any longer, stole the torch from the official torchbearer and returned the flaming stick to the woodpile below Joan. Tom and Shirley reluctantly began the chant.

As he slowly suffocated on the smoke, the flames licking agonisingly about the heels of his borrowed body, Tom wondered what was worse: being burned alive or breaking the trust of the only friend he had left? (It was still being burned alive, but not by much.)

Goat

Tom awoke to an orange sunrise on a beautiful, wind-swept mountainside. Surrounding him were a herd of grey, brown and black goats with thick coats, each still soundly asleep, dreaming of endless grass fields and eating all the aforementioned grass in said fields. He looked at his feet. Hooves. At this stage it seemed safe to assume he was a goat.

He rose on all fours and tip-toed closer to the edge to gain his bearings. Right on cue, flashbacks of his earlier life as an infant ibex falling to his death from a cliff made him reconsider his proximity to the edge. He was at the top of a valley of some sort, with patches of tall pine trees rising here and there in the valley below. He saw no buildings despite the valley's vast swathes of land. Tom tried to recall where exactly home was. He caught glimpses of clay brick, hardened by heat, though it was a frosty morning.

He turned back to the herd and waited for more memories to rise to the surface. A herd usually had a shepherd, so where was his? He looked left and right, seeing a boy higher up along the valley, sitting on a rocky ledge. This was his shepherd. A young teen in clothes too big for his slender frame. He was bowing in prayer, the sunrise behind him. The boy rose from his knees, eyes still closed. Shirley, once more.

Tom edged closer as she finished her prayer. When she saw him, the serenity of the sunrise and the peace of prayer dissipated, replaced with a sunken soul. A sigh. Not a terrific sign, but Tom had recovered from worse. *Shirley, I'm so sorry about before...*

Shirley stood and folded her mat quietly. She grabbed the wooden staff lying beside her. Tom flinched. It wasn't out of the question that she could use that staff for more than guiding the flock. She walked down the path toward him, but ignored his cries for attention and instead addressed the rest of the goats. "Wake, my lovelies, it's time to return home."

"Shirley..." Tom bleated.

She regarded him with nothing in her eyes. "Come, Baptun, Father will be displeased if his favourite does not return."

Tom tried to recollect whether she meant herself or him. He looked at the other goats, their bodies nowhere near as strong or sturdy as his. The favourite, through sheer luck of DNA dominance, must've been him. How fortunate.

The rest of the herd awoke and the bleating began. They grazed among the grass at the edges of the path, wandering off without reprimand from Shirley. Tom approached Shirley from behind. *Where are we?*

"Why, Baptun, we're in the Korengal Valley. How funny of you to forget." She spoke in English, but refrained from using telepathy, avoiding the more intimate form of communication they had once savoured.

Shirley, I'm really sorry about before. I did a stupid thing and even dumber things to try to fix it, like when I lied to you.

"Lying is a sin, Baptun, especially to those who *cared* for you," said Shirley, deviating from the path to corral a wanderer from some less than savoury dark berries.

Stung, Tom returned to the rest of the herd, sparing his energy for another shot later. He did not stop to feed like the others and merely took in this Korengal Valley. Tall pines adorned the rolling hills of the valley floor, while further below, dry rock beds of sandstone snaked through.

Where and when was it exactly? From the scenery alone, one could think he was in the Canadian Rockies, but Shirley's funny flat hat and goat-herding vocation suggested otherwise.

Further down the valley, he decided another reconciliatory attempt was in order. Part of this was the realisation that most of the other goats couldn't stand him, a stark deviation from their standard indifference; something about the favouritism heaped upon him by their farming patriarch.

Why are you acting this way?

"I don't know what you're talking about, Baptun. For a goat with simple needs, you sure seem confused by things."

Tom bleated. He decided he would have to go on the offensive to win her forgiveness. *Why were you praying before if you know what really happens when we die?*

Shirley flinched, scratched at her wispy moustache, and kept walking. Tom persisted. *Why do you herd goats when you have the knowledge to do so much more with your life?*

Shirley's grip on her staff tightened.

Tell me that lying is a sin, then why are you lying to yourself? Tom shouted, telepathically. The fire in Shirley's eyes suggested this had done the trick.

"I've lived so many lives since our last time together. So many lives. Endured hardships much worse than my time in prison. Do you know what it's like to be locked in a cage, immobilised, experimented on with nasty chemicals with long names that made your fur and eyes burn? Or watch as your family and others drown when your rickety boat sinks on a desperate quest for freedom? I didn't enjoy a dignified life for so many lives, and I blamed you, Tom, for a very long time... But then I realised what I was doing wrong. I was getting stuck in the past—blaming you, trying to be old, Canadian Shirley. That's not what this gift is about—and it is a gift—despite the hardships. It's a chance to learn about the world from many viewpoints. To endlessly try to reinforce one life or one set of beliefs would be pointless... You ask me why I pray when I know what really happens when we die? It's because that's what I, Tashfeen, like to do. And the more I follow the life I'm supposed to live, the more I enjoy it and the earlier I remember each previous life..."

Tom groaned. Lectures always rubbed him the wrong way.

You're right. Of course you're right, he said to appease her, *but I'm not in a position to do that with Sal and his CARROTA. I need to do some good deeds; I need to see the Dalai Lama or something, whatever it takes so I can win this trial and start over—and then I'll definitely be incorporating that stuff about being grateful for life and stuff.*

Shirley stopped and stared into Tom's eyes. "I'll be honest. I don't want to help you. No good will come to my family from helping you, and yet the universe keeps throwing us back together. I will only honour its wishes by making sure your life as a goat is as good as it can be. That's what I will do for you. That's all I will do."

So you haven't forgiven me?

"Not yet." Shirley rushed off, stopping more goats from eating more unsavoury dark berries further down the track.

Tom held onto those last words while he chewed on some dry bush leaves. Not yet. So maybe one day? There was hope there, some faint chance of fixing the things he kept breaking. Helping Shirley would be his good deed. In fact, she wasn't going to help him, no, *he* was going to be the one to help her. That's how he'd fix it and fix everything else.

Tom's grand plans for redemption were interrupted by the other goats, who began bleating and huddling together in panic. Shirley looked up to the sky. Tom looked up too. The whirring blades came next, as a black military helicopter rose into view.

Then began a chorus of gunfire that cracked and rippled across the valley and was capped off with the helicopter launching several missiles into a hillside opposite.

Oh, Afghanistan! Tom realised. *We're in Afghanistan. Terrific.*

They passed some loggers stacking the severed remnants of what had once been a tall and majestic pine. The loggers stopped to gaze at Tom and the other goats, carefully studying their thick coats and admiring the robust health of the herd. One logger, an arrogant, grizzled brute wearing the same flat pakol hat as Shirley, waltzed up to her and promptly offered his daughter's hand in exchange for a dowry, making it clear he had a particular interest in Tom. Shirley waved this off and a terse discussion soon followed, very little of which Tom understood. The logger eventually trudged off, disappointed, and Shirley picked up the pace of the herd along the valley, rounding up the stragglers busy demolishing any stray blades of grass they encountered.

What happened back there?

"A wife in exchange for yourself, twelve of the cashmeres and eight of the sheep we have in the village."

And you said no, right?

"Father would not have allowed it."

Tom gulped. He glanced back at the loggers in disgust. *How can you stand that?*

Shirley gritted her uneven teeth. "It is what it is…"

Their village was on one of the more peaceful ridges. Marasta Naw. The family's dwelling was made of solid sandstone and was slightly bigger than the leaky wooden shack Tom had called home during the Middle Ages. Several families, all related, lived in the seven houses that made up the village. Tom and the other goats were herded into their pen. Shirley entered her house and did not emerge for the rest of the night.

The life of a prize goat in Afghanistan wasn't so bad. Shirley's father Mahmoud was especially warm to Tom and treats were dispensed whenever possible, usually in the form of sweet biscuits or even opium seeds. Tom got the feeling this extra attention wasn't viewed kindly by the other goats, given their open gossip about how he had received his impeccable genes. Very much outnumbered, he tried telling stories of his previous lives. The other goats particularly liked the one about the monkey fooling all the people and the pigeon that flew around shitting on infidels who incurred his displeasure. All the stories were embellished with "ride off into the sunset" endings.

Most seemed to soften in light of this entertainment, but for one cantankerous old goat, who hated both Tom and Shirley with a passion, it only intensified his aggression, ramming into Tom's gut and biting at his legs whenever the opportunity arose. One night he went so hard the other goats woke and told him to knock it off because they were trying to sleep, but the grumpy bastard persisted.

"Your stories are bullshit, there is only the valley!"

"That doesn't make sense!" Tom countered. "How can you know a valley is all there is, if you've never even left it? It literally requires the existence of surrounding areas to make it a valley."

The wily goat thought about this briefly before cruelly nipping Tom in the eye and repeating his assured belief. "Your stories are bullshit, there is only the valley!"

Tom was limping the next day. He was also likely blind in one eye. Father Mahmoud, displeased by this, took it out on the rest of the family. Aware of the phrase "snitches get stitches", Tom offered nothing when Shirley questioned who had done this to him. To channel her father's blame elsewhere, Shirley suggested it could have been one of the jackals roaming the valley. In anger, Father Mahmoud took his rifle and went off searching for jackals to hunt with Shirley's older brother. Both were killed by US forces after being mistaken for militants.

Shirley and her mother and younger sister wept for days. The entire village came to pay their respects. They arranged for three days of mourning, with the funeral carried out as soon as possible, in accordance with Islamic tradition. As a goat, Tom did not attend. The herd grew sullen amid the continued weeping that carried throughout the night. The other young males in the village and Tashfeen's extended family debated retaliation against the US military, but Shirley and her uncle were quick to call for calm. Tom saw in Shirley a quiet anger he'd not seen before, not even aimed at him. She wanted to fight, truly she did. It was then that Tom understood that Shirley had really lost a father. Because with each life she wasn't looking toward the next, but giving everything to the now. And that meant getting hurt; being thrown across a rolling van in a doomed rescue mission, being burned alive at the stake by the side of a friend, and being inconsolable for days when your father who raised you since birth was shot to pieces not five hundred metres from home.

Tom had never truly experienced that kind of pain before. He'd been too wrapped up in his own world, saving his own skin. It begged the question: was his soul worth saving?

The last time the Americans incurred similar "collateral damage", they'd made a discreet payment of cash to Shirley's aunt for compensation. This time there was nothing. Tom wanted to help Shirley and her family, but the only way he knew how was a radical deviation from this life in the valley and completely disregarded the small moment of enlightenment he'd just had.

On the third day of mourning, late in the evening and shrouded in moonlight, Shirley stood by the goat pen, staring at Tom. The valley was silent, not a bullet fired nor tears left to weep. Without a word, Tom walked to the gate of the pen and Shirley let him out.

They seated themselves on some nearby rocks. It was just like their midnight rendezvous during the ill-fated life of Joan. Despite the sombre occasion, Tom practically wagged his stumpy little tail in anticipation. It felt like years since they'd connected in this way, reminiscing about lives past and present. Shirley spoke about her father, both fathers in fact, and Tom talked about his parents and his amusing uncle who made misguided impressions of Thanksgiving turkeys. Tom waited until the right moment to offer Shirley and her family a chance at freedom, a chance of experiencing life outside the valley, away from its hardships.

Shirley snorted, "Okay, Tom. We'll try it your way, again..."

***

Tom had watched the film *Zero Dark Thirty* one hungover Sunday, many centuries ago, curled up in bed. He didn't know exactly how truthful the Hollywood account of hunting Bin Laden was, but he assumed that the location where they discovered Osama, a large urban compound in Abbottabad near the Pakistan Military Academy, had to be correct. He told this to Shirley, omitting the fact he remembered the location from a movie. They decided to leave the next night. There were American units all around the valley, but they needed to go to Kabul to find a bigger base with a commanding officer who would take their story a little more seriously. Shirley told her mother she was going to go look for work in the poppy fields and her poor mother, reduced to a mere shell by grief and loss, mutely nodded her assent.

An hour before they planned to leave, Tom grew faint. It was his eye, the one that his cantankerous pen-mate had gnashed at with his horrid rotten teeth. Shirley leaned in close to inspect it and almost fainted from the smell. "It's badly infected. I'm sorry I didn't address it before. I was, well, distraught."

You worked in a zoo. You can fix it right?

"Not with anything here."

Kabul?

Shirley took a second inspection of the infection. She grimaced. "I don't think we have the time, Baptun."

It's Tom.

"Right, sorry. I think we may need to go closer. I think we need to find an American patrol in the valley."

Without the Taliban catching wind that we are cooperating with the Americans or the Americans mistaking us for the Taliban?

"It's going to be just fine."

Eye hope you're right, said Tom, but Shirley didn't spot the pun.

They set off for the nearest outpost toward Kabul, walking along the valley floor rather than traversing its ridge. They happened to pass the two loggers who had offered Shirley a wife for her prize goat. The man asked if this was the same goat he'd fallen for previously and laughed when told it was. Further along, they passed two Taliban fighters making their way home from a day of shooting at infidels. They stopped Shirley and asked her where she was going. They told her she needed to be careful—that she was walking toward the firing line of an American outpost.

"The Americans killed my father and brother last week," she said. "I'm going to ask them why they killed my family."

One of the Taliban fighters laughed, thinking her foolish, while the other one felt sorry for her naivety. The one who felt sorry for her reached into his sack and gave her a grenade, like an Afghani Father Christmas. "When you get the chance, don't bother with words."

"Thank you. God is great."

Shirley threw the grenade away first chance she got.

Tom was overjoyed that Shirley's relationship with him was on the mend, but he was also fading in and out with his head going dizzy and his hooves feeling heavy. At one stage he collapsed and Shirley had to carry him. *I'm alive right now,* he muttered.

"I know you are," she said.

No, I mean, somewhere in New York is the original "me". I'm just out of high school, got the whole world in front of me...

Shirley seemed taken aback by the notion. She didn't think it was possible, but here they were. She didn't say much else for a while. When they took a break at the foot of the main incline, a casual question escaped her.

"So, this boy in New York, has he met the girl he talked about before? The girl that started it all?"

Tom lifted his head and it swayed uncontrollably. *Nope. She's much later... lot of failed starts.*

"And if you get your freedom, what are you going to do? Tom? Tom?"

***

Tom woke up to US Marines pointing a variety of guns in his general direction. The Americans were screaming for Shirley to put the goat down. She placed Tom on the ground and he was left looking up at her wispy, teenage chin. Her hands were up, and even down in the dirt Tom felt her heart pounding, her mind going straight to the chant as a reflex.

Shirley spoke in English with her Canadian accent. She explained that her goat required urgent medical attention. The Americans, many of them initially shocked at the sight of this dirty Afghan boy speaking perfect English, took her Canadian accent as a swipe at their own. The charming phrase "goat fucker" was uttered a few times too many. The only one beguiled by the fact an Afghan teen in the Korengal Valley was speaking perfect English luckily happened to be the commanding officer. He asked her where she learned to speak English and she told them she was raised in Kabul by a Canadian aid teacher. Shirley repeated her request that they save her goat, and in exchange she would provide them with information relating to "the world's most wanted terrorist".

If it had been any other day, the commanding officer would have entertained her claim, but on this particular day, it just so happened that the commanding officer was in the midst of an impending personal crisis: he was thinking about all the well-intentioned things they'd been trying to do for these people and the indifferent (occasionally explosive) responses they got for their troubles. Because of this, he quickly concluded that he didn't want to risk losing another human life, specifically an American life, to this war. They had no way to properly treat the goat at this remote outpost, other than painkillers from the medic. A helicopter would have to be called, which would put Americans at risk, all for this little dying goat with a bung eye and its keeper with his far-fetched claim. None of his men would ever trust him again if he pursued a foolish thing like that. (Though incidentally, he would think about this moment when they later found Bin Laden in Pakistan, right where that Afghan boy had said he was hiding.)

Unfortunately, Shirley's lies about how she knew English were also so believable as to warrant no further questions. His curiosity satisfied, the commanding officer gave Shirley a small vial of morphine, which could ease Tom's pain but not cure his infection. Shirley begged for proper care, antibiotics at the very least, but was given none. The rest of the soldiers told her to get lost. Tom watched Shirley's chin quiver as she stood her ground. Desperate, she rattled off more facts only an American would know, saying she lied and that she was in fact once a Canadian citizen. Finally, it culminated in her revealing where Bin Laden was hiding.

Where? they asked.

Tom fed her the answer.

"Pakistan!" They laughed. "Tell us something we don't know. Everybody knows that's most likely the case."

"That's because it is."

"Yeah, sure," they dismissed.

And then the commanding officer said he'd had enough and told her to make her own way to the hospital (seven klicks out of the valley).

To her credit, Shirley remained defiant, even when they fired a warning shot over her head. Finally, Tom asked Shirley to take him back. She carried him back down the valley, but they had to stop because the adrenaline had worn off and Shirley was crashing.

If I were as brave as you, we'd never be in this mess. Tom whispered.

"I don't know why they wouldn't believe me."

A Canadian-accented Afghan boy knowing the location of Bin Laden may have been too much for them to handle.

"Do you think we should try for Kabul?"

I'm not going to make it that far. I've told you Bin Laden's location. When I'm gone, you can try again in Kabul. Hopefully, you'll find someone that believes you and gets your family out of this war. They deserve it. I had a daughter once. She was a good person. Still is... You'll be able to save your little sister and she'll become someone amazing like you... I didn't save my daughter. She managed it on her own... Tom realised he was rambling and apologised. *I think it's time for that chant now,* he decided.

Want me to sing it with you? Shirley kindly offered, this time telepathically.

Sounds good.

And they both did, which proved fortuitous, as a drone strike ordered by one of Sal's CARROTA had been launched mere moments before, without the usual gentlemanly warning sign offered. (The only rule stipulated in the war against Tom.)

How lucky.

Vegetarian progress: a goat will eat almost anything.
Who was Tom to stop this?

Human V

A field of cotton. Little white clouds suspended in small trees.

A field of cotton, waiting to be picked.

Like when he was an Austrian art teacher, Tom came to being in the midst of his work, only this time he was not standing in an auditorium with an audience of students hanging onto his every word. This time he was being shouted at like a dog, and promptly ordered to get back to work. The heat of the blazing Southern sun hit him all at once and he was suddenly desperate for water. He turned to the man who had shouted at him.

"Water. Please, I need some water," he rasped.

The hatred in the response was palpable. "What makes you think you deserve water, boy, when you taking a break the way you are now?"

Tom thought fast. "I need water so I can stay strong and pick cotton better for you, boss."

The others in the field flinched. They were smart enough, however, to keep picking. The overseer flinched too, though for different reasons. "I will require some water myself, after all the whipping you gon' make me do..."

The overseer, who wasn't the big boss of the plantation, was a sadistically cruel man who treated beatings like Monet considered water lilies: with a purposefulness in his strokes. Oscar Benjamin, the illiterate slave whose body Tom now inhabited, had been beaten by the overseer many times before, and this latest indiscretion, asking for water, was to be given the overseer's full and undivided attention. Five lashes were administered to Tom while the other slaves were forced to watch. The overseer then asked Tom if he needed some water. Tom glared at him with murderous eyes, but merely whispered, "No, thank you, boss."

Later that night he was laid down in his cot beside thirty other crammed cots, in a room full of slaves, a rural version of the shelters he'd stayed in during his comparatively blessed times as an orphan in Mother Russia. Lying on his side to not aggravate his throbbing wounds on the rough hessian, Tom wept for Shirley, who had died once again because of him. The trial was three lives away (including this one) and not a single good deed had been carried out by Tom in his last two lives, or those further back for that matter. Lying in his cot, sporadically scolded for his idiocy by the other hardened slaves, Tom wondered what counted as a good deed in this new slave life of his. Was it to not rock the boat? Serve his Master with the will of an ant for his Queen? Or teach his fellow slaves how to read and write? Convince Southern society on the merits of the abolitionist movement?

Or, and this was perhaps a blinding aneurysm of rage, lead a slave rebellion like Nat Turner and kill as many slave owners as possible? A sordid revenge to make up for the bloodlust he was denied during the Middle Ages.

The slave in the cot next to him was whispering his nightly prayers. He was one of those who had scolded Tom before. This slave's adopted name was Peter. Peter was Tom's cousin. They did not get along. Tom had to roll over, groaning at his wounds, to face Peter. "What year is it?"

"It's the year of our Lord—and fools who don't do what they're told."

Tom rolled back painfully again to ask the person in the cot next to him. Her name was Henrietta, and her scowl reminded Tom of Helena, very much so in fact. It was then he remembered his own wife in this time: Abigail, but she and their two children were scattered in other plantations, and any chance of ever seeing them again would almost certainly be denied him.

"Henrietta, what year is it?"

"Same thing Peter told you. Goodness, did the boss whip the sense out of you too?"

"Henrietta, please, what year is it?"

"What year would you like it to be?" asked Henrietta, "Because it ain't gon' make much difference."

The man on the other side of her told them both to shut up. Peter echoed this sentiment. Henrietta sighed and whispered what Tom needed to know. "It's the year of our Lord, 1832. Year of the fool, too."

***

Antiseptic, not soap. That's what he was thinking of. They already had soap. They didn't have antiseptic, and Tom knew what with the civil war some thirty years away, there was going to be a lot of need for it. The only thing he feared was inventing a solution that fell into the hands of the Confederacy and changed the course of the Civil War, much like his sneaking suspicion that he'd inadvertently helped the nazis build a better airforce. That was one thing he did not want to change.

This was the plan, laughable as it might have seemed to the powers that be. He would teach his fellow slaves to read and write (Illegal and punishable by death) and convince the Master of the plantation to embark on a radical journey of racial awakening, or something of a similar manner. How was he to do this? By offering some invention of modern advancement he had the skills to recreate in exchange for greater liberties for his people. Precisely what invention or innovation he could shamelessly steal and pass off as his own escaped him, but with the trial looming, the pressure was on to do something so groundbreaking that it would improve society immeasurably and earn him untold amounts of karma. A flawless get-good-quick scheme. And if not antiseptic, then something a little simpler, like tampons? the brassiere? Electricity? (Maybe not electricity.)

While he settled on an invention, Tom taught the others in his cabin to read and write, letter by letter, one by one. Convincing them he knew what he was talking about was harder than encouraging them to do something that could very well lead to their painful deaths.

They managed to obtain a book from their church, which was a stuffy revivalist tent erected close to their living quarters. More specifically, Henrietta got the book. The preacher, a free black who travelled between plantations and only gave sermons under white supervision, didn't accept Tom's request for reading material, brushing him off. "The only good book is the Good Book, and I'll preach that to you every Sunday."

Tom asked Henrietta why the preacher was acting cagey. "He's teaching us to free our souls, can't he also help us learn to read?"

"He's part of the Underground Railroad," said Henrietta. "He don't trust you, he don't know who you working for."

So that's how Henrietta got the book. The Good Book. A real worn version. Tom taught Henrietta first, and she then taught others herself. This took a whole season, from planting to harvest. The only person unwilling to learn was Peter, who didn't see the point of it all. When they were too exhausted, Tom told them stories of his other lives. As expected, they told him he was crazy, yet they listened all the same.

Based on local slaveholder surveys, a Master's greatest fear was the threat of a slave rebellion, so it was prudent the overseer was occasionally dispatched to listen in on their workers at night. On one particular night the overseer just so happened to catch Tom's tale of a monkey that routinely beat humans at checkers. The boss heard Tom explaining the rules and finally give in to the others demands that they play a game or two.

"We'll just have to make ourselves up some pieces and a board," Henrietta encouraged.

"Massa wouldn't allow it," one of the children moped. That brought everyone back to reality. Yet learning to read and write gave them pride. When their bones were too tired and their souls too battered and bruised and they asked what was the point of any of it, Tom told them stories of the future, told them of their children getting a better run of luck, of each generation getting a little more freedom. This they liked. It lifted their spirits. Out in the fields they would hum and sing, and the songs soon came freely at night too.

The overseer did not appreciate their soulful offerings, but they chanced his arm and whipless they remained, for now.

A few weeks later, Tom was summoned to the house. Tom had to chuckle internally when the Master mentioned how privileged Tom was to find himself in a house as wonderful as this. Wonderful no doubt for the time, but lacking the A/C of Tom's rent-stabilised shoebox almost two centuries later. The Master was not the richest slave owner in town. An unfortunate spate of low yields had transpired into heavier spells on the drink, further weathering his declining health and causing the house to follow suit. The Master told Tom to sit at the table.

"They look up to you. Yes, they do."

"Yessir," said Tom.

"You were born on this land, wasn't it?"

"Yessir."

"You don't run errands like Henrietta, do you?"

"Nossir."

"And at the nigger church we let you attend—for now—there ain't no orientals?"

Tom was taken aback by the unusual question and thinly veiled threat. "Nossir."

The Master motioned to Henrietta, who stood at attention by the door. She was shaking. Henrietta went into the other room and returned with a board. She placed it on the table. Tom saw the white and black markings and chuckled. A checkers board, hand-crafted.

Naturally, the Master was white, and Tom black. Tom considered losing on purpose at first. But then he grew bold in his vision. "I won't go easy on you, but what I will do is keep my victory to myself. No one else will know. I will give you that, Massa."

The Master laughed. "You really think you're going to win?"

"I used to play for food, liquor. Used to beat travellers from all over."

"When was this?"

"When I was a monkey."

The Master chuckled to himself. "*Was?* What's changed?"

***

The trick with checkers is sacrifice. Forcing your opponent to strike but in doing so leaving themselves vulnerable. Tom did exactly that. Swept the Master three for naught. The Master stopped sipping his grain whiskey by the third game.

"If you ain't never left this land, where did you learn?"

"Thailand... Maybe it's called Siam now."

"Where's that?"

"In Asia."

"How'd you get over there?"

"Well," Tom laughed uneasily, "you wouldn't believe me if I told you."

The Master was uneasy. "They teaching these stories in church? Because I'll tell you, there ain't no monkeys playing checkers in the Bible, and if they telling you tall tales like this, then I wonder what else they filling your skulls with?"

"Nossir," Tom backpedaled, the cockiness evaporated. "I made the whole thing up. I learned checkers from one of our older brothers, one who went panning for gold before they captured him." Tom was referring to one of the older slaves who had already died, dead men suffering no consequences and all.

"He wasn't one of them free blacks, was he? That's one hell of a slippery slope, I always said."

Tom was almost offended the Master wasn't up to date with the origins of his "property". Then he remembered that the Master owned people, so a complete disregard for their general existence should have already been expected. "Yessir, he was."

The Master shook his head in disapproval. "Where'd he teach you? Wasn't in church, was it?"

Tom shook his head, raising a hand in deference. "Was in the quarters. The others told him not to teach me. They burned the board up when he died. Didn't want no trouble. I wasn't happy about it, but I get why they did it."

This was a turning point, a small cog set loose in the Master's ingrained understanding of the world. He wanted to believe Tom because he liked Tom.

"Lying is a sin," said the Master. "I don't want to pull your people out of church. Even the niggers deserve their chance at salvation once they earn their keep."

What a generous concession.

"And I don't want you to take away the church," Tom pleaded, still somewhat bemused by the Master's obsessive fear of a black church left to its own devices. "They shouldn't be punished because a runaway told me how to play checkers and tell silly stories about animals..." The silence that ensued was excruciating and Tom felt sick to his stomach. The Master eventually nodded in agreement. "Good. I just wanted you to remember your place. You're a smart one, I'll give you that, but don't make me have to punish you for it..."

Tom sensed something else in the Master, perhaps a man tiring of the hate he inflicted? After all, it was all he knew. Surely it ate him up. "Shall we play again sometime?" he asked.

The Master was thrown off by the tone. Henrietta too. No nigger ever said "shall" like a Southern genteel. But the Master was happy with the offer. "Yes."

Tom smiled. The Master smiled warily, wondering what the heck he'd got himself into.

***

They played chess next. Tom played dumb about the rules and the Master was quietly pleased when Tom seemed to catch on quick. Worthy chess combatants were few and far between in the rural south.

"What else you good at?" he asked Tom once, a few weeks into their little games. Tom's gaze drifted to the walls, deep in thought. The Master wasn't much of a decorator, his walls plain like a blank canvas. The sight reminded him of an old skill. And he got to scheming. "I can draw," said Tom, but the Master seemed unimpressed and remained silent.

"Painting," Tom offered instead. "I know how to paint."

Intrigued by his new pet, the Master obliged.

Tom was sent into town to obtain the needed supplies. He arrived clad in his rags, utterly terrified to be amid the townsfolk, clutching the crumpled and, by now, sweat-stained letter that gave him permission to be outside unattended. They murdered him with their eyes and their prayers; men, women and children alike. The few free blacks who passed him dared not acknowledge their mutual suffering, small talk between coloureds being widely considered a sure-fire sign of conspiracy.

The inner Austrian art teacher in Tom scoffed at the brief list his kind wasn't meant to grasp. A single pencil, one or two brushes, a few cheap oils and some canvas for stretching. He was resourceful but he wasn't a magician. There wasn't even enough for a rudimentary easel. He'd need to construct one himself back at the plantation.

The shopkeeper was willfully rude to Tom, but acquiesced to the Master's written, if somewhat unorthodox, instructions. Walking back laden with his meagre supplies, it occurred to Tom that any failure to paint satisfactorily could well incur some violent punishment. This was terrific for his already frayed nerves.

Taking on board the time-honoured advice to "paint what you know", he painted the plantation on a sweltering summer's day. For style, naturalism was a safe first bet. This was well-trodden territory from page 34 of the Viennese art textbook Hubert helpfully co-authored. Took him a week, an hour each day after his ten in the field. He finished it on the Sunday and nearly collapsed thereafter.

The Master was blown away.

Encouraged by this reaction, Tom did another, this time employing daring hints of impressionism into the composition. A depiction of humanity's fallen state: man reaching out for God, begging for mercy and forgiveness. This man was, of course, white. The Master did not like the lack of detail used in this style, the technique informed more by laziness than artistic choice. He tutted and clucked his tongue. Unlike Tom's "Southern plantation" picture, this failure was not hung up in the house and Tom didn't see it again. Tom was told to do it over, this time with more detail.

Tom lobbied for less time in the field to devote more time to his painting. This request was immediately refused. The Master had grown bitter. The astounding surprise of his slave's latent talent had confounded him, not least because the Mistress had loved the impressionistic painting and taken it to town, where it had caused a sensation and sold for a pretty penny. The townsfolk had literally never seen anything like it in their lives. Herein lay the true reason for the Master's souring favour: a bitterness at his own deficient perception of art, and that a slave might just know more than him. The painting of the Southern plantation was duly reproduced, and once again sold in town for more pretty pennies.

All the while, Tom siphoned off writing implements to Henrietta, who passed them onto the other slaves to aid in their lessons. Unfortunately, due to the gruelling demands placed on Tom, he had barely any energy left on Sundays to teach them to write like he promised, and their progress slowed.

Tom didn't play checkers or chess anymore, either. Now it was just painting this or that masterpiece on demand. His chance to gain the Master's crucial friendship was slipping away, cotton picking replaced with creating art and treated almost as one and the same. Tom knew nothing of the additional money he was turning over for the plantation, but he sensed it was considerable: shortly after handing over his fourth or fifth painting, the Mistress took to wearing a pretty new dress with red rubies sparkling round her neckline, and the Master started puffing away on the finest imported cigars. How wonderful for them.

So it went. Tom alternating between naturalism and impressionism, one for the Master, one for the Mistress, capturing Southern life in its simple glory. The Master scolded Tom for his slow delivery and the Mistress, suddenly a connoisseur of high art, began to criticize his impressionism (despite each new work selling quicker than a glass of water on a North Carolina summer's day).

And just when Tom was thinking about snapping the brush and putting it to both their throats, there came the arrival of an old friend…

Out in the cotton fields his bitterly unsocial cousin Peter suddenly stiffened as though being struck by lightning, then immediately demanded water. The overseer, as custom dictated, responded to the request with a whipping. Tom arrived late on the scene and asked Henrietta what Peter had done. And when Peter looked at him between the fourth and fifth whipping, Tom's face went slack. *Hello, comrade!*

***

Later that night, in the cots where they slept, Napoleon on his side and Tom on his, a reunion was held. While Tom had found himself in a string of restricted lives, Napoleon had been extending himself in all directions; learning skills and inventions to transform into a time-travelling MacGyver. He even casually mentioned he'd sold 40 million copies of his first album. But for all the new things Napoleon carried with him, there was one thing that stayed the same: a steadfast belief in the tenets of communism.

Communism? Weren't you living in America in the '80s as a religious leader?

Yes, and I was sending information back to the USSR, where possible. Don't tell me you've given up the fight?

I've been preoccupied with survival. I'm a marked man, remember?

Ah, yes, that cretinous coalition.

Indeed.

Surely with your amassed knowledge, you've learned ways to defend yourself?

Tom drew an embarrassing blank. *I really haven't had the chance, unfortunately. And now I'm to stand trial.*

Ah, yes, the trial.

You've heard?

Yes, they tried to dissuade me from acting as a character witness! But I laughed in their faces—what kind of monster would I be if I didn't stand up for my old friend?

A capitalist? Tom offered.

The word itself drew Napoleon's blood hot. *Exactly!* His eyes exploded in passion. *But still, you need to learn to defend yourself in the meantime. Me, I know how to make explosives and weapons in more or less any timeline.*

I don't want to hurt anyone, Tom clarified.

In the name of revolution sometimes blood must be shed.

Sure, Tom muttered.

Napoleon looked around the cots, inspecting them with a cold, calculating demeanour.

We're in the 1830s, said Tom. *Times are cruel for people with black skin.*

Napoleon grinned. *A place ripe for revolution!*

Tom was all for revolution, but not the kind he knew Napoleon liked to lead. *I don't know if that's such a great idea...*

Well, what else did you have in mind? We cannot stand idly by while our brothers and sisters suffer!

I teach my friends to read and write, while befriending our Master and convincing him to change his mind about holding slaves.

And how will you do that?

By offering him the medical invention of antiseptic or tampons or the bra, once I set aside some time to figure out how to make any of them. I've been a little slack in this department...

I know how to make all three! Napoleon exclaimed.

That's excellent.

But I also know how to make a machine gun, given the right components.

Uh-huh, said Tom, increasingly uneasy. *Well, maybe let's sleep on it and we can discuss the best method for attaining freedom for our people another time?*

Napoleon grinned. *Tomorrow, comrade, we begin our revolution.*

Thoroughly unsettled, Tom was relieved to end the conversation at this point. Unfortunately, Napoleon was not finished. He startled Tom, metaphorically hitting him in the face with a bottle of shoe polish. *Do you remember that falcon I owned back when I was leader of the USSR?*

Tom's heart raced. *Yes...*

Napoleon's lip quivered, and a thousand-yard stare coalesced in his eyes. *Sometimes I forget, which is good, but then I remember: I have never bumped into her since then... Are you absolutely positive she sang the chant?*

Tom gulped the guilt down, same as before. *Of course, we sang it together,* he rasped, hoping Napoleon could not see his hands trembling in the dark.

***

The ultimatum was simple. Tom had four weeks in which to either free the slaves his own way or support Napoleon in revolution. How did Napoleon come up with this timeframe? This was roughly how long he felt it would take him to source the materials and build a machine gun with which to ignite his revolt. Tom asked Napoleon how exactly he intended to source the necessary components.

Why, our friends in the church, I'd say. That preacher's a nice fellow, isn't he?

Tom had only two minutes of alone time with Henrietta while church wrapped up and Napoleon was busy giving Peter a personality makeover, effortlessly making friends with the preacher.

"Stall him," Tom said to Henrietta.

"Who?"

"Peter."

"Peter?" she asked, bemused. "What's he doing that I got to stall?"

"Building an advanced weapon to utilise in a slave rebellion."

"We talking about the same Peter?"

"Trust me. He changed. Like I did."

Henrietta's eyes widened. She clicked her fingers. "You did change—I knew it!"

"Yes, I did. But that's not important right now. Peter. He's going to lead a slave rebellion and it won't end well."

"Why can't *you* stall him?"

"I... It just can't be seen coming from me, OK?"

"OK, but when we going to continue lessons on writing? The others are getting restless."

"Napoleon knows how to read and write. He can show you."

"Who is Napoleon?"

"Huh? I meant—Peter!"

"OK..."

Unfortunately, instead of distracting him, Tom's suggestion drew Napoleon an audience for which to gain influence. Later that afternoon, when Tom returned from his horrific excursion with the Master, Henrietta took him aside. "Did you know that a group of slaves overtook their masters on an Island in the Caribbean? A place called Haiti?"

They returned from church to their living quarters, Napoleon eagerly boasting to Tom that he was already well underway at making an impression with the preacher and securing some of his components. "And don't you worry," Napoleon continued, "he was unsure about you, Tom, but I set him straight. Looks like he'll be willing to help out with a few more books for the others to read while I prepare us for war."

The overseer was waiting for them. He eyed Tom with that indignant scowl he was so good at. "Master wants to see you."

"It's my day off," Tom reminded, as peaceably as possible.

"Don't matter. He's got a job for you. Big job. Something in it for you too apparently, not that I agree with that last part."

"Do you disagree when you get paid for your whipping?" Napoleon retorted, finger raised.

"I do it for free today," said the overseer, whip raised and fist clenched.

Tom came between them and urged calm. "I'll go see the Master, sure thing."

***

It was an excursion by horse-pulled cart. The Master sat by Tom's side. In front was an artist's toolbox and canvas. The Master thought their sitting side should impress Tom. After all, it wasn't everyday one of Tom's people got to ride alongside his owner. Tom dutifully feigned gratefulness with an undercurrent of Oscar-worthy conviction. Along the way, the Master revealed their reason for travelling. "My reputation as an artist has spread to Wesley—that's one of the neighbouring towns—so much so that they've commissioned me to paint them a picture for their town hall. The money is good, boy. Very good. I would even like to pay you."

"I appreciate it, Massa. What would they like you to paint?"

"Justice."

***

The "justice" his Master spoke of was not, naturally, a blindfolded lady holding a pair of scales, but rather the body of the negro hanging from a grand old tree in the town square of Wesley. This was somewhat more confronting than the Southern plantations and accomplished impressionist knock-offs that Tom had grown accustomed to painting.

"What was his crime?" asked Tom, sick to his stomach.

"He disobeyed his Master," said the Master, himself a master of the thinly-veiled threat.

The Master engaged in a meet and greet with his fellow gentlemen compatriots: the lawman, the mayor and various other townsfolk who deemed it both fashionable and prudent to hook their thumbs thoughtfully through their suspenders and exchange idle, self-important chitchat while a lifeless body hung not thirty yards away.

Tom set up and the Master instructed him to memorise the scene and discretely scribble his required outlines in a small drawing book. Meanwhile, the Master made his own series of fake strokes on the canvas while looking deep in concentration. The other esteemed members of Wesley gave him space and gossiped among themselves of the allegedly amazing transformation of the Master. "I heard he was a drunk, but then he found the Lord—and a knack for painting too."

"The Lord has truly blessed him with an eye for detail."

"Hey, wait, what's that nigger doing next to him?"

"Is he... Is he writing?"

The lawman was first at the scene of the crime. The Master had to defend Tom and made the excuse that Tom could only draw. The lawman seemed to settle and both were allowed to continue with their painting of *Justice*.

Once Tom had completed the requisite prep work, capturing all the outlines and general minutiae of the scene, the ridges of the tree, the jovial righteousness of the crowd, the slackness of the bare feet, and so on, the Master announced loudly he would complete the depiction from the comfort of his home. On their ride back, the Master scolded Tom for almost giving the game away. "This better be your magnum opus."

***

Tom's hours in the field were reduced from ten to seven, so he could spend more time on his artistic pursuits. This did not sit well with the others, but Napoleon was quick to restore their confidence, assuring them that Tom was still working to gain the Master's ear and ultimately help them escape.

"Sure," said Tom, the morbid image of the hanging brother swaying like a pendulum before his eyes.

"Don't worry, comrade. I will teach them while we wait for the necessary parts."

Tom sat down in the Master's living room and painted with dead eyes. He painted the background first, a picturesque townscape of ivory and brick storefronts. He then recreated the self-righteous townsfolk, their gaze cast upward, the sight of the dangling body impeding their view of God. He gave the grand old tree its trunks and leaves next, imagining what he'd think if he was the tree they used, with all that rope and hate burning his boughs, knowing there was nothing he could do about it. Finally, it was time to paint the figure of the hanged man. A modest rebellion quashed with fatal fury. Tom considered his own rebellion, reversing the skin colour of each of the people, but his cowardice, that deep-rooted vine that snaked throughout his soul, that trait for which he was always meaning to finally sever, remained intact. Even daring to ask again what exactly this man had done to deserve such punishment never made it so far as clearing his throat.

Four Sundays and a few disciplinary whippings later, Napoleon received his final component from the preacher. He'd been running off in the night, sourcing things the preacher couldn't get himself. Tom had no idea how he found the energy. The lawman came round and talked to the overseer and Master about a masked nigger stealing some peculiar things. The other slaves were questioned, and maybe if it were any other plantation they would've tattled, but there was a sense in the air that change was coming and for this they held firm.

"I thought I told you to stall him!" Tom seethed to Henrietta later when it was safe to do so.

"I did, I told the preacher to withhold a few bits from him but Peter, *whoever* he is now, is quite...resourceful."

"Merde," said Tom.

"How's the painting going? Master said how much he's going to pay you?"

Henrietta, despite being one of the Master's house servants, had not seen Tom's painting of *Justice* yet. Tom had made that provision clear to the Master and he was obliged on this one request. Tom shook his head. "No, he hasn't..."

The deadline for *Justice* was scheduled to coincide with the unveiling of a new public building in Wesley. There would be many important white folks there. To make matters worse, harvesting season was coming up, and, with all those people in England needing endless supplies of cotton for their textile mills, the overseer was forcing everybody to ramp up the workload. Everyone else's hours increased while Tom's decreased, to allow him more time to paint. No one said anything to Tom's face, but disgruntled rumblings from afar suggested his standing had taken a dip.

His final brushstroke was applied two days before the harvest period began. It was a bona fide racist masterpiece. Tom gulped.

If ever there were evidence of his awfulness, this was at the top of the pile.

He was rewarded with his first ever payment of three dollars, reduced, of course, from four dollars, due to the "scene" he'd allegedly caused back in Wesley when sketching the outlines of their painting. The grin on the Master's face as he handed over the coins was one of genuine absolution. "You earned it," he said. "Now you can focus more on helping with the harvest."

That night Napoleon told Tom and the others he was going to leave the plantation for a few days to make the ammunition for his weapons. He promised he would return, and when he did, they would start their revolution. They would harvest the cotton for the profit of the people this time. Several he'd helped teach were willing to follow; others said they wanted to flee to the north, but Napoleon convinced them it wouldn't be better up north anyway. They were going to have a Haitian-style revolution right here in North Carolina.

Napoleon deferred the floor to Tom, asking for his support.

"I... I think we just try to escape," replied Tom, a tiredness creeping in that made him wonder if he even wanted that.

Napoleon gritted his teeth and clenched his fist but was undeterred. He would not give up on his friend. "When I return, I hope you will have changed you mind."

And then he was gone. Left Friday night, discovered missing Saturday, with interrogations commencing immediately and continuing bright and early Sunday morning at church. The congregation was shocked by the brazen boldness of the once-obedient Peter. The gall of it! The older slaves who didn't bother with dreams of escape claimed he was just being lazy, skipping out a couple days out from harvesting season.

The lawman came around and did his own interrogating, but with little incentive to talk other than not being whipped, everyone held firm. That afternoon, Tom was summoned to see the Master. To his surprise, the checkers table was set up. There was also some corn whiskey poured, dare it be said, for Tom.

The Master motioned for Tom to sit.

"Drink."

Tom sipped the drink.

"I found it peculiar how no one seemed to see this individual sneak out, days before the most important work of the season. You'd think they'd want an extra pair of hands helping them. Wouldn't you think?"

"Yessir."

"Don't yessir me, boy. You're one of the smart ones, what do you think it will take to make those accomplices sing? Do you think we should take away your church privileges? Take away your salvation?"

"That'd be a pretty evil thing to do," said Tom.

The Master was taken aback. "Evil? Boy, skipping out on work is the fruit of the devil. It is not my fault the actions of one man condemn the rest of you..."

The situation was at boiling point now. It was only a matter of time before Napoleon returned and chaos ensued. In his heart, beaten down from this life and all the others before, Tom knew that when you fight the system, it cost not just your life but those of the ones you love. The backlash after the inevitable failure would be catastrophic. A deal had to be struck.

"If I bring him to you, and you do what you have to with him, then after this crop is harvested, you free all the slaves, except for me."

"Sorry," said the Master, almost falling out of his chair. "What did you just say?"

"The man who escaped, the man whose name you don't even know, he's not going to escape north. That's not his style. He's coming back here to free the slaves, and he will not be asking nicely like I am for this inalienable human right."

The Master grabbed the drink from Tom's side, sipped it as though deep in thought, then spat its contents in Tom's face.

"How dare you!" the Master scolded, as Tom wiped the whiskey from his face. "Free all my slaves? I'm not freeing anyone. Guess you aint so smart after all."

The Master rose, and Tom did likewise. The Mistress and Henrietta peered in from the door, but they were waved away.

"Massa," said Tom, "the reason why I'm smart is because I come from a time and place where humans realised the evil that went on in these plantations—and it wasn't no skipping out on forced work they were concerned about, neither. In thirty years there will be a civil war between the south and the north and your side will lose. If you don't agree to free the slaves, that masked brother on the lam will kill you and your family."

The Mistress approached, having been listening in from the hallway, and demanded the Master punish Tom for speaking with such insolence. The Master agreed. He told her to fetch the overseer, then reached across the table and smacked Tom in the face.

"How dare you threaten my family! I ain't freeing your people ever—don't you know how valuable you dumb bastards are to me—you're all worth more than the damn crop!"

Tom held firm. "Listen, I'm not asking to be freed, I can keep painting for you, for free, I'll make you all the money in the world. I'll paint things that will keep your name spoken for hundreds of years to come. I'll return your fugitive peacefully. All I ask is that you free the others. This is the best deal for you, you've got to trust me on that."

The Master laughed. "This ain't checkers, boy. You don't have any moves to play." The overseer came rushing in and launched at Tom with the cat o' nine tails. Tom did not fight back, but cowered into a ball, clinging to the checkers table until he was dragged outside by his legs.

***

The other slaves were beckoned out from their living quarters. Tom was tied to the whipping post. The left side of his face was badly bruised, his left eye puffy and swollen. He expected a whipping, and a bad one at that, but Henrietta's scream drew his attention to the seasoned oak between the house and their living quarters. There a noose hung. He then heard the Master's voice behind him. "This negro has disobeyed his Master. This is what happens when you speak in a manner that displeases me..."

And then Henrietta screamed and the others gasped. Tom closed his eyes, awaiting the first blow, but none came.

He opened his good eye, and looked at the faces of his compatriots, arrested in a state of pure disgust. They were looking beyond him. He turned his head and there he saw it, his magnum opus. *Justice.*

"As many of you may know, your friend here has been doing a few paintings recently. Been given a few hours off work each day, in fact. His latest one was so good, I thought I might share it with you lot. Such a remarkable talent..."

The Master made other observations about the painting, commenting on the superior brushwork and impeccable eye for detail. Those gathered switched their contempt between Tom and the painting, back and forth in disbelief, until the Master dismissed them.

Once everyone had dispersed, the Master approached Tom. He noticed Tom glance at the noose on the seasoned oak. "That noose is for your friend when he returns... Gee, you know, I think your friends really enjoyed your painting. I'm sure they'll be dying to let you know what they think of it..."

If this were an action film, Tom would have spat blood and said, "Last chance to accept my offer." But it wasn't, and Tom could only manage the "coughing up blood" part.

"I want you to think about how you want your future to look. You keep up this attitude and I'll be happier to sell you along to folks who really take a shine to a beating. Thirty years from now there may be a civil war, but till then..." The Master chuckled as he and the overseer left Tom tied to the post, where he passed out.

***

He was shaken awake in the dark of night by Napoleon, who illuminated Tom's face with a torch that resembled a primitive, homemade maglite. Napoleon examined his eye with concern. "Can you still aim a rifle with this one?" he pointed at Tom's good eye.

"You came back," Tom muttered weakly.

"Of course! I never leave a comrade behind. So, how about that revolution?"

Tom sighed. The rest hated him, clearly. All his efforts thus far had resulted in little apart from whippings, beatings, and the production of a racist (if technically accomplished) masterpiece. Napoleon had in his hand a homemade, battery-powered light source that would only come to exist over a hundred years later.

Maybe a successful revolution wasn't a far-fetched notion after all.

"Sure," muttered Tom, "Why not? Let's kill everyone. I know a public unveiling we could make an appearance at."

"Excellent," said Napoleon, cocking something mechanical in the dark.

Cow II

A cow.

A bloody cow. Again.

Better than being yet another chicken, of course. Anything was better than being a chicken. But what good deed could a good cow do?

Provide milk and meat for humans! one part of his brain offered.

But what good is that? another part countered. *It will only give them more fuel to help them proliferate their hate.* And on the scale of doing good, how did selling his body for human consumption rank in light of all these other nasty things he'd done, especially his time in the antebellum south? His stomach (all four compartments) went queasy and his udders shuddered. Not good for much.

So what was he to do? And where was he? It appeared to be some kind of closed-in yard; corrugated iron and the tall, decaying, sky-blue wall of another building hemming him in. It was nothing like the open fields and meadows of before—not that he could say he rightly deserved that. There was a poster of a serious man on the sky-blue wall. The supporting message was provided in a language Tom couldn't understand. Indian? He wasn't sure. He'd never been Indian before. The man in the poster looked Indian, but honestly Tom could never tell the difference between

Indian, Pakistani and Bangladeshi, no matter how racist that sounded. (Good to see that after all this time, he'd evolved into a beacon of worldly understanding.)

And then he remembered a most telling fact: India worshipped cows. After all the horrible things he'd done with Napoleon in North Carolina, he'd still ended up reasonably well in the reincarnation lottery. Not a bad outcome. There were far worse, as he knew only too well. So Tom sat and waited to be worshipped.

An old lady came out and offered him some fresh grass. She was cringingly old. Babu, she called him, not too dissimilar to his name as a goat in Afghanistan, not that he fully recalled this. North Carolina, that's what saturated his memory, like oil in a pan, covering everything like a burning sea. Belatedly, it occurred to him that he was alone. Usually, there were other cows, diseased or otherwise. Where were the others?

A young boy fed Tom hay in the morning and the old lady brought grass in the afternoon. This was relatively peaceful, if not udderly boring. They kept feeding him and feeding him until he remembered where he was headed: as a sacrifice for an Islamic feast, Eid-al Adha. He was showcased there last year, taken along a superhighway into a big tent where he was tied to a pole and people decorated him with paint to make him more attractive to potential feasters. He had not sold that night, perhaps due to his smaller frame at the time, hence the extra feeding from grandma. Being fed and fattened up for food was not new to him, but the smile on the old lady's face now took on a distinctly sinister shade.

Tom studied his confines, scanning for weaknesses in the corrugated iron. Perhaps there was an opportunity to plot a *Shawshank Redemption*-esque escape using the poster of the local political figure tacked onto the sky-blue wall. Yet he had no tools nor fingers to use tools even if he had any. Even if he were to develop a method, concealing a cow-sized hole in the wall presented a few logistical issues. It was only in staring at the poster for an entire afternoon that his brain sparked another idea. A crude idea, but an idea nonetheless.

The time to strike was just after his first feeding. Tom waited for the boy to return inside before he got up on his hind legs and began licking the bottom edges of the poster with his fat tongue. Once both edges were free, he gripped the poster in his teeth and carefully tugged until the poster was separated from the wall, then placed the poster along the ground, but upright so that the old lady would notice it. He sat down facing the door and waited.

The old lady came out and had eyes only for him. She was muttering something in a language Tom was still trying to grasp, but was certain it revolved around getting a good price for his dissection. He threw his head over to the poster and it took several flailing nods before the old lady noticed and changed course.

Once her hobbling frame had cleared the door, Tom rose to his hooves and charged like a bull. He burst through the wooden door and found himself squeezing through the squalid kitchen, pinballing along the hallway and over the top of the young boy of the house. *SORRY!* Tom mooed.

Because he didn't have enough momentum, he had to unlock the front door with his teeth, all while the old lady, who had caught up to him, smacked his backside with a saucepan while furiously tugging on his tail. But once he pried the door open, that was it. He was free. Out into the world of the impoverished; a main strip of food vendors cooking up a storm right by the roadside, while fume-spewing cars rolled along beeping each other with vigour. He looked left and right and trotted in the direction with the fewest people (this was only marginally less crowded).

The old lady followed and screamed for someone to stop the cow. A nearby policeman, dressed in green khakis with a large belly, heeded her call. Tom's eyes bulged in fear. The policeman rushed over but was knocked off balance by a whizzing motorbike, the unwitting driver becoming the policeman's new target of choice.

Tom turned at the nearest corner and saw a clearing of farmland further down the dirt road at the bottom of the hill; perfect for getting away from the old lady, who persisted alone in her mission, saucepan in hand, out for vengeance. It was at this stage he found his fitness tested (cows not being known for their speed, endurance or general fluidity of movement) and though he began to gallop like a horse down the hill, this pace did not last. Heaving, he turned corner after corner to escape the old lady's sight, slowing down when trotting past people who went about their day, unperturbed by a wandering cow.

He trotted until he found himself in the middle of the clearing. He looked behind; no sign of the menacing old lady nor of any passer-by who had heeded her pleas. He was free, again. (In truth, the blistering action had proved all too much for the elderly woman and she'd had a heart attack and collapsed on the hill shortly after Tom galloped out of sight.)

Beyond the wheat field he sneakily chewed on at select intervals, Tom wandered the land, mooing at any field workers who eyed him funny. And just when he was finding his legs ready to break down and the light of the day beginning to dim, he spotted some shrubland in the distance he could hide in without being disturbed. He nestled in behind a thin tree and decided he would need to find water tomorrow. Thoroughly spent, his eyes grew heavy and he was ready to fall asleep…

Tom.

Tom's eyes burst open, though the rest of his body remained in shock. He couldn't identify the source of the noise, but it was right in front of him, up real close.

Tom.

Who is it?

It's Rudiger.

Ah, merde.

It's OK. I'm not going to kill you this time.

How kind. To what do I owe this sudden leniency?

Rudiger sighed, which came out like a hiss that made Tom's blood curdle. *I've temporarily fallen out of Sal's good books, after what happened in Afghanistan.*

It took Tom a while to recall what had happened: chanting with Shirley, in her arms, as a bright light flashed his end.

That was you, he finally said. *You almost killed Shirley forever!*

Yes, and Sal said he was very sorry. I am also sorry.

So you will call off your vendetta, the trial is no more?

No, I should clarify. Sal is very sorry—that you weren't given prior warning, as is usually the custom. But he was more upset that I tried to wipe your soul's memories before you were taken to trial.

So the trial will go ahead?

Yes. He wanted the trial to go ahead after we found your character witness list. He said your defence is laughable. He wants to use the trial to publicly crush you.

Can't we just let bygones be bygones? I made a mistake, you made a mistake… Tom suggested.

And that's why I'm not going to kill you this time. This reprieve cancels out my mistake.

Did you find me just to tell me that?

Rudiger hissed, the relief clear in his voice. *No, I just happened to see you stomping through the wheat field. See, our meeting was fate, the universe giving me a chance to atone for my mistake and return to Sal's good books once more.*

Delightful. I'm thrilled for you.

Where is your owner? asked Rudiger.

I escaped, Tom triumphed.

There was silence for a while. *Where to now?* asked Rudiger.

I don't know. Where are we?

We're in Pakistan.

So, not India... No wonder that old lady was planning to sell me for food. Well, this settles it then: I'm going to India.

Why?

Because they worship cows in India.

There was a hissing that sounded like a conceited *tsk. They don't worship cows in India. They simply don't eat them.*

You're lying, but even if you're not, and they don't eat cows, I'll take that. Mind if I follow?

Tom was surprised. *Are you just going to wait until I'm India and then kill me?*

Rudiger said this would not be the case but Tom didn't believe him. Tom suggested they sleep on it, though in reality little sleep was accomplished; something to do with the fact that an old foe with a troubling history lay a forked tongue's length from his face.

***

Tom awoke to the sight of eternal dark eyes and that rhythmic flickering tongue. White hoops played at intervals on a scaly black body. Probably venomous.

Good morning, hissed Rudiger.

You didn't kill me, Tom noted.

Wasn't easy, old habits dying hard, but no, I did not kill you.

Thanks, I guess. You wouldn't happen to know where I could get some water?

Rudiger proved most helpful in this regard, dutifully leading Tom to a camp lodging of farm workers. There was a well. Not being the most inconspicuous of animals, Rudiger offered to distract the field hands while Tom lapped up some water. Rudiger snaked his way over and raised his head like his enemy the cobra to the field hands. Warning shouts soon turned to playful cheering as Rudiger threw on a frenetic display of dancing for the locals, all while Tom made a long arc to the well and stole a filled bucket with his teeth. They reconvened in the shrubland, where a more leisurely slurp could be had.

Thanks, said Tom.

You're welcome.

I guess you can come with me, Tom schemed, realising this was his best chance at gaining a character witness from the enemy camp. Road trips always brought together strange bedfellows, if the films were to be believed.

Rudiger hissed, perhaps excited, though it was hard to tell with those cold, dead dark eyes. *Excellent—but full disclosure: I will still be testifying against you at the trial.*

Tom's smile faltered. *That is perfectly fine.*

***

Rudiger knew the way, having once been a local politician in a Pakistani town in the south (using his meagre wealth to fund an African safari to hunt the most deserving prey known to man). They were approximately 200 kilometres from the border. Hourly, Rudiger made it a habit to remind Tom that cows in India weren't worshipped; just left to their own devices.

Tom always replied that being left alone was all he was asking for regarding Sal's CARROTA anyway...

They snaked around towns, avoiding roads where they could. The few farmers and field hands that saw them either witnessed a snake leading a cow, or a snake draped over the cow's back. Anyone who got too close received a warning hiss from Rudiger and an aggressive moo from Tom.

One time, as per his plan to flip Rudiger, Tom asked Rudiger what he did when he wasn't busy killing Tom. *You're loyal to Sal, I get that, but surely there are better things to do. After all, you don't want to do this forever, do you?*

Rudiger laughed, which also came out as a hiss. *I'm not always killing you. We take turns. I tend to be a horse most times after I kill you. And not even war horses anymore. Can't argue with that kind of karma. So why stop?*

Tom cringed. He thought he'd try another way. *Well, my favourite so far was being a pigeon, but if I had the chance, I'd be a majestic whale.*

Rudiger said he was a whale once, it wasn't too bad—he even helped a polar bear get to Antarctica. Tom exclaimed he remembered that, before it slowly dawned on him why Rudiger helped a polar bear travel to Antarctica in the first place...

Well, what about when the trial is over and I've won—or even lost? I bet Sal will be like a rudderless boat.

He will continue to seek justice for the oppressed, Rudiger said with a little more party-line gusto. *You're not the only bad apple, Tom.*

I've reformed, honest.

The evidence suggests otherwise.

Well, I've been trying! The effort is there.

That makes it all the more concerning, given the number of chances you've had.

***

Their mistake was not being inconspicuous enough. It's not often one comes across a "snake and cow" duo, and it wasn't long before the Pakistani media were packing into vans from Lahore and heading for the rural districts, searching for a feel-good story of the "dog befriends cat" mould instead of overdone territorial disputes over land soaked in generations of blood. This was to be the local feel-good story of the year, before it sadly deteriorated into rioting and renewed tensions between Pakistan and India.

The person who spotted them first was a lonely boy known for stretching the truth. But on this particular occasion, his well-connected father indulged his claims. At the time, both Tom and Rudiger extensively mooed and hissed at the boy, who'd followed them for a considerable distance with his mobile phone. When the boy stopped following, they thought that was the end of it. No extra precautions required.

The Punjab countryside in Pakistan was a flat sprawl of busy farms, health crops, shrubs and dusty dirt roads. The going was slow, given that the perpetual hunger of a cow necessitated grazing at frequent intervals. Rudiger used these intervals to remind Tom that this was the only time he was going to help him. These reminders came up against their greatest test on the fifth morning of their travels. They'd only progressed one hundred kilometres; Tom's wayward grazing a major factor. Tom had woken from a terrifyingly lucid nightmare in which he was feeding Napoleon glowing rounds of ammunition inside a bell tower in the 19th century. He woke in a sweat and thanked God he now had hooves and couldn't deliver glowing pieces of lead into a whirling machine at the behest of a madman.

The arrival of Sal's CARROTA swiftly shattered Tom's relief.

This time they came in the form of a street dog and a little girl missing one arm. Tom's old friend Deborah, who had killed him when he was a tree and a sunflower, was the girl holding a Tom Tracker with her only remaining hand.

Stand down, said Rudiger.

What is the meaning of this? asked Deborah. *Why haven't you sunk your fangs into his hide yet?*

We're giving him a break this life. Normal operations will resume the next life.

Deborah was indignant. *The Tom Tracker hasn't been updated with any amendments to current orders.*

This order has come from me.

So, you're disobeying Sal then? You've gone soft, Rudiger.

Rudiger slithered forward. The street dog mirrored his approach; like two pawns ready to collide.

One life, that's all it is. I made a mistake and I'm making up for it. Sal will understand.

Deborah waved her ghost arm around, presumably giving Tom the ghost finger. *That's all well and good, but I need the karma. I don't want to wake up with a missing limb again in my next life. It's not my problem you made a mistake. It's not Sal's, either. I'm not going to fuck up when I kill Tom because I know what I'm doing.*

The street dog cheered, *Hear hear.*

Rudiger bared his fangs. *Sal and I go very far back. Don't talk to me about killing Tom. I've killed Tom more than anyone. I was hunting Tom before you even had Tom Trackers—that's how long I've been hunting Tom. He's all yours in the next life, but for now: back the fuck off.*

Deborah threw down the Tom Tracker and drew a machete. Tom suspected a Mexican standoff was in place and planned accordingly. He'd do OK against the little amputee, Deborah, while Rudiger would handle the mangy street dog.

Deborah eventually relented. *Let me at least punch him a few times in the nose. I came all the way from Sri Lanka.*

Rudiger allowed this. And a few bites from the street dog, who may or may not have been rabid.

Once the two defeated members of Sal's CARROTA trudged off, Tom thanked Rudiger for standing by him. Rudiger used this touching moment to remind Tom he was still taking the stand against him in the trial.

Of course, sighed Tom.

***

They kept moving eastward, grazing their way through foothills and shrubland, oblivious to the growing media sensation lighting up television sets across Pakistan. The Boy who Cried Snake and Cow had just wrapped up his second TV interview for the day and this was followed by a cross to an old lady in a hospital bed, who claimed that the cow who had violently escaped her backyard was the same cow teaming up with the snake. Calls were made from locals to return the cow to its rightful owner. The news anchor's passing remark that the pair were heading for more cow-friendly pastures in India was beamed up via satellite and swallowed by cow vigilante groups living on the border. A public statement from the vigilantes was issued and a bus charter organised for that night. Rewards were offered for more footage of the odd duo. Several emerged, but these proved false upon greater scrutiny, the imposter cow being frightened to death of the deadly white-hooped snake and the pair not getting along famously.

Fifty kilometres from the border, they were spotted. Several white news vans appeared in columns struggling up the dirt path and slowing to a very conspicuous crawl. Tom and Rudiger, who was hanging off Tom's back, strained their necks to stare at the cameras and news presenters dressed in outdoor gear, ready to reveal this latest animal friendship to the masses.

What are they doing? asked Rudiger.

I think our friendship has captured a few people's imaginations.

Friendship? They are surely mistaken.

Thank you, muttered Tom. *What do we do?*

Keep going, I suppose.

So they did. And the media vans and various news teams followed. The closest a human came to the duo was a lawyer who claimed the cow belonged to his client, the old lady. This caused a bit of a stir, with a lot of pushing and shoving between local law enforcement and the legal team. Tom and Rudiger turned their heads and paused their pilgrimage to observe the kerfuffle. When everyone else noticed they'd stopped, the fighting ceased and Tom and Rudiger continued on their way. The sun was setting and the news crews continued their tracking, like covering the world's slowest car chase.

Shouldn't they be bored by now? Tom mooed to Rudiger.

That's the Pakistani media for you, Rudiger said with toneless familiarity. They sat down for the night and it appeared the news crews settled in too. Tom discussed with Rudiger the possibility of slithering over to the crews to spy on what they were saying. Rudiger was amenable to the idea but before he could make a move, a shouting voice stopped them. Tom and Rudiger turned to see a woman wearing grey khakis and a white business shirt, holding a clipboard with calm authority. Tom couldn't make out her face in the dark but he got the feeling he knew who it was and let out an excited moo.

"Shhh," motioned Anna. "Listen, there's not much time. I'm

supposed to be observing a bread thief in Victorian London."

It's great to see you! said Tom.

"You too, Father. So, I have good news and bad news. The good news is that I've figured out a way to be your lawyer for the trial. The bad news is that you can't cross the border into India."

Why not?

"There is a group of cow vigilantes on a charter bus intending to kidnap you and take you over to India themselves."

What's wrong with that?

Anna, pressed for time, was a little dismayed by Tom's lack of trust. "Because a fellow Auditor has done a favour for me and run the probabilities of an Indian vigilante group kidnapping a Pakistani cow—the results are violent clashes leaving many dead with the potential for escalation to miniature skirmish or small war..." Anna flipped her pages on the clipboard. "That possibility is running at 79% at the moment."

What do we do then?

"Give yourselves up. Go back to the old lady. It'll be the best thing in the long term."

But I've only got one life left after this!

"And you can still do good with it."

Tom sighed and turned to Rudiger. It was too hard to tell from his cold, dead eyes if any sympathy was escaping his scaly body, so Tom decided to imagine this was the case.

May I speak to my legal counsel in private?

Rudiger dutifully slithered away. Tom turned to Anna, his inner voice shaking. *You haven't seen my most recent lives yet, have you?*

Anna shook her head. "No, I haven't reviewed them yet. The Bureau is keeping me extra busy—I suspect on purpose. Anything you want me to highlight?"

<h1 style="text-align:center">Cow II</h1>

Tom's eyes flashed North Carolina, 1832. A high-pitched scream wailed after an explosion. *Nope. It's all good.*

"Great, well, I must go. Keep trying to do good things—and write them down when you can!" And then she was gone.

Rudiger returned shortly thereafter.

Guess I better turn myself in then, muttered Tom.

Do it in the morning, said Rudiger.

***

At the dawn of a beautiful new day, Tom awoke to see media hiding in the shrubs. There were more people now, locals who had travelled with banners and flags. Tom looked left and right for Rudiger, but the snake was nowhere to be seen. The camera crews were on both sides this time, the Indian media in front and the Pakistani media behind. Tom watched them all whisper to one another. He stood. The crowd went silent, each holding their breath as Tom turned in circles, deciding his direction. It was futile though, there was no point going to India if it meant more suffering caused by himself. He'd done enough of that.

I hope someone is noting this sacrifice I'm making, writing it down and underlining it multiple times and highlighting it... for whatever little it's worth... he said to the sky. He turned back toward the Pakistani media and took his first step towards them. The Pakistani media cheered. The visiting Indian media groaned in disappointment until one of them noticed that the snake was missing. They started laughing and the Pakistani media grew quizzical at this laughter until they too noticed that they were filming a lone cow on a shrubby hill.

It was then that everyone came to their senses and plans to leave commenced in rapid succession. As they packed their cam-

193

eras and the locals wrapped up their banners, in came the busload of cow vigilantes from India who demanded the relevant Pakistani institutions release the innocent cow from this oppressive country. Despite the fact that the story was over and the cow was worth little to anyone but the old lady, the Pakistani law enforcement and fifty or so locals would be damned if any Indians were going to tell them what to do. The lawyer for the old lady threw the first projectile and it all kicked off from there. Cameras were pried from their cases as soon as they'd been clasped shut. Tom stood in the middle of it all, tiredly singing his usual chant.

Moo Moo Moo. Daba dee daba doo.

Human (Last life)

This was it. He needed a miracle, a Hail-Mary type of life to undo all the damage he'd done.

A local Mother Teresa (if not the original).

A billionaire who could give it all away.

A neurosurgeon who saved life after life after life.

The universe, sensing his previous intentions of getting to India and ignoring his other requests, gave him that wish: A Bollywood starlet.

He came to life in a dressing room on the day of the big dance sequence. The final number. The makeup artist noticed an immediate change in his demeanour.

"Do you not like the makeup?" She tensed, traumatised by the raging tantrum Tom had thrown earlier that day. Tom simultaneously studied her face and the tantrum that caused it. The part of him that was Jacinta Khapour felt the need to scream at the poor diminutive woman, for the makeup *was* too smudgy—even Tom agreed it wasn't evoking the kind of beauty the star of the show deserved. But the new leaf had already been flipped. Tom suppressed Jacinta's boiling personality and, with some effort, calmly said it was fine. The makeup artist nervously continued, taking extra care as tiny droplets of sweat rolled down her brow.

The set opened onto a lovely domed palace. Despite all his lives spent swimming in expanses of deep blue sea filled with plastic garbage, playing checkers on the beach in Thailand, and very briefly finding himself in the heart of the Amazon rainforest, Tom had never witnessed so many vibrant colours invigorating his senses all at once; swirling about, making him downright dizzy. The assistant director was busy with the choreography of Jacinta's backup dancers, who were dressed in suits as per the big-budget, Westernised story the director and studio were aiming for.

Tom was called over by the director, who paused when he noticed Tom's face.

"Did you not go to makeup?" he said bluntly.

The Jacinta part of Tom screamed inside, preparing to demolish the foolish little man standing in front of her.

"Yes," Tom said with restrained eloquence.

The director eyed him with suspicion but decided to take the pleasantly less-than-hysterical Jacinta at her word. Besides, they could fix it all in post. Hopefully.

Tom was thrust into the lights, centre stage. Her love interest, who hated Jacinta and was just as much, if not more of a prima donna, faked a grin that said "let's just get through this".

The cameras began rolling and Tom tried to remember his lines but it all came in a blur just like the lights, their clumsy attempt at a final segue into the big dance number met with awkward silence. Jacinta may have been a prima donna, but when it came time to perform, she was the best in the game.

"Something wrong?" the assistant director queried from his chair. "Have you got food poisoning or something?"

"Yeah, what's up?" her love interest echoed, looking annoyed. He suspected this was one of Jacinta's attention-seeking ploys.

"Apologies," said Tom. "Let's start again."

And then Tom let the part that was Jacinta take over, the Jacinta that was a paragon of otherworldly beauty when the lights flicked on and it was time to shine. Her delivery was perfect, and when it came time to dance the choreography was executed so effectively it was as if they shared a single heartbeat. Jacinta's lip-synching was likewise flawless. The entire effect was one of pure magic and Tom had front-row seats to it all. At some stage during the energetic sequence, the thought occurred that Napoleon would be thrilled with this display; its boundless energy and gravity-defying theatrics not dissimilar to those displayed by the Russian ballerinas of the Bolshoi. Confetti cannons capped off the last notes as Jacinta and her on-screen lover became seductively entangled.

Everyone froze in end-scene poses. "Your breath stinks like porcupine dung," Jacinta whispered through smiling gritted teeth before Tom could stop himself. His love interest merely glared. Cut was finally called, and they all returned to their real selves. Tom went back to being Jacinta the tempestuous, "painful to deal with" star of the show. She asked the assistant director if they had finished for the day. The assistant director, finding a few minor faults in the first take but deathly afraid of upsetting the talent, said they had got it in one. Everyone else quietly disagreed, but Tom, still acclimatising to the dizzying energy of showbiz, was happy to call it a day.

Jacinta's PA guided Tom to her waiting black knight, a formidable tinted SUV, the driver speeding off to join the thronging Mumbai traffic. Jacinta's PA kept glancing at Tom, who stared out the window in wide-eyed wonder at the frenetic energy of the streets. In every direction, chaos narrowly avoided further chaos. Beeping replaced lanes, as tuk tuks snaked around their car with brazen assuredness. Streams of people flowed along the sidewalk, sidestepping endless building construction, little Hindu shrines and haggling stall vendors, while children with fruit to sell desperately flagged down cars. At one stage, Tom saw a young amputee crawl across the dirty pavement carrying his money pan between his teeth. Everyone had places to be.

"Is something wrong?" the PA finally asked, when the sight of a cow shambling about along the sidewalk, not a care in the world, sent Jacinta beaming with joy.

"Huh?" said Tom.

"Is your phone broken? Do you want to use mine?"

"No," Tom shook his head, before realising he ought to investigate more of this Bollywood life he'd been thrust into.

"How long until my part in this film wraps up?"

The PA began to panic. "Filming wraps up in two days—why? Was there something I missed in your calendar?"

Jacinta waved her hands about, trying to calm the startled PA. Her next request did little to soothe the poor girl's nerves, however. "Can I arrange a meeting with my accountant?"

As the PA set up a meeting, Tom rolled down the window, taking in the smog of overcrowded scooters, tuk tuks, buses with no doors, and the sickening contrast of hi-rise mansions neighboured by patched-up tin shacks. His eyes gleaned, mania evident, as an opportunity to do good presented itself. *That's the answer: poverty! Large-scale, heartbreaking poverty! Perfect!"* He would tackle one of the greatest problems in human history. Maybe not a dent would be made. But no one could tell him he hadn't tried.

***

The idea to visit the Dalai Lama came to him while re-watching Jacinta's favourite film, a film that, unsurprisingly, starred herself. Tom had played the DVD with the hope it would jog his memories. It was the simple simile, "As Buddhist as the Dalai Lama," uttered in reference to one of the more pious characters that sparked Tom's lightbulb moment. His eyes opened wide. Here was a real chance at getting the best character reference, possibly in the history of the human race.

The new and improved get-good-quick scheme was three-fold:

1. Give away all his wealth, except the amount needed to get to the Dalai Lama.

2. Meet the Dalai Lama and get a character reference, and possibly a signed picture.

3. Perform charitable deeds toward the less fortunate for the remainder of Jacinta's life.

This was perfect and would definitely go towards making up for what happened with Napoleon in North Carolina.

Sitting in her luxurious mansion, Jacinta browsed the internet, something Tom hadn't done in over three-hundred-odd years. Looking to play some of his favourite songs while he surfed the web, he stumbled onto the famous playlists of the rock icon of the 1980s–2010s: his good old friend Napoleon, who's unprecedented time at the top was a testament to his uncanny ability to predict and capitalise on each new trend. The biggest loser from Napoleon's behemoth career appeared to be Eiffel 65, who's electronic cover of "Blue (Da Ba Dee)" was widely panned, though they still had success with the hits "Move your Body" and "Too Much of Heaven". Disturbed by this discovery, he decided to see what else had changed and what hadn't, though he deliberately avoided the events of 1832. Everything appeared more or less the same, people being notoriously people, except for Stalin replacing Hitler as the endpoint in Godwin's law. Once he confirmed the non-existence of Hitler, Tom searched for footage of his highly-publicised journey as a cow in the short-lived "Cow and Snake" duo of Pakistan. He found nothing and assumed it hadn't happened yet. There was still Facebook, though it was coloured green instead of blue. And like a drunken teenager stalking his crush, Tom unashamedly searched for Lily White. There among the lilies, he found her. As beautiful as ever. Lily White. The girl who started all this mess. The girl he wouldn't kill Hitler for. She was alive anyway, World War II or not. The butterfly effect had done zip on her. Tom laughed. Was she worth all this? He didn't even know her well enough to answer, and it was this unknown quality which filled that stupid heart of his with fantasy: Lily and himself, living in domestic bliss in a modest mansion such as this...

Not entirely for narcissistic purposes, Tom performed a search on the words "Tom Robinson". Born 1988. Attended Biggie Smalls High School (it had been called Robert Smalls High the first time around), then Rutgers college. Liked funny pun meme pages. He scratched his head in self-awareness, his nostalgic trip revealing the remnants of a very bland existence. Was this really the life he wanted another shot at? Maybe if he all he asked of the judge was to return to his old life, they'd chortle and grant him his wish. Maybe they would consider that punishment enough.

Tom then searched for images of his parents, finding very few family pictures, but those that he stumbled upon made him weep, the innocence of those times unreachable as long as he sang the chant. Depressed, he stood up in his mansion, dropped his pants and started watching porn. The part of him that was Jacinta was petrified. The part that was Tom was certainly not.

The next morning Tom called his PA to ask her again if she'd organised a meeting with his accountant. "Yes, it's scheduled for two days after the wrap party," she offered, meekly.

Tom gripped the reins on Jacinta's fury and through gritted teeth said this was acceptable.

The wrap party was attended by most of the cast and crew, along with the film's financial backers, some of whom were notable figures in the Mumbai underworld. Like the big dance sequence, the wrap party was extravagant in every conceivable way, the unrestrained opulence a slap in the face to all those doing it tough in the surrounding slums.

Napoleon would have a field day with this, thought Tom, who then unfortunately recalled a Napoleon "field day" consisted of luminous glowing bullets tearing limbs from torsos, with everyone screaming and—

Let's not dwell on that again, he decided, happy to take advantage of Jacinta's highly-selective memory.

Most of the party was spent dancing with people who secretly despised him and delicately knocking back high-end executives and producers who offered Jacinta opportunities beyond their capabilities. Fruity libations were consumed from fancy glasses as Jacinta edged each conversation into how one could arrange a private audience with the Dalai Lama, and what they might ask him if given the opportunity.

"I could get you an audience," one producer claimed, "in exchange for a private audience elsewhere."

"I'd ask him how to attain enlightenment," said one of the other actresses.

"I would ask him how best I can help the world," said her love interest, acting worldly and compassionate while thoughtfully sipping his champagne.

"I think I will create a charity and ask him to endorse it," declared Jacinta.

"Oh, and what would this charity be in aid of?" asked the other actress, humouring Jacinta.

"Helping the poverty-stricken children of India," Jacinta stated proudly.

"Do you mean like my charity that you turned down on numerous occasions?" said the love interest, leaving the rest of the group speechless.

The diplomatic Tom wanted to say yes, that he'd changed his ways, but Jacinta acutely fought back, her strong personality overwhelming Tom as she uttered an exasperated, "Yes, except one that would be far better than yours, you *chod!*"

This went down wonderfully.

***

"What do you mean I can't give away all my money?"

"I'm sorry, Ms Khapour, but you simply cannot do that. It is not financially sound. It is what we in the accounting game refer to as being 'financially stupid'."

"But it's my money!"

"Yes, but your career investors require significant payments and if I don't oblige, both of us will be in serious trouble."

"Who?!" screamed Jacinta, and the accountant flinched backward in his chair, truly shocked.

"Well, principally, Mr Tendulkar, a man I'm sure neither you nor I would want to displease."

As Jacinta recalled that most of the producers at the wrap party and in most of Bollywood were financed by the Mumbai underworld, her dawning recognition elicited a smile from her accountant. "Yes, that is the one! Let us not displease him, lest we find a cow's head in either of our beds."

Tom resisted the urge from Jacinta to call it a day and instead claimed he wasn't scared at all (though he was), to which the accountant replied, "That's all well and good for you, Ms Khapour, but I am also indebted to Mr Tendulkar as well as scared of him, so I will not be doing that, please." He smiled and shuffled his papers away to signal this was the end of the discussion.

Tom's eyes narrowed. "You're going to sell the shares and assets I don't need and we are going to put that money into my new charity or so help me Shiva I will beat the living shit out of you."

The accountant was a timid, rather tubby man, but he sized up Jacinta and, despite her notoriety for emotionally decimating assistants, saw no immediate physical threat.

So Tom reached across the table and took the first swing.

They underestimated one another. The resultant tussle was long and scrappy, but once again Tom's experience as an ant helped him employ the chemical kamikaze attack technique that no human could possibly prepare for.

"What the hell was that?" gasped the accountant, clutching his windpipe and wiping the spit off his face. "OK! OK! I'll set up your stupid charity."

To allay the accountant's fears, Tom said he would talk with Mr Tendulkar and smooth things over. The accountant doubted this but let Tom go while he nursed his bloody lip and aching ribs.

Returning home, Tom did more research on how to set up a charity. This primarily involved googling the phrase "how to set up a charity". After much internal debate between dealing with the laborious administration pains of creating a charity from scratch versus simply donating his wealth to an existing organisation (other than love interest's), Tom determined that in order for him to do good deeds he probably had to do more than just give money. He would name his charity Good Karma, if that wasn't on the nose enough. At Jacinta's urging, it would have to be the exact same cause as her love interest's charity, so that there would be a measurable opportunity to show him up. Tom reluctantly agreed and wondered to himself why, on his last life to do some good, he was saddled with the headstrong personality of an insufferable prima donna. Were things not hard enough already?

The doorbell rang and Tom's housekeeper helpfully let in several goons flanking a large man with a combover. Tom made a mental note to remind the housekeeper in future to not let in any goons unless they had a decent reason for being there.

The man with the combover wore a scarlet suit, his shirt unbuttoned to reveal a tacky though presumably expensive gold chain, while ruby, sapphire and emerald rings adorned his thick fingers. Mr Tendulkar had worked his way up from the packed slum pits of Dharavi to become what he always dreamed: A Bollywood kingpin and sophisticated purveyor of the arts.

"Ms Khapour, I have been told you wish to turn most of your growing wealth over to a charity for less fortunate children. I've come here to tell you not to fret about these things: my organisation gives many opportunities to children already, so you need not worry your pretty little head, my dear." The opportunities he referred to were offloading electronic goods smuggled from the docks, begging in the wealthier parts of Mumbai, or good old-fashioned sex trafficking. He was a regular Father Christmas, all right.

With the help of Jacinta's superior acting talents, Tom hid his repulsion and instead spun a naïve tale of how he'd come to think it unfair that he got to live in a mansion while children scavenged in the streets and slept in stoops and gutters and God knows where. The goons were swayed but Mr Tendulkar held firm. "You're a star, Ms Khapour, you deserve this mansion, people admire you *because* you own nice things, because of your wealth and your lifestyle. This is your power and you must show it if you want to continue to be the jewel of Bollywood." He drew closer, his cologne overpowering, and reached out a hand to brush her face. "People at our level deserve nice things."

Tom nodded, clearly being reminded that Jacinta herself was one of Mr Tendulkar's "nice things".

Mr Tendulkar advised that if she wanted to persist in this fool-hardy endeavour, she could make small donations to charities like her love interest's (but amounts so insignificant they would offer little in terms of karmic recompense, and certainly do nothing to impress His Holiness the Dalai Lama). Tom outward-ly agreed to this pitiful compromise and a part of him wished Napoleon were there to take care of matters, as ugly as they would no doubt turn. Mr Tendulkar then rambled on about another film opportunity while Tom weighed his real options: somehow escape the financial chains of Mr Tendulkar and set up a successful charity to precipitate a meeting with the Dalai Lama, or keep with the meagre donations until Sal's CARROTA made their inevitable appearance.

Or, and this was a little more practical: escape the financial chains of Mr Tendulkar, skip the charity-building and just straight up give the money to the Dalai Lama to donate to the charitable endeavours of *His Holiness'* choosing?

Ding ding ding. We have a winner.

Tom abruptly stopped the conversation and said that it was an amazing film idea that he would be happy to start as soon as possible, perhaps after a luxurious R&R escape that the Mumbai tabloids could lap up. Mr Tendulkar went giddy at the prospect.

"Wonderful! I'm glad you've seen the light. Let's discuss this further over dinner sometime—perhaps I will even join you on this promotional break too, my darling…" He made the same eyes at Jacinta that the knight back in the Middle Ages had made at Joan. Seemed nothing had changed regarding excited men in all this time, neither the looks they gave nor the object of their desires.

***

First, Tom needed a gun. Getting a gun would have been easy, if not for the fact Jacinta needed to hide the acquirement of said weapon from Mr Tendulkar's many eyes and ears. Her PA was thus thrust out into the Mumbai heat, tasked with obtaining an untraceable firearm. She returned in the afternoon with a nicely compact 0.38 and a traumatised psyche from the ordeal. Pleased, Jacinta then instructed her driver to take her to the accountant's office once more. The accountant was surprised to see her.

"Ah, Ms Khapour, I'm so sorry for our misunderstanding previously. Don't worry, I didn't go through with any of your prior requests and we are now both thoroughly safe from Mr Tendulkar."

That was when Ms Khapour revealed the gun.

"OK, let me just go right ahead and bring up the relevant files, you crazy bitch."

***

Much like they had during Tom's journey as a cow through Pakistan, storms outside his immediate periphery began brewing the moment he stepped into Ms Khapour's dancing feet. The final cut of the big dance sequence was not working for the director, in no small measure due to the poor makeup on Ms Khapour's face defeating the collective talents of the editing room. The assistant director was now ruing his initial cowardice at not demanding multiple takes. The inefficient footage was shown to Mr Tendulkar who agreed wholeheartedly and commended himself for having sufficient restraint to not break the director's legs on the spot. Calls were made to all involved parties immediately, but Mr Tendulkar found it troubling when Jacinta did not pick up her phone to confirm cancelling her luxurious R&R to return to the studio for a reshoot and dinner with his handsome, powerful self. The only call he did receive was from one of his Bollywood accountants...

***

Jacinta took two suitcases and a backpack full of money and gold jewellery to the Bandra train station, a place someone of her upper caste seldom visited. Assuming her newly transferred funds to a scarcely-attended savings account in New York were not frozen, she had over 1.35 million US dollars to donate. Many offered to help carry her bags through the sweaty, packed station. She refused their help but gave them a few rupees nonetheless.

The online ticketing system was down but luckily for her the train was to be four hours late. She got to the ticket line and the queue stretched for miles, with many jostling at the front, trying to cut in. A headscarf concealed her face. Shuffling along, she glanced at the weary bodies around her. A commute in blazing heat was a draining affair no matter what country you were in.

On the other side of the station a train pulled up and a mass of workers streamed in, jamming themselves inside until the carriage could take no more. Middle of the day, yet still overcrowded. The Jacinta part of Tom was repulsed and Tom admitted he wasn't too keen on the idea either. A first-class ticket was quickly determined to be the safest means of travel, given the precious luggage and all.

Tom needn't have worried, though. The Swaraj Express to Chakki Bank was known for being all class and ultra-fast (once it finally departed).

The ticket officer at the front desk only needed to see Jacinta's eyes to recognise Ms Khapour. To confirm her suspicions, she made up a document Ms Khapour had to sign for the first-class ticketing system.

Her eyes bulged when Jacinta mindlessly signed the paper like she would any other autograph. The moment Jacinta saw the recognition in the ticket officer's eyes, she grabbed her ticket and marched off, while the ticket officer madly quoted her favourite lines at the fleeing actress.

The train was beautifully functional, a modern marvel compared to the rusted contraptions adorning the other platforms. A fourteen-car bullet. Jacinta got herself a booth seat with plenty of legroom and plonked her luggage on the seats opposite. First class was relatively empty, made up of the odd tourist and a few extended families; no locals seemed to recognise her. She was a bundle of nerves until the train departed from the station, Tom and Jacinta having seen too many Hollywood films where the bad guys hopped aboard just seconds before the doors closed.

Once the train shot out of the station, Tom breathed easy and tried to take in the Indian landscape; the rivers and trees and the hazy sky. Pretend he was a tourist on a spiritual journey. At first, all he noticed was poverty and pollution. So he looked harder and saw scatters of people scavenging along the rubbish-laden tracks, persisting with it all because that was life, for better or worse. It occurred to Tom that maybe Shirley was out there somewhere, living her life, respecting it. If Tom had another chance, he'd do just the same.

"Chai, chai," the child waiter cried. Tom sipped the tea and took in the aromatic flavours.

Anna visited him briefly in the afternoon. All she had time for was a question and a yell.

"WHAT THE HELL WERE YOU THINKING IN NORTH CAROLINA?"

You'll have to be more specif—

"DON'T PLAY DUMB WITH ME, HUBERT MULLER! YOU DO SOMETHING LIKE THAT *AFTER* WE SET THE TRIAL? FOR FLIPPIN' SAKE!"

I'm sorry, Anna!

"YOU'RE MAKING THIS ALMOST IMPOSSIBLE!"—she sighed heavily—"DO SOMETHING VERY GOOD VERY SOON! FOR BOTH OUR SAKES!"

And then she was gone.

"Chai, chai," the child waiter cried.

After the Anna interlude, the express train returned to its top speed of 110km/h, blurring the sunset-drenched Indian countryside once more and serving as a fitting metaphor for Tom's multiple existences passing him by. When the sun began to set (another life metaphor), he confirmed with a tourist their likely arrival time in Delhi, the train's next major stop. Turning in to his sleeping cabin, Tom hoped for deep, peaceful sleep. Some small reprieve. He was granted none.

If it wasn't the chainsaw snoring of his two elderly cabin companions or the random jolts of locomotion, then it was the endless replaying in his head of all his awkward, embarrassing, rude and deadly mistakes. Any brief patches of sleep were converted swiftly into nightmares; Shirley bleeding profusely from her forehead before burning at the stake, while Anna berated over and over "What the hell were you thinking?" and "Do some good!"

As form would have it, he didn't have much time to dwell on this, the train abruptly changing gears (final life metaphor) and slowing down to enter the bustling city of Delhi. It was 6.30 in the morning.

Bleary-eyed, Tom absconded to the lavatory to hide from any potential assailants, and also apply makeup. He waited until the train had taken off and picked up pace to blur the countryside anew, before carefully edging his way back out to the seating area, luggage in tow. An old Chinese woman with a butch haircut had taken a seat facing him in his old booth. A shoebox studded with tiny holes was on the foldout table. Tom thought to turn and keep walking but a voice in his head implored him to take a seat and face the old Chinese woman and her breathing shoebox.

Hello, Tom.

Hello, Sal. Who is in the box?

Hello, Tom.

Tom scoffed at the voice. Sal was a little hurt he didn't receive the same amount of scorn.

Hello, Rudiger. I'd like to thank you for abandoning me to the mercy of Pakistani nationalists and militant Indian bovine rights vigilantes.

Rudiger was silent.

That hasn't happened yet, said Sal. *It won't ever happen, in fact. I picked up Rudiger before your little trip began.*

So Rudiger didn't leave me to die in a field?

No.

No, I did not, Rudiger hissed. *But I certainly would if you gave me another chance.*

No, you wouldn't, objected Tom, *we became pretty tolerable travel companions as cow and snake. Friends, you could say. Well, sort of...*

Sal, who was once again a good-looking human, even in her advanced age, threw her hands up. *Look, forget about your little trip with Rudiger. None of that happened.*

So you mean those riots didn't happen? I didn't start the fire, so to speak?

No. Once again I had to erase your "good deeds".

Gee, thanks, said Tom.

Now that this has been settled, let's move on to the end of your current life. Your last life.

"Chai, chai," the child waiter cried, pushing his cart down the aisle. Sal accepted the tea and Tom found some small relief in this, at least he had until the end of the tea, hopefully.

So, here we are, said Sal. *Where you off to?*

Dharamshala.

Going to see the Dalai Lama?

Yes. A bit of a Hail Mary, I suppose you'd say.

You packed a few bags...

Full of money. For charity.

Sal smirked. *A little too late, don't you think?*

Will you let me have it?

Sal's face went cold. *Why should I, Tom?*

Tom thought about this for a long while, even Rudiger tried to poke his head up from the shoebox lid, intrigued by Tom's response. Tom gazed out the window, the train back to full pace, the outside world a fleeting blur.

Because, if you kill me now, you'll stop me from completing a mission with potential life-saving implications... Does this sound familiar?

When it dawned on Sal what Tom was getting at, Sal almost gasped. The nerve of this slimy little schmuck. He ought to have blown Tom's brains out then and there, leaving no time for the chant, but his sense of righteousness and innate moral superiority restrained him once more. There was no way he'd stoop to Tom's level, not when the trial was so close and a humiliating, total victory was so near at hand.

What if we kill him and then perform the charitable act ourselves? Rudiger suggested, always looking for a workaround.

Sal snapped at the shoe box in Hindi, turning heads. "Then we'd just be stealing his good deed!"

If it's any consolation, I probably won't last much longer once I give the money over.

Yes, because we'll kill you.

Or the Mumbai gangsters will... Tom countered.

This furrowed Sal's brows. Of all the things Sal detested, organised crime was right up there, only a few rungs below Tom Robinson and the Holocaust. Sal slammed a dainty, age-pocked fist on the table.

Mumbai gangsters. I hate Mumbai gangsters...

Sal picked up the shoebox. *Rudiger and I are going to have a word. Don't you dare think of escaping. If you move, I guarantee you won't get to perform your last good deed.*

Of course, Tom agreed, then frantically reached for his gun and aimed it from under the table. His eyes were also drawn to the calm surface of Sal's tea. Would it be so bad to lace it with poison, if he were to find some? It was probably OK relative to the array of misdeeds he'd already committed, and it would also feel really good. Or maybe if he shot him in the head while his back was turned, he could erase Sal's presence forever, eliminating star witness and lead prosecutor in the process. *It'd be worth it,* Jacinta's subconscious joined in, urging spiteful action. But Tom sighed and put the gun away. What was the point? It'd only prove Sal right, and he'd be damned if he was going to throw it all away at this late stage.

Sal and Rudiger argued in animated mute fashion at the end of the cart, Sal oblivious to the strange looks he received. Nevertheless, they returned with a compromise—they *were* the good guys, after all, Sal made a point of reminding Tom.

They decided they would fight these Mumbai gangsters, let Tom donate the money and then kill him. The only restriction: he wasn't allowed to talk to the Dalai Lama. This seemed merely punitive, but Tom agreed to it anyway, acquiescing to his enemy for the thousandth time because what else was he supposed to do?

Sal pulled out his Tom Tracker and pressed a few buttons on the side of the contraption. A call-out for reinforcements.

***

They reached Chakki Bank by noon. The air was muggy and the midday sun scorching; not exactly ideal conditions for a final standoff with a group of heavily-armed mafiosi. As they pulled up to the station, Tom was ordered to look for the gangsters and did so with his face pressed to the window, but this proved a fruitless exercise, as Tom could recall only one face, that of Mr Tendulkar; the other goons, no disrespect to them, having never previously been given the time of day by Jacinta.

How was I supposed to know I'd be picking them out for a fight at a decrepit train station? Jacinta sullenly impressed onto Tom's consciousness as he tried to compose himself.

The train finally came to a halt at the platform and Sal motioned to Tom. "Did you see them?"

"No," replied Tom with a shake of his head.

They waited for the other passengers to disembark before Tom was forced out in front of Sal, his arms laden with the suitcases of money. Tom was then instructed to stand there as a perfect example of a sitting duck while the Swaraj Express slowly rolled towards the next station, exposing both sides of the platform. There was no one there, but Sal insisted Tom stay put for a little while longer, with which he complied, as Jacinta's once-silky hair quickly dried out in the heat.

"They better have Philip B. Imperial Conditioning Crème in this shithole," said Jacinta haughtily before Tom could stop her.

They waited for another ten minutes to no avail. Tom asked Sal and Rudiger (who was still in the shoebox) if he could sit on a nearby bench. Sal gruffly relented and had another quick strategy session with Rudiger.

It was decided that they would wait at Chakki Bank for reinforcements to arrive before heading to Dharamshala, a three-hour car ride away. In the meantime, they'd wait in ambush at the station, in case Mr Tendulkar and friends came via the train. There were six hours until reinforcements arrived and eight hours until the next train rolled in. Tom wryly congratulated Sal on his grand planning, before kicking at the loose gravel like a petulant child.

"This is your last life, Tom," Sal reminded him. "Try to remember the good times, or the times you were good, however few there were, even if only for Anna's sake."

Tom grunted in a very un-Jacinta-like fashion, fed up with all this introspection.

"What about you, Sal?" he said, thrusting his judging finger out, an instinct well-established by Jacinta. "Soul like you, telling everyone else how it should be—when did you really LIVE? And while we're at it, since when did you give a shit about Anna? Seems like all you care about is screwing over one little insignificant schmuck while everyone else gets away with murder—or, well, other, equally bad stuff that I don't do anymore, and didn't even mean to do in the first place!"

Sal and Rudiger were both taken aback, though they should hardly have been surprised.

"I lived!" Sal defended himself. "I lived and died in awful times because of awful, selfish souls like yourself, and I made an oath, long ago, to serve justice."

Tom threw his hands up in frustration. "Jesus Christ, you're a broken record. We get it. You're all that stands between good and evil. Kudos to you."

"And Anna shouldn't be wasting her time on a wretched creature like you," Sal added.

"What? Why do you keep bringing Anna up, you got a thing for her or something?"

Sal's strident denial was a dead giveaway.

"She was my daughter at one stage, you know," Tom offered, somewhat boastfully. "I passed on the knowledge of reincarnation to her."

Sal narrowed his eyes at this inference. "You didn't make her good. How dare you take even the slightest credit. She could be doing so much more with her time, helping build a better world. Instead, she's thrown away everything to save a greedy, self-interested pile of shit. You don't deserve her. You had all the possibilities in the world available to you, Tom. And this is where you ended up. You're going to drag her down with you."

***

The next few hours crawled by with interminable slowness, and even Sal lost focus in the stifling heat and sought a nap. They remained on the train platform, the harsh sunlight bouncing off the cement and practically smacking their cheeks. Tom picked up a local tabloid paper that detailed the disappearance of one of Bollywood's leading lights, the vendor who sold it to him failing to recognise that the actress on the front cover was standing right in front of him. Jacinta, somewhat starved for attention, sulked at this lack of recognition, but Tom told her to suck it up. They settled for slow dancing on the heat-baked concrete of the railway junction, much to the delight of the odd individual or two taking a shortcut across the tracks.

The arrival of Guneet Hatar, Bollywood's greatest agent, by way of a rusted taxi to the Chakki Bank Junction was a most unexpected surprise. A flashy suit and a motor mouth that was roaring from the get-go, Guneet squealed with delight at the sight of his next big coup and launched into a movie pitch and an assurance of riches in the same quick breath. But when Jacinta Khapour, the last big fish he hadn't netted, ignored his offer of cinematic gold and instead questioned how he found her, Guneet reaffirmed that it was just himself being himself, always finding the talent.

"No, but seriously—how did you find me?"

Guneet glanced over at Jacinta's company: a wizened Chinese

woman holding a shoebox poked with holes.

"Hardly the matter at hand, but I heard rumours you were talking about the Dalai Lama at the wrap party for Rhopti's *Tale of Love*, a subdued affair compared to the illustrious role I could secure you in *Saadvika*—did I mention you'd be playing the heiress herself?"

"HOW DID YOU FIND ME?"

Guneet was momentarily nonplussed. "Well, I couldn't find you in Dharamshala and then I got a hot tip you were spotted at Mumbai Central Station, so I thought it was maybe that you were still on your way to Dharamshala—"

"Wait," interjected the Chinese lady in perfect Hindi, surprising Guneet. "Where are her underworld friends?"

Guneet's eyes darted between Jacinta and the old Chinese woman. "Are you her new representative? Jacinta, let me tell you I have the connections to take you straight to the top, and I can assure you that you won't need to reduce yourself to the Chinese film market to get there!"

Sal leaned in, and once again in flawless Hindi stated, "We're not interested, sorry. Please go."

Guneet was surprised the foreigner's accent was so perfect. He was also more than incensed at the response itself. "You're not interested, but maybe Mr Tendulkar *will* be interested in hearing exactly where his talent has fled to!"

Sal turned to Jacinta. "Who is this Mr Tendulkar?"

"He's the underworld film producer I'm running from."

Sal nodded with great interest and the shoebox hissed in excitement. "OK, you can call this Mr Tendulkar."

Here is where Guneet faltered, his bluff inexplicably called. He sized up Jacinta and the small Chinese grandma with the funny shoebox. "You wouldn't want me to do that," he said, to state the obvious.

"No, I think we do. Please call him now."

Guneet reached for his phone and then put it away, shaking. He rubbed the sweat from his brow. "No, this is crazy. Jacinta, let me tell you about this wonderful role I can secure for you that will protect you from—"

Sal lifted her shirt to reveal the pistol. "Make the call."

For the first time in a long time, Guneet struggled with his words. Even Mr Tendulkar sensed something was gravely wrong when a rapid-fire machine gun such as Guneet was lobbing soft peas. "I know where your runaway starlet is... I thought you should know..."

"Why are you telling me this, Guneet?"

"I'm, I'm not sure..."

"Have you tried to steal her away from my agent? Because I didn't think you'd be that foolish, Guneet..."

"..."

In the ensuing silence, Sal's patience wore thin. He gestured for the phone. Guneet handed it over, relieved. Sal's first question was simple: was the person on the other end of the line a leading figure of the Mumbai criminal underworld? Who wanted to know? came the cagey reply.

"The unstoppable force of karmic justice," said Sal.

"Stop wasting my time and put my star on."

"Your manners are truly reprehensible," Sal observed, "Nevertheless, we'd like to discuss the film career of...what did you say your name was again?"

"Jacinta Khapour," said Tom.

"Yes, Jacinta Khapour."

(It was at this stage Guneet almost imploded, silently seething that Jacinta's new agent didn't even know her name.)

"We're in Chakki Bank," Sal continued, "on our way to Dharamshala... Yes, it's true, Jacinta would like to meet the Dalai Lama and donate all her money... Well you'll have to come up here and stop her yourself if you want it back..." Sal then told Guneet to write an address down for her. "...Yes, OK. See you tomorrow."

Once the call was over, Guneet's gaze flitted back and forth between Sal and Jacinta.

"Can I go now?" he asked, still not fully understanding what was happening.

You can't let him go now, Rudiger pointed out, *he will call the police.*

Tom wasn't sure if it came from him or if it was Jacinta's slim prospect of furthering her career, but he knew he had to convince everyone then and there that Guneet would never mention this meeting to anyone for as long as he lived. Jacinta took a deep breath and grabbed Sal by the arm, her eyes puppy-dogging, tears swelling, believability at maximum level. "You *can* let him go. He won't tell anyone about us going to Dharamshala, not the *Mumbai Star* or the *Daily News*." Jacinta then turned to Guneet. "Believe me when I say this: You cross that grandma, and you will learn a pain so frustratingly unending, you're going to wish death was the end. You stay silent, and that grandma will take care of Mr Tendulkar for you. Then the rest of Bollywood is yours..."

Sal chuckled and shook his head. "No, he comes with us."

***

Jacinta arrived in Dharamshala squished between Guneet and a large silverback gorilla at the rear of a convoy of old rustic trucks and vans branded with all kinds of faded corporate sponsorship from the 1980s. This was a far cry from being chauffeured in a limo to all manner of locales, parties and film premieres, her obedient driver now replaced with a Delhi muscleman in a singlet and a baboon riding shotgun. As nightfall approached, the baboon asked Sal if he could have a turn at the wheel. Sal obliged and everyone except for Jacinta and Guneet cracked a howling laugh as the baboon carted them along the perilous, winding road ascending the mountains.

"Why is the baboon driving?" asked Guneet.

"Because he asked nicely," Sal replied.

The city of Dharamshala was an assortment of coloured flags, temples of ancient wisdom and thickly-wooded cedar groves known for their serenity. The exiled Tibetan government and its figurehead, the Dalai Lama, were based in the city's upper suburb of McLeod Ganj. Jacinta and Tom's last night on earth was spent in the back of the van; an oven that reeked of gorilla, baboon, mongoose and "human in 34 degree heat" odour. Not to mention the gorilla hair was unrelentingly itchy against Jacinta's once-beautifully-soft skin.

The meeting was to take place at a derelict temple on the outskirts of town, abandoned for the promise of greater enlightenment in the more popular tourist temples where His Holiness spoke.

Reaching the temple three hours before their showdown, Tom and Guneet were permitted to wander through the abandoned, crumbling monastery while Sal and his CARROTA secured their ambush positions. Tom came across a plaque caked with dust. He wiped the dust away, and the resultant plume made him sneeze. The sign read: *Please be quiet as you enter the state of peace.*

No fucking shit, thought Tom, disappointed with the rather generic advice. He got on his knees and began muttering a prayer, not to God but to Anna. *Please, Anna, I really need your help today. Please help me achieve my last good deed—the only one I've ever done.*

Once certain the others were out of earshot, Guneet nudged Jacinta. "This is our time to run," he said. "We can go into town and get the police, and we'll use your kidnapping to make you an even bigger star—not just in Bollywood, but Hollywood!"

His eyes practically glazed over at the prospect.

"The money is locked up in the van," said Tom. "I only get the money once Sal nabs his Mumbai gangsters."

"Who is Sal?"

"The old Chinese woman."

"You said she was a he?"

"She is. It's complicated."

Guneet scanned their surroundings once more. "I'm leaving. When I save you, you must work for Real Mumbai Studios."

"I'll help you escape. I'll distract them," said Tom.

Guneet nodded.

Jacinta gestured beyond the wall with the sign encouraging one to remain quiet, which under the circumstances wasn't such bad advice after all. There was a steep descent behind the abandoned temple. A chance for Guneet to escape through the cedar forest.

"I'll aim for the suitcases. They're not going to hurt me just yet. If you escape, don't mention me until the day is over."

Guneet nodded again. "I have no idea what the hell is going on, but I admire your new-found spirit, Jacinta." *You're also less of an unpleasant bitch,* he thought, but did not say aloud.

"Be safe, Guneet," said Tom, and they both split off. Tom burst through the front door, past the stymied gorilla and Delhi muscleman and leapt over Rudiger's fangs, before making it to the truck with the suitcases inside. The truck was unsurprisingly locked, and the roar of a tiger and a shriek from behind the temple moments later likewise failed to bode well for poor Guneet.

Sal emerged calmly from the temple and joined the rest of the CARROTA in surrounding Tom.

"That was unnecessary," said Tom.

"I could say the same thing to you," replied Sal.

"There's almost two hours to kill before the gangsters arrive. Could I please go to the temple to drop the money off, talk to the Dalai Lama then come back here and you can have your showdown to finish the job?"

The CARROTA deferred to Sal, who seemed to find his hip going funny at this higher altitude. He was in a bit of an ethical pickle. On the one hand, letting Tom do this task was objectively a good thing to do, but on the other, all eight of the CARROTA members who had showed up would find it strange for Sal to show mercy against the one irredeemable creature who had brought them all together in the first place.

Could we perhaps kill him and then have the gangsters for seconds? suggested the Bengal tiger, evidently having finished mauling Guneet.

No, Rudiger hissed, *we already agreed that killing him and stealing his good deed was wrong.*

What if we don't do the good deed then? the baboon offered.

"Don't be ridiculous!" shouted the Delhi muscleman. And then they all started arguing with one another, just like the time Sal's hyenas fought with a pride of lions over Tom.

It was all getting a bit too much really, so Tom stopped them with a high-pitched scream that only Jacinta's vocal cords could reach. He pulled out a gun, the one he had all along and that no one had bothered to search him for. A gun that, in hindsight, could have helped Guneet quite a lot.

Very much outnumbered, Tom had to settle on one target. Sal was the obvious choice, seeing as how he also had a gun and a funny hip.

Give me the money or I'll shoot Sal.

You really can't afford to do that, said Rudiger. *It would negate giving the money to charity.*

Panicking, Tom then turned the gun on himself.

Now what are you doing?

If you don't let me take the money, then I'll shoot myself without saying the chant and all your chances of humiliating me won't work.

Sal found this threat pitiful. *Go on then. Be the coward you always were.*

Tom was lost for words, his bluff called. It appeared to be the end of the road, the end of all his memories—more bad than good at this stage, if one were counting. But luckily for Tom, another aggrieved party showed up just in time. Everyone was early and everyone was surprised—the Mumbai gangsters more so because their opposition for the morning included a Bengal tiger. Everything happened so fast, like a chemical kamikaze attack on crack. The Mumbai gangsters, led by Mr Tendulkar, frantically opened fire as the animals in Sal's CARROTA launched themselves in brazen assault. Seizing his chance, Tom shot out the passenger window and threw Jacinta's dainty arm over to unlock the door. Toppling over the front seats, he grabbed one of the suitcases and the backpack and kicked his way out the back of the van, just in time to witness the outlandish exhibition of a baboon firing a bazooka. Tom scrambled around the gangsters on the road and slipped into the forest, aiming for what he thought was the town centre, bullets ricocheting off the trees all around him.

Jacinta was a fitness nut, but lugging the heavy suitcase while simultaneously avoiding being peppered with lead took its toll.

To add to her good fortunes, the clouds overhead had turned monsoonal and the sky water came down with force. The undergrowth she was hopping across almost instantly began oozing mud, and one loose footing later Jacinta's ankle was painfully wrenched in the wrong direction. She flung the soaked suitcase to the ground and screamed at the sodden sky, asking what other calamities the universe intended to throw her way, her howls of frustration lost amid the caterwaul of the storm.

Out of options, a hopeless Tom decided to pray, not necessarily to God but to Anna once more, asking for something, anything, to help him out of his current predicament. He was met with more rain. And the roar of thunder. Then a lightning bolt that cracked a large cedar nearby.

Before Tom could say, "Hah, you missed me!" the wooden giant fell with an almighty crash, and this was soon followed by the screeching of tyres. Tom scrambled upright and realised he wasn't far from a bend in the road. Hopeful his prayers had been answered, Tom retrieved his luggage and hobbled over. The driver of the little beaten-up yellow car stood scratching his head in the pouring rain at the sizeable act of God, the results of which now blocked his path. He wondered to himself what he'd done to deserve this, before a bedraggled young woman lugging a suitcase hobbled into view. Despite her filthy state, the man was smitten and thought it fate until Jacinta pointed a gun at him.

"I'm sorry," said Tom. "I just really need to see the Dalai Lama."

***

Jacinta caught her breath in the blissfully dry interior of the cosy little car, just as the rain was beginning to clear. The drive was slow and treacherous, but the view of the valley was

223

awe-inspiring, stretching for miles in sheer, unbounded majesty. She had produced a wad of damp cash from her backpack on the climb up that had helped ease the driver's tension somewhat. On her instruction, he was now taking her straight to the main temple. When they arrived, several tourist buses and their accompanying adventurers were standing around laden with cameras and wonder. Tom hobbled up to the entrance dragging the suitcase. He found the first monk he could and asked, "Where is His Holiness?" The monk was wide-eyed and vow of silence-y, so Tom hobbled to the next. "Where is His Holiness? I need to speak with him at once!"

"I think he's off sick today."

Tom blinked incredulously. "What?"

"He's often unwell these days. He is 89 years old, after all."

Tom looked around at the small scene he was causing. "Well, I still have to see him. I've got over half a million dollars to donate to Free Tibet."

"Maybe tomorrow he'll be better..."

"NO!" shrieked Tom, pulling out the gun. "Take me to him now, I'm not going to hurt him. I just need five minutes of his time."

The monk stood firm. Other monks began to circle, their bald heads overwhelming Jacinta. They knew kung fu, Tom assumed, based on what he'd seen in the movies, long ago.

"Wait," said one of the monks, his eyes squinting at Tom. "Aren't you Jacinta Khapour?"

***

The Dalai Lama, true to the monk's word, was indeed unwell. He was on the bed in a tiny, no-frills room similar to Tom's shack back in the Middle Ages. The room was lit by candles, though this was just for aesthetics: there was a light fitting in the ceiling. The Dalai Lama had a coughing fit then turned to Tom, agitated by the interruption of his dying.

"I brought money," said Tom, kneeling and fumbling with the latch of his suitcase. "Money to donate to the cause of your choosing. There's about 40 million rupees in this suitcase."

"Why have you done this?" asked the Dalai Lama.

"I needed to do a good thing. I haven't lived a good life, and this is my last chance to do something of note. And if you think I'm worthy, I'd like to ask your Holiness to be a character witness for me in an upcoming trial..."

The Dalai Lama chuckled then coughed, a lot. "Is that you, Tom Robinson?"

Tom's head dropped. This couldn't possibly be good. "So you know who I am..."

"What kind of person murders someone trying to kill Hitler?"

"An idiot, Your Holiness."

The Dalai Lama realised he was being a tad harsh. "Not necessarily," he retracted. "Killing is wrong, yes. It should only be resorted to when absolutely necessary. Sometimes it may be the only option available. Do you believe you killed only because it was absolutely necessary?"

Tom thought long and hard about this. For the longest time he'd protested his innocence and pitied his unfortunate circumstances, but in the face of his Holiness he knew this was insufficient. He shook his head. "No, I stopped Sal out of fear for my own interests. I was scared things would change for me. I'm starting to see that Sal was right. People don't change, not really. Hitler was always going to be Hitler, and I'm always going to be selfish. I had so much time to change, but I haven't."

"Well," the Dalai Lama coughed, "compassion is one of the

great virtues, and forgiveness is a part of compassion. Have you shown compassion in your previous lives?"

"I, uh, tried not to hurt anyone after that?"

"Wonderful!" The Dalai Lama sat up, reaching for a pen and paper. "Any specific examples of you showing compassion and helping others?"

Well, I, uh, I've become a vegetarian."

The Dalai Lama smiled politely but kept his pen still and Tom cursed himself for leading with that example again.

"I taught my fellow slaves to read once!"

"That's good!" The Dalai Lama wrote it down.

"But then I kind of undid my good work with what I did next... I guess I can't claim I didn't hurt anyone after Sal."

The Dalai Lama chewed on his pen pensively. "Well, at least you've brought some donations to help us reclaim Tibet. The gesture may not be entirely without self-interest, but at least the act itself is commendable. How much money did you bring?"

Tom opened the briefcase and his eyes bulged. He threw his hand into the suitcase and the soaked money crumpled softly in his hands. He checked his backpack too. Same situation. All of it soggy, the colour beginning to run.

"You can dry it! And there's some gold jewellery here you can have too!" Tom offered, not a hint of desperation at all.

"Thanks..." said His Holiness the Dalai Lama. "Well, the main thing about forgiveness is the forgiving, allowing those that ask for it the chance to redeem themselves."

"So... you'd be OK with being called as a witness for my trial?"

The Dalai Lama shrugged. "Sure, why not?"

It was a small piece of compassion, a very touching moment; completely forced, but nice nevertheless. Tom was shaken with relief. He thanked the Dalai Lama profusely and walked outside, his damaged feet floating on air, before being very much arrested by a swarm of local authorities.

***

Many lawyers and flashing cameras came from all over the country to unpack Jacinta Khapour's wild kidnapping ordeal. Sordid details emerged about Jacinta's involvement in the brutal gun battle between exotic animals, a Chinese national and members of the Mumbai criminal underworld. The whole country was engrossed. In response, Tom provided a fourteen-page handwritten statement, categorically detailing his past lives, Sal's CARROTA and the events as they happened. Needless to say, most commentators suggested it was a ploy for some kind of insanity plea. The only thing they had on her was threatening a poor driver with a weapon and obstructing the peace. While this likely amounted to a few months' home detention and compensation to affected parties, a high-profile trial was in the works, and Jacinta Khapour stated she would plead guilty and not seek bail. She was happy to wait in the tiny McLeod Ganj holding cell.

Sal came to him a month later, this time as a rainbow lorikeet accompanied by a high-powered, Croatian prosecution lawyer. Jacinta seemed at peace, despite the sewage smell of her confines. The Croatian prosecutor reached through the bars and opened his palm for Sal to perch on. "I'm told that what remained of my CARROTA after the firefight passed on the rest of the money to the Dalai Lama, so that's good for the people of Free Tibet, but we lost a few souls in the battle…"

"Rudiger?"

"No. He died. But he's fine now."

"So you're going to let me see out the rest of this life?" asked Tom. "I still have a chance to do some good here."

Sal shook his head. "You'll see out your sentence, and then we'll come for you, for the last time."

Tom laughed and sat down on his bunk. "While you're here, maybe you ought to see the Dalai Lama and learn something about compassion and forgiveness..."

"There are some who deserve nothing of the sort," said Sal, taking his leave, before Tom stopped him.

"Hey, Sal."

"Yes?"

"I forgive you."

Sal stiffened with discomfort. "See you in court."

Daba dee daba daa...

The Trial

The trial was expected to take both months and only the afternoon. Such a contradiction of time was part and parcel of the kind of place where a trial like this could be held. They came from all manner of time zones, bodies and memories (both good and bad), each piling inside expecting a show. A quick headcount numbered the total souls present at over sixteen hundred, including the ants. Tom wasn't sure how he'd arrived at this place, a courthouse in the jungle. The judicial commons was the size of an outhouse on the outside and a gigantic bureaucratic maze on the inside. Animals and Auditors with clipboards criss-crossed one another in a hurry. Tom stood in the entrance, allowing his confusion to amplify to the point of chuckling madness. When the lions and Auditors realised who was laughing like a madman, they all stopped to glare. And that's when Tom realised he was plain old Tom again. He clutched at his clothes, the same crummy business shirt and slacks he died in all those lives ago. He even had his work lanyard hanging from his neck.

"Good luck!" said an elephant, and the rest of the Auditors nodded in quiet agreement before returning to their ceaseless schedules of scribbling and note taking.

A small pair of clawed feet dug into Tom's shoulder and, wincing slightly, he turned to see a mockingbird. Rather than communicate telepathically, the mockingbird opened her mouth and spoke perfect English with an Austrian accent.

"Tom, I've done all I can. It's time to face the music," said Anna. "Can you help Shirley carry the files?"

Tom turned to see Shirley in all her past forms he'd crossed paths with; in her zookeeper uniform, in her Korengal Valley goat herder garb, before she finally solidified as a little black cat with muddy feet. They stopped and smiled, before Tom took the ropes Shirley had been using to drag two large filing cabinets along.

"It's good to see you—*great* to see you... Did you find the life you deserved in the end?"

"Yes, I did," Shirley replied softly, smiling at Anna and Tom, a great peace emanating from her.

They had been appointed the main courtroom. Outside, Tom observed the room schedule, headed "The Trial of Tom Robinson, Case #3244444245". Next on the agenda was a committee meeting to discuss the renaming of the term "reincarnation rememberers", which although usefully descriptive was widely held to lack pizzazz.

Tom asked one of the kangaroo guards if he could go to the bathroom to wash his face before the trial commenced, but the kangaroo at the door said there were no bathrooms. "You don't need to urinate in this realm, mate."

"Good to know."

The empty courtroom where his destiny would be decided was enormous, each footstep echoing across its ancient wooden foundations, with leafy trees flourishing here and there out of the floorboards. There were two levels, with rows of seating for an audience on the balcony. Aside from the trees sprouting from the floor and its cavernous size, the rest of the room was much like Tom had pictured a courtroom would look and feel: stately and intimidating. The trio were briefly the only ones inside, but Anna assured him it would soon be a packed house. "A lot of souls want to see you burn and me fail. More than a thousand, actually, last time I checked ticket sales. They're fans of Sal, even if they aren't officially in his little army."

Tom and Shirley set up the filing cabinets according to Anna's suggestions, then sat down to face the empty podium where the judge would preside. Tom looked at Shirley and Anna. "OK." He rubbed his clammy hands together. "Where do we start?"

***

Their audience came wagging their tails, blowing their trunks, roaring with pride, chirping with delight and barking like seals. The air was electric with excitement and positively heaving with pheromones. Once both levels of the audience were packed in tight, the prosecution entered and were unsurprisingly given a home team reception.

Sal's CARROTA comprised a wide assortment of creatures: Deborah came as the lumberjack, there was the polar bear who'd travelled a legendary amount of miles to assassinate Tom, and in terms of experienced lawyers they had a black widow spider who had practiced law for over 608 years and had twice attended the Nuremburg Trials, according to Anna. Last to enter was their leader, in the guise of the slick-haired revolutionary Tom stabbed in an Austrian field all those lives ago...

Everyone cheered when they saw Sal. Tom thought it surprising no one had booed him in complementary fashion, but this honour was saved for when the bailiff of the court formally introduced him. Tom's paltry legal team tried to stare down the imposing prosecution, but with ten different souls, one of them a spider, the prosecution had more eyes with which to burn holes.

The bailiff called for all those present to rise for the entrance of the judge...

Despite being a vulture, Judge Talbot knew how to wield a gavel (he grasped it in his beak). Feared throughout the Bureau for his sharp wit and even sharper beak, the judge had a knack for breaking defendants who would collapse and concede under the relentless stare of those beady, remorseless eyes.

"Well, Mr Robinson," said the judge, fixing Tom with one of his sterner gazes. "Shall we get on with it?"

Opening Prosecution

Sal took the stand and they dimmed the lights. An all-encompassing and at times nauseating hologram experience was then beamed into the centre of the court, *The Legend of Sal*, a heroic tale of Good vs Evil, narrated by David Attenborough.

"Aah," muttered most members of the crowd appreciatively throughout.

"Ooh," said some others.

"That Sal sure is one heck of a guy," said a bonobo to a chimp, to which the chimp could only nod mutely, so overcome was he with feelings of admiration.

It was disheartening to hear his favourite presenter lending his support to Sal and yet, at every triumphant and tragic twist in the almost two-hour running time of *The Legend of Sal*, even Tom couldn't help but find himself being swept up in the epic.

Here was a soul who'd convicted over five thousand felons in the short span of five lifetimes. A soul who'd saved countless men, women and children from being horrendously raped, pillaged and burned at the stake.

Each life prior to meeting the worst soul to have ever existed (Tom) was spent joining the local ranks of authority and rising to the top on the back of countless thwarted criminals locked behind bars or sent to the gallows. They went through five incredible (though Tom would stress "repetitive") police procedurals before they got to the part about the Holocaust. *"And there she was, skinny as a toothpick, a girl defiant against a horrific regime that must be stopped at all costs..."*

Anna was covering her eyes with her wing. Shirley was holding back tears and glancing guiltily at Tom. "You can't deny how badly Sal suffered," she offered.

Tom stuffed his face in his hands and tried to appreciate the fact that they were his old hands for however long left he'd have them. He was brought back to the propaganda reel when a new Sal, scarred by the horrors of Dachau, wandered into that small Viennese beer hall and locked eyes with a down-and-out art teacher, the greatest monster who ever lived. The booing was immense. Someone from the audience threw a carrot. And a bowl of popcorn. (Neither of which were edible in this realm.)

"How long can their opening statement be?" Tom lamented to Anna. Anna then chirped and chirped in objection but Judge Talbot said he was going to allow it as the prosecution's case against Tom was about to come to light. The audience clapped at this astute decision and then subsequently booed en-masse at the part where Tom stabbed their hero in the field, giving the opportunity for another budding tyrant to escape. Shirley wrote something on a piece of parchment and slid it over to Anna, who chirped once more at Judge Talbot, who ordered the broadcast paused. The audience didn't take kindly to this decision and it took some time for order to be sufficiently restored to allow Anna to voice her objection.

"I'd like to interject with some counter-perspective to this matter: Tom was a victim of poor mentorship from a fellow reincarnation rememberer and with that said I'd like to transport our first witness to the stand."

"Jim Caputo?" asked the judge.

"Yes, your honour."

The Old-Timer Chicken

Jim Caputo, or the old-timer chicken as Tom knew him, was far from pleased when zapped into existence inside the courtroom's witness box. He did not waver in his glare.

"Why'd you pick *him?*" Tom queried to Shirley, who reassured him Anna knew what she was doing.

Anna fluttered to the branch of a leafless tree that had sprouted abruptly between their defence table and the witness box. "Jim Caputo, is it true that you advised Tom Robinson, during a shared stay at the Farmer John egg farm, not to do anything stupid, making particular mention of not killing one Adolf Hitler?"

Jim Caputo squawked. "Yeah, I did. Why do you need me to be here? Can't you just review the memories or something?"

"Thank you for the suggestion," said Anna, "but we were hoping to ascertain a motive from you, if possible?"

"You could have played the memories back—I guess I'm pretty sure I said it—but whatever... I told him not to do that otherwise he'd screw up the time continuum and end up in a bad place, which is where he is now."

Anna nodded thoughtfully. "Why didn't you want him to screw up the time continuum, Mr Caputo? Was it so you could continue to use your retained knowledge of the future to make monumental gains in the stock market whenever you became human again?"

"Yeah. So what? That's not a crime. I'm just smart."

"Not only smart, but *greedy*. Some might even say avaricious. Something that an impressionable first-timer like Tom was unable to truly grasp..." Anna then flew to another branch to address the rest of the room, the additional height of her vantage infusing her words with a greater sense of drama. "And I think we all remember what it was like that first time, how crucial it was in shaping the beginning of our journey. I remember when Tom, as my Austrian father, Hubert, told me that there was a better future for me out there. It was this hope he instilled in me that helped me believe in the contents of a letter, left locked away by my mother and returned to me on her deathbed. A letter that taught me the secret of the chant and allowed me to reach the position I am in today. I'm here because Tom Robinson saw something in me, believed in me, nurtured and encouraged me. *This*, ladies and gentlemen, is the true importance of having a great first influence—something Tom was deprived of when he encountered Jim Caputo..."

Tom looked around and from the silence felt they'd clawed something back. He looked over at Sal, who appeared conflicted, either by Anna's words—or Anna herself—it was hard to tell. A conniving thought popped in his head: *If Sal does like Anna, then perhaps there is a way to exploit this?* Tom shuddered, disgusted with himself.

Sal's next witness, a mosquito named Bzz, happily replaced the brief peace created by Anna. It appeared Sal was content to let the memories do the talking for now, and the sound of Wagner's "Ride of the Valkyries" sent a cold shiver down Tom's spine, as the judge and all those present in the gallery watched a powerful bloodlust overtake him on a trip to a hospital in Indonesia.

Both Shirley and Anna had missed this little bite-sized life. Shirley whispered that they could argue it was another case of Tom being a victim of a gang mentality, but Anna decided it was best not to comment on this at all. "Let's pick our battles. Besides, it looks like the judge isn't a fan of Bzz..."

They all turned to see Judge Talbot, his wing gripping his gavel like a fly swatter, as he eyed Bzz with disdain. It was undeniable; mosquitos, maybe moreso than Tom, were universally despised. It didn't help that Tom had been one, but as Anna said, this wasn't entirely his fault and he had to pick his battles.

No counter arguments were offered, and the prosecution continued, comfortably transitioning to Tom's next indiscretion with a seamlessness that impressed Judge Talbot greatly.

This particular indiscretion occurred when Tom was a cobra and an unfortunate little girl crossed his path. The crowd once more gasped in horror, recoiling as one. "He's an abomination!" shrieked a platypus, before fainting. It didn't help that the prosecution had cut together a heart-warming montage of the poor girl from Bangladesh going about her innocent, hard-working life before she crossed paths with Tom.

"Tom, can you please inform the court why you used venom on this ill-fated girl, when a warning bite, or indeed even a loud hiss would have sufficed?" asked the black spider, speaking into a microphone.

Shirley and Anna looked at Tom, who threw his hands up. "It was a surprise, an accident! She caught me off-guard! You can plainly see! It was just instinct!"

The spider chortled, an awful screech. "I put it to the judge, and everyone else here today, that you used venom, not because of your snake form at the time, or because of any primitive drive, but because you yourself are in fact filled to the brim with toxicity of another kind. This is what happens when your soul is allowed to continue wandering the earth. The eventual decimation of all innocents crossing your path. Your own venomous nature is to blame here, sir! Why, us spiders overcome our instincts all the time. Everyone does. You don't see me biting anyone at this moment, do you, sir? Do you?" The spider puffed out her chelicerae indignantly, and many of those present nodded in agreement. Tom's head dropped. Two distant incidents, both almost forgotten, and there was plenty more to come. But then he remembered that wasn't how the story ended, at least not with the little girl.

"Wait! I tried to save her! I alerted her brother. The auditor watched! I tried to save her!" he pleaded.

"But you didn't, Tom. Her brother didn't save her in time and their family was ripped apart in the exponentially negative paths their grief and torment led them down... This is something your counsel should have told you: intentions can only count for so much after the fact. Your redemption came up very short in this instance and while we're at it..."

Tom anxiously tapped his toes on the floor, causing a miniature volcano to emerge and erupt, scorching the nailed offend-
ers. Everything in this realm was alive and out to get him. They
were doing poorly. Very poorly indeed. There was still the Pakistani grandmother he gave his back hooves to. And they hadn't
even got up to the bad stuff yet.

"Exactly how long is the prosecution allowed for their opening
statement?" Tom again queried, feeling nauseous, before Shirley
herself was called up to be questioned.

"What? Why?" shouted Tom in disbelief.

"To put your friendship under the microscope, as it were," said
the spider, "that is, if the honourable judge will allow it?"

"I'm going to allow it," said Judge Talbot, eliciting another
round of applause from the audience. The judge dipped his beak
in gracious recognition. He certainly knew how to work a crowd.

"Doesn't this seem a little vindictive? Can't you leave my friend
out of it?" Tom pleaded.

Finally, Sal broke his silence. "Oh, but would it not be beneficial to
see how you treat your friends? Judge Talbot has already witnessed
how you treat strangers, surely you'd treat your friend a little better?" said Sal, breaking his silence and ending it with a snicker.

Tom and Shirley exchanged fearful eyes. *Merde.*

Shirley changed shape in the witness box. She was a human
again, wearing her zookeeper uniform. Her horribly disfiguring
scar was gone. Tom dropped to the floor on all fours as he painfully shifted into a tiger, the very same "Raj" enclosed in the big
cats quadrant of the Vancouver Zoo in 1983.

Sal was front and centre of the attack. "How would you describe your relationship with the accused at this point in both of
your lives?"

Tom and Shirley gazed at each other, tiger and zookeeper once more, and the world rolled back to those first few moments. Shirley explained as innocently as she could Tom's intentions, manipulations... "I know why the caged bird sings," she explained, trying to keep upbeat as the horribly disfiguring cut slowly emerged again, dripping blood and forcing Shirley to wipe it away casually like a tear.

"That may be, but we also have footage of a conversation Tom and yourself had quite a few lives later, where our telepathic recorder picked up a definite vibe that something wasn't right. Can you recall that conversation, Shirley? I believe Tom had misled you somewhat? Is that fair to say?"

Shirley stared at the broadcast hologram hovering above in the centre of the courtroom. The memories flooded through her and she transformed back into Emmanuel the cat. The first thing she felt was betrayal. The gut-wrenching feeling that the only old friend left in this big universe of errors had lied to her about a very simple thing. When the hologram of them burning at the stake vanished, Shirley was left to respond to Sal's question. She meowed, unable to hide her hurt.

Satisfied, Sal was prepared to leave it at that, but Shirley would not let this happen. "I remember these things, sure. I remember a soul who abused my good nature, took advantage of it wherever he could. I spent many years, frankly speaking, getting fucked over by karma for supporting him, and I will continue to do so, because he *is* sorry for what he's done, and he sincerely wants to change for the better. I believe he can, but I don't think you've given him a real chance. That's all he wants."

Even the hard-hearted of the audience members couldn't help but be moved by Shirley's impassioned defence of her friend. In response, Sal's CARROTA gathered together in a huddle as Sal consulted with the spider, Deborah and the other members of his anti-Tom coalition. There was barking and hissing, but eventually they emerged with a counter.

"Judge Talbot, based on the advice of my counsel, I wish to mulligan Shirley's testimony, citing rule 52," Sal announced.

Anna swooped up to her speaking tree in flapping fury. "That is ridiculous! *You* brought a member of my defence team to the jury and then didn't like what you heard! Deal with it!"

"But she has a clear case of Stockholm Syndrome. Her opinions regarding the accused are therefore invalid."

This was a bit of a stretch, given that at no time had Tom kidnapped Shirley, but the spider on Sal's team argued it was more of an *emotional* kidnapping, furthering the "destroying every hapless innocent in his path" theme that appeared to form the crux of their argument. This descended into more shouting and goading between the hundreds of animals present until finally it got so loud and angry Tom did what he usually did when a full-blown riot was about to explode: he started chanting. When everyone else noticed this they all quietened down. When it dawned on them why he was chanting, the heat in the room was replaced by the howling jibes of the highly amused. Judge Talbot was laughing, inasmuch as vultures could laugh. Even Sal appeared to find it rather quaint.

"Sorry," said Tom, "force of habit."

"That won't do anything for you here," Sal promptly changed tune, trying to return a sense of gravitas to proceedings.

"Your honour." Tom faced the judge. "Can we have a break?" His request was met with confusion. "Food break? Recess?"

"We don't require the intake of food in this realm."

"Of course you don't..." Tom sulked.

"I'd like to request seventeen squids," said Anna.

"Why would you need that, Anna?" the judge said snootily. "Your auditing days are over, need I remind you."

Anna flew back to her desk and chirped at the audience. "It's not for me, it's for them!"

"Very well then, we'll take seventeen squids."

The captivated spectators begrudgingly agreed this was for the best. Tom turned to Anna. "What did we just request?"

"The closest thing to a recess."

***

The story goes that seventeen giant squids had once tried to overthrow the Bureau. Everyone had to stop their filing and fend off the marauding sea creatures. When the ink-soaked battle was over, they returned to filing much behind schedule. So to call seventeen squids was to take a break from filing to catch up on more filing. This was unnecessarily explained to Tom by Anna, shaving off precious moments of their requested break.

"So, are we doing well?" asked Tom. "Because it doesn't look like we are."

Shirley and Anna glanced at one another like parents who had just seen their child ingest a handful of poison berries.

"It's not...terrible," said Shirley, looking for support from Anna, who fluttered her wings, unable to hide the trepidation in her answer. "It's more or less what we expected so far—it was always going to be a tough ask getting the judge not to hate you."

"Thanks. So when do we get to bring out our own witnesses?"

"After the prosecution is finished presenting their evidence."

"And when does that happen?"

"You've lived quite a few lives, Tom..."

"OK, OK. I get it. So *who* do *we* have on *our* witness list?"

Shirley handed him a sheet of paper. There were the expected names, Tenazz and Quartz among them, but others conjured painful memories he'd kept locked away for decades: Natalia and, even more perplexing (especially from a trial standpoint), Helena, Anna's mother.

"Are you sure we want Helena up there? I wasn't always the best husband..." said Tom, as if Anna hadn't been present during Hubert's alcohol-fuelled rants.

"You'll have to trust me," said Anna.

Much like the cursory list he wrote in the Middle Ages, it was still embarrassingly brief for a lifetime's worth of lifetimes. A glaring omission was also apparent, perhaps for the best.

"It's probably a smart move he's not included." Tom laughed nervously. "We could even get the Dalai Lama in his place, if need be."

Shirley was surprised. "You met him?"

"Briefly," Tom boasted, before Anna cut his story short.

"Just because *he's* not on *our* list, doesn't mean he won't be on theirs..."

Opening Prosecution Continued

The first witness Sal's CARROTA called after a brief seventeen squids was, perhaps not surprisingly, Napoleon.

Tom's old comrade came as his original pig self and, to Tom's astonishment, given a rousing reception. Napoleon often divided opinion in the Auditor realm, given that he'd done things like revolutionised rock music, promoted reincarnation remembering and advocated for an equal split in the means of production. But he was also Joseph Stalin at one stage, and his unbridled penchant for leading bloody uprisings meant he revolutionised violence itself.

When he saw Tom, his eyes lit up and he squealed with unabashed joy. "Comrade, it's so good to see you!"

"Likewise," Tom nervously replied, glancing over to Sal and the members of the CARROTA, who seemed to delight in Napoleon's complete misreading of the situation.

"I've been waiting a long time to help my oldest friend give that Sal schmuck the spanking he deserves. Now, where is this moron?" Napoleon challenged, looking around the courtroom.

"Napoleon," began Tom, his face pinched, "I didn't call you as a character witness..."

"But why not?"

"I just didn't..."

"Then who brought me here?"

"Sal."

Napoleon was shocked. "The moron? Why would he call me to testify against you?"

"I guess we're about to find out..."

Sal paced slowly in front of the witness box. In fact, it was more of a waltz, the kind of swagger a smug victor indulges in when he knows he has his opponent beaten. He glanced back at Tom's legal team and another miniature volcano erupted under Tom's tapping feet.

"Napoleon, you and Tom go quite a way back, correct?

"That is correct, you capitalist swine."

The audience snickered.

"Funny you mention swine—given your current state. Was it not also the case that you met one another as pigs at a farm?"

Napoleon said nothing, but stared daggers.

Sal took it in his stride. He told the audience and Judge Talbot the story of Tom and Napoleon's first friendship, talking about their shared love of the trough, and it was obvious to Tom, Shirley and Anna the backstory and cliff-drop Sal was roping the room toward. Even Napoleon saw right through it. "Yes, we were comrades and Tom shared with me the secret to remembering my past lives. For that I will always be grateful!"

"Were you also *grateful* that he led you away from sparking your revolution on the farm?"

Napoleon puffed from his snout. "It wasn't the time."

"But I think we all know here that you have a history of sparking revolutions. You're the revolution king. On numerous occasions in different lives I have multitudes of sources that claim you said 'revolution is always the only way'. Seems pretty black and white to you, is all I'm saying..."

Napoleon turned to Judge Talbot. "This clown got a point to his rambling?"

"Just reminding you where you stood with Tom. Or at least, where you thought you stood... Let's skip forward a few lives to when you were Stalin..."

Napoleon morphed effortlessly into the moustachioed former Soviet leader as Sal kept talking.

"Do you remember a fellow reincarnation rememberer called Cedna? Tom might better recall her as your beloved pet falcon..."

Napoleon swallowed his pain. He rushed to dismiss the path Sal was leading them all down, keen to dispel and move on. "Yes, Tom killed my friend. It's OK, I know. It was an accident."

"Yes, we know you're well aware of the accident. But let me ask you something, Napoleon. Have you ever come across Cedna since then? Doing some research into our witnesses, we've noted that in several points within your recalled existence, you've asked other reincarnation rememberers if they've ever come across a soul called Cedna. But no one has seen her since…"

Napoleon looked at Tom, his cold dictator eyes dark like a crow. They both knew where Sal was slowly, painfully dragging proceedings.

"We looked at her file, and found no remembered lives beyond being a national pet for the Soviet Union in the winter of 1956. So it begs the question, why were you asking others if they'd seen Cedna, if Tom had already explained everything that happened?"

Sal turned to the audience, feigned surprise failing to mask his glee. Not a roar or howl was released from the audience as they watched Tom's lie finally take its first breath out in the open. The witness box shook. Napoleon stood and pulled the very same pistol he was cleaning when Tom was dragged into his Kremlin office. He pointed the gun at Tom and cocked back the hammer with a loud click.

"What did I say that day, Tom?"

Tom, Shirley and Anna all froze. The other souls in the room didn't seem to mind the gun; they were merely excited by the theatre of the show. Judge Talbot remained cold and indifferent, suggesting that true to form, he was going to allow it. "I'm going to allow this," he confirmed.

Shirley nudged Tom. "You should probably answer him." But Tom was tongue-tied and the excruciating silence continued unabated. To the audience's disappointment, Sal offered to read the extract Tom was too fearful to speak, but Napoleon refused.

"I want to hear it from *him*," Napoleon said with gritted teeth underneath his famed moustache.

"Couldn't agree with you more, though I fear how long it will take for a coward like Tom Robinson to face the music he chose to play."

Anna turned to Tom, and her defeated eyes told him this was it. Time to unload. "OK, Napoleon. Yes. I killed your bird friend. And I lied about her singing the chant. I'm sorry about Cedna, but not for your sake. Truth is, I was scared of you. Terrified. Every life. I may have made some bad mistakes, *but they were nothing compared to you.* You are a monster and we were never friends. And because I didn't stand up to you, more people died. That massacre in North Carolina would never have happened if it weren't for you. Kowtowing to a bully. *That* was one of my worst crimes. You deserve to be on trial every bit as much as me…"

Everyone was stunned. Their attention turned to Napoleon for his rebuttal. Napoleon still had the pistol aimed at Tom. But his rage was gone, withered. He dropped the pistol. Hurt.

Sal paced back and forth as he waited impatiently for the rage to return. He welcomed blood, retribution of any kind. But none came. Napoleon remained in shock. Sal tried to prompt him, but to no avail. Others in the prosecution suggested broadcasting the massacre to spark something further, but Napoleon cut them off.

"It was my first time being a human too. I came into control just as young Joseph joined the Bolsheviks. A perfect match, so I took it from there. I never accepted things the way they were and I may have terrorised those unwilling to accept my lack of acceptance. Everything you've said is true. It hurts deeply that my Cedna is gone, but it hurts even more that my oldest friend was never a friend at all. I'm sorry. You deserved better."

Napoleon stood and addressed Judge Talbot. "If you grant Tom mercy, then I will cease all my revolutions."

The judge waved him off with a deft wing. "You can't bribe judges."

Apparently there was at least one thing the judge *wouldn't* allow.

"Well, for Tom, I will stop anyway," Napoleon declared.

"What about your music career?" shouted one of the llamas in the audience.

Napoleon stiffened with resolve. "The music revolution will always continue!" The gallery erupted into cheers, and the judge simultaneously slid a copy of Napoleon's multi-platinum album across the bench for him to sign.

Sal was furious and the prosecution scrambled to broadcast Tom's pivotal role in the bloodthirsty Southern revolution, but the sting had already been taken out of this damning evidence, with the horror and carnage given crucial context.

Anna and Shirley were quietly relieved, while Sal's CARROTA tore fur out and growled at one another in frustration.

Napoleon left the witness box and crossed paths with Tom on his way out. As they met, both morphed into portly pigs.

"I'm sorry about Cedna," said Tom.

Napoleon swallowed his pain. "I'm sorry about forcing you into my ceaseless revolutions. We live and we learn, I guess. If you end up winning your freedom, just try not to oppress your fellow man through the means of production."

"Of course, comrade." They bumped snouts and Napoleon left the courthouse to continue his journey on the wheel of life.

Murmurs abounded from the audience. The trial of Tom, the trial of the century/afternoon, was not turning out to be the slam-dunk case that would usher in the new reign of Sal at the top of the Bureau. Sal and his CARROTA discussed fervently where and how to try and hurt Tom next. Deborah postulated they'd done enough, even if their case wasn't as open and shut as it had first appeared. "This coward is a murderer, and not the good kind. He literally participated in the massacre of hundreds of families, slave ownership notwithstanding."

Sal tried to restore calm. "It's OK, we'll still get him. We know all his witnesses. All his weaknesses. We are exceptionally prepared."

In Tom's Defence

Tom's defence was simple arithmetic. Good deeds plus bountiful examples of suffering equalled a lesson sorely learnt. Anna was to be commended on her straightforwardness. Her mockingbird voice didn't project particularly well, but it forced everyone in the courtroom to listen carefully.

Their list was heavily reduced since Tom's time in the Middle Ages. Tom's parents were stricken from it—nothing was to be counted from before his reincarnation remembering, at least for the purposes of this trial, and Shirley had already been in the witness box. All Anna had to work with was a few ant friends, fellow slaves, and ex-lovers and wives, the latter of which were still some cause for consternation.

Quartz and Tenazz were transported to the witness box first, with a large magnifying glass held by the bailiff enabling all parties to see them. It took a few moments to corral them into understanding the situation at hand. A translator box was brought in. They spoke of Tom's commitment to Queen and Colony, albeit while disparaging what they perceived as his inferior lifting ability. Anna chimed in, suggesting that this limited strength only further proved his testament.

Professions of willpower aside, the redoubtable spider in Sal's CARROTA didn't take kindly to the presence of his sometimes on-again, off-again prey. He promptly constructed a web over the witness box and time and time again belittled the purpose of ants as small fry in the larger scheme of things. Shirley called this unprofessional. Tenazz and Quartz didn't appreciate the spider's tone and challenged him to a fight. The judge allowed it.

While they rumbled, Shirley explained to the judge that Tom stuck by his friends to the end, in some instances enduring a gruesome death for his loyalty. Shirley then used this opportunity to elucidate other ways Tom had suffered: being exploded, skinned. Eaten alive. Most of these were at the hands of Sal's CARROT agents, so his suffering came as no great surprise.

Sal scoffed and the audience followed suit. Tom died many times, but had he truly known pain? Was he ever born blind? Deaf? Missing limbs? Maimed? How many winters did he endure in the wild, each comprising a daily struggle for survival? Was he ever given the lucky lottery ticket of his bones filling with cancer? This was part and parcel of when reincarnation rememberers face the wrath of karma, so why wasn't Tom receiving any "love"?

"Because you're standing in the way of natural justice," Anna rebutted.

The fury exploded from Sal. "This monster became a tree after he killed me! Do you think he deserved to be a tree after doing the thing he did? Forgive me for saying this, but karma got it wrong then, and it's moments like this that make me realise our

Auditors are not doing enough to correct the mistakes karma is clearly making. This is why we need to start with irredeemables like Tom and get to work on the rest!"

Cheers followed, but not as loudly as before. Anna was appalled by Sal's nerve and she flew around the courthouse until she was out of breath. Who had the right to challenge karma? Was this really the direction the Auditors were heading in? Because if that was the case, she was glad she'd given up the honour to help Tom.

In a room full of Auditors and judges, Sal's speech did not go down well.

The spider emerged from the fracas victorious; Tenazz and Quartz once again bodily dismembered before their time. Tom did not notice, for he was wrapped up in the revelation Anna was no longer an Auditor.

"You gave up your role for me?" said Tom.

"Not just for you..." replied Anna, her beak aiming at Shirley. It was only then that Tom noticed the clear chemistry between the two of them. "Oh, I see," he said, an unexpected inkwell of sadness spilling inside him. "You found a soulmate."

Sal also didn't seem to enjoy this revelation and tried to move past this by attacking Anna some more, suggesting it was probably for the best that an Auditor with a complacent view on troubled souls had called it quits.

Anna threatened to peck Sal's eyes out, but the judge refuted her threat, calling for peace and order.

"A member of the prosecution just dismembered two of my star witnesses!" Anna retorted.

"You know I don't like ants in the courthouse, Anna. You should have done more research on that," the honourable vulture patronised.

Anna flapped her wings in a flurry of frustration, so Shirley requested another seventeen squids.

"I'll allow it," said the judge.

Second Seventeen Squids

"You two?" said Tom.

Shirley, still in the form of Emmanuel the black cat, gazed forlornly into Anna's eyes and purred. "Yes."

"How? When?"

"Tom," Anna huffed, "there's no time. We're not doing absolutely terribly—there's still a chance we could win, but we need to discuss—"

"Hang on just a second! Hang on. Wait. This is important. You two are *very* important to me. So tell me how you met. What happened? Please."

Anna sighed. "I needed to interview some of the souls on your list. One day between audits, for the briefest minute, I was able to observe Shirley. She was in a makeshift emergency ward, trying desperately to save the life of an earthquake victim. She had blood all over her shirt, soaked thick from trying and trying and trying again. I didn't talk to her that life. But in that brief minute I did more than scribble down a note of commendable effort for trying when all hope was lost. In that brief minute I fell in love. Have been ever since."

Shirley transformed into the doctor, blood still soaked into the fibres of her scrubs. She rubbed at the deep red stains, not in disgust, but curiosity and sadness, transported back to an awful day so long ago now. Tom and Anna were left breathless by the tremendous light in Shirley's spirit. When she noticed them both staring, Shirley put her hands away and smiled sheepishly.

"I guess I see what you mean," said Tom, coughing awkwardly to change both the conversation and the uncomfortable feeling overtaking him. "Let's focus on the case. For instance, why in God's name did you include Helena?"

***

Helena, as Anna explained to the rest of the audience, was someone Tom *did* very much owe an apology to. Even if he deserved a second chance, he wasn't a saint, and this was a chance to confront a painful past and address it the proper way. This was inescapable—and admittedly personal for Anna. So when Helena Muller appeared in the witness box, surrounded by all the inquisitive animals eagerly awaiting a penny or more worth of her thoughts, a deep-set fear rose from within and gripped her skin tight, reminiscent of the many times a drunk Hubert, or in one instance Tom, had yelled and threatened her.

Tom transformed into the Austrian arts teacher once more, and Helena froze when she saw her former husband. *Of course,* thought Tom. *Of course.*

"I wrote you a letter before I died," Tom began, his hands trembling, "but you didn't believe me. I was right about the afterlife, and wrong about everything else."

Helena's face scrunched up. She was on the verge of tears. Everyone in the room was silent, ears upright, tails stiff.

Tom approached the witness box with caution. "I never treated you right. I drank and got angry. Whenever I was drowning, I pulled you in too. I had affairs with students. I abandoned you. And yet you still raised two wonderful kids. One of whom believed me enough to live many wonderful fulfilling lives more, based on the values and strength you instilled... I can't undo what I've done to you. I will never be able to. I'm truly sorry."

It was at this stage that Anna transformed for the first time, briefly, into her younger Austrian self; child of Helena and Hubert. Helena's eyes bulged when she saw her daughter. She clutched at her chest, tight and ready to explode. Luckily the courtroom didn't allow for heart attacks. "It's true, Mother. Father was an awful man. But he's tried to make amends, to help others wherever possible..."

Helena spat long-dormant venom when she finally responded. "You got to live so many lives, when all I can remember is the life of suffering you put me through. You don't deserve an afterlife. You don't deserve a second chance."

Sal, who had remained gamely silent, exploded with agreement and zealous pointing. "And, just after he wrote you that letter, he murdered me AND stopped the assassination of a future German dictator!"

The audience erupted wildly at the juiciness of it all. Tom said sorry over and over amid the chaos. But nothing could take back what he'd done, and Helena vanished with hatred in her soul.

Sal was agitated Helena hadn't stuck around for cross-examination, but the damage was done. He requested the court photographer plaster Helena's scowl above Judge Talbot to serve as a reminder of the kind of reaction one ought to have when thinking about Tom Robinson. Judge Talbot thought this highly irregular, but decided in this instance he was going to allow it.

Anna felt guilty she'd miscalculated her mother's capacity for forgiveness, but Tom consoled her. "No, you were right," he said, "it was still the right thing to do."

Henrietta was next, and after the usual explanatory spiel, Tom's long-time confidant was quick to note his various attempts to give his fellow slaves a modest education. Sal interjected and requested immediate cross-examination. Despite this realm not containing the ability for one to ingest or excrete food, Tom's bowels took another turn for the worse when he realised what was to happen next. Sal apologised for not bringing this up before, as he proudly unfurled a grotesque painting, the last stroke of paint still drying. The audience gasped. This was more than enough to jog Henrietta's complete memory. She started screaming and ended her outburst by pointing an accusing finger at Tom. The audience continued with their gasping and Sal successfully argued for *Justice*, as the Master had called it, to be placed alongside Helena's scowl.

Tom glared at Anna and Shirley. "We were doing well before the defence!" he seethed.

"We have Natalia next," offered Anna, her wings twitchy, little feathers frayed. "From my notes, Natalia will return the course."

Natalia was indifferent, her eyes dull, like she'd just woken for a gruelling shift at the depot. Tom was a good partner, reliable, yes. It was sad when he died. Very sad. But Natalia had to strengthen her bones and move on with haste.

"He was a friend of Stalin," the spider in Sal's CARROTA informed Natalia.

Natalia's expression did not change. "This soul called Tom does not deserve another chance. Disregard whatever I said about him being good in any way."

Desperate, Tom pleaded that he was, at the very least, a passionate and generous lover.

Natalia considered this, but ultimately decided to stick with her abrupt change in testimony.

"Looks like all the bad things that happened to you were your own doing." Sal smirked and the crowd followed.

Tom turned to Anna and Shirley. His gaze lingered on Shirley. There were no witnesses left. This was it. They'd shot themselves in the foot and gone out with a whimper. Sal's CARROTA were already busily shaking hands and tails with one another. As he grimly considered these proceedings, looking at each of his past killers, he saw that Rudiger was missing. For the first time, this struck him as significant.

He hushed Anna's mockingbird tune of sorrow and shouted at Judge Talbot, "I have one more witness!"

"You don't need to shout," said the vulture.

"Sorry. I would like to call to the witness box the soul known as Rudiger!"

The audience gasped and the CARROTA members flinched. Tom didn't know what it was that made them uneasy, but he knew it was the key to swinging everyone back to his side. All he had to do was figure out why very, very quickly.

Rudiger

Rudiger had killed Tom more times than Sal, Deborah and that polar bear combined. He was there during the first betrayal and he was almost the first of the CARROTA to kill Tom (it had been some other horse, but Rudiger laid the groundwork by spreading the word to other horses).

Rudiger was Sal's right-hand man, so why hadn't he been present? That was the first question Tom asked, hoping to strike gold.

Rudiger, once again a snake, slowly draped his body along the edges of the witness box, before he raised his black head and flicked his forked tongue. He considered Sal with lifeless serpent eyes and said, "A courtroom is not my place."

"So where is your place?"

"I told you, my place is being a horse."

Tom's eyes widened. He clicked his fingers. "Yes, I remember! When you weren't killing me you said you liked being a horse... But you're not a horse now. You're a snake. Which is what you were when I was a cow..."

At this stage Sal called objection, claiming Tom was rambling at the witness, but Anna chirped to let him get to wherever it was he was going. "Please, Tom. Get to the point. Quickly."

"Right, my point..." said Tom, wondering what his point was, though, really, what was the point? In his search for this elusive point, it was his inability to find one that saved him. "Yes! That's it!" he finally exclaimed, doing a self-congratulatory fist pump. "You fell out of favour with Sal because you tried to kill me once without letting me chant. *Because there was no point letting me relive this nightmare over and over.* You realised I'd never give up and Sal would never give in. We'd just go on and on about the same mistake till we made more mistakes. Deep down, you knew that at some stage I didn't deserve what was happening to me..."

Tom dared to meet the eyes of Sal before he resettled his focus on the judge, the Jacinta in him compelled to insert a dramatic pause for effect.

"Rudiger has changed. I have changed. Even Sal has changed. Sal used to be good. But his fixation on destroying me has changed that. He doesn't deserve to spend the rest of his life punishing me. His punishment has already worked. I changed because of him, whether I liked it or not. I was in the wrong and he was right—but now it's the other way around and he refuses to see that. We both deserve to live separate lives."

It was at this stage that Rudiger, monotone as he always was, helped Tom one last time. "The rambling aside, Tom is correct. I stopped because what we were doing was unnatural, and I believe Tom's karma was kept low but not as low as it should have been, because of what we were inflicting. The only benefit to our punishment was that Tom learned."

Sal shot daggers at Rudiger, before turning to Tom, a more familiar target. "What's changed, Tom? What have you really learned while you destroyed every life you crossed?"

Tom looked at Anna and Shirley, certain he'd changed, but unsure how best to express it? This certainly looked like the big speech. A chance to redeem himself from that garbled mess earlier.

"What have I learned? I guess, truth is, I *don't* want to experience everybody's story. It's just too painful. And no amount of time, no amount of lives will ever cover all the perspectives of this world. It's too damn big and too damn scary. But I've tried my best, because there's something worth living for in every life, even it's just being good friends with a cat in the Middle Ages or spreading hope on the plantation. And I will continue to search for the worth in each and every existence, if given the proper chance..."

Tom glanced at Shirley, with a "how did I do?" gesture.

She smiled. This was enough.

All eyes fell on Judge Talbot. An audience member lightly tapped their jungle drums in anticipation. The vulture extended his wings to stretch, before reaching for his gavel and slamming it down on the piece of wood it was designed to pound for reaching a decision. "Guilty!"

Sentencing

Judge Talbot emerged from his chambers after only half a seventeen squids. Before the judge reseated himself, Sal was quick to make his recommendation of punishment known, a true sign of his future capabilities as a judge and beyond in this realm. His grin was wide, his 19th century Austrian teeth relatively gleaming.

"Judge Talbot, before you hand down your punishment, I would like to offer the punishment Tom feared the most: being a factory chicken, over and over, for the rest of time."

"Does it concern him where and when the factory is located?" asked the judge, as if Tom weren't in the room, standing before him at his mercy.

"I believe the time and geography will be irrelevant, as long as the chicken factory retains the same due level of *care* for the chickens."

Shirley became her zookeeper self again and hugged Tom, who turned into the tiger Raj. Anna hovered near his ear and whispered her apologies over and over.

The judge considered Sal's recommendation for a moment. "Good. Very good. You would have made a great judge."

Sal was surprised. "*Would have?* Are you implying I won't be?"

"That discussion is for another time, as for Tom..."

"—What do you mean another time?"

The judge squawked loudly. Sal's CARROTA, their bones only moments ago made of steel were now the density of coconut water. "Let me finish with the sentencing, Sal. This is an important part of the trial, which is something you would have learned were you to become a judge."

Sal and his CARROTA threw their arms and forelegs up in protest, but the judge remained steely in his determination to continue his deliberation. "Tom Robinson, please stand."

Tom morphed back into his original, pasty self.

"You have been deemed guilty of being a selfish soul that deserves punishment and correction. Despite your trial being very entertaining for the audience of vacationing Auditors, we are rather busy and I don't particularly want to have you turning up at the Bureau again. Therefore, I sentence you to live out only one more life as your original self and you are to promise us here today that you will not recite the chant at the completion of this last life."

The disbelief in Tom's eyes extended to Shirley and Anna and the rest of the Auditors.

Sal was beyond outraged. "How is that a punishment?"

"Punishment was deemed served after the 45th death carried out by your party. Everything else was excessive."

"Excessive? Have you not heard of the Holocaust? This cowardly, pathetic reprobate was going to enable it! I stopped it! My CARROTA killed Hitler and eventually Karl Kaiser too."

"Yes, so it didn't happen. So he's not guilty of a thing that didn't happen."

"But it's... attempted enabling of genocide!"

"Which was already taken into consideration."

Sal slammed his fist on the prosecution table. "This will not stand!"

"Well, like a great musician once sang, 'Stand up we must, comrades...'" said the judge, still elated by his signed CD copy. The audience got the reference and started chanting one of Napoleon's greatest hits with rhythmic zeal. His fury uncontainable,

Sal turned to the audience, launching a tirade against the Bureau itself for its soft stance on justice and how it was he, Sal, who was the only one who could fix it. Most in the crowd, once vocal supporters of Sal and the CARROTA, remained ashamedly silent. A judge's decision was final. An open and shut case had been butchered, and with that, Sal's CARROTA dealt a powerful blow.

Sal pleaded his case for his own kind of justice to prevail, but karma, for better or worse, was not to be tweaked any further than it had already been. Another decisive factor was the paperwork. Maybe Sal's way of justice meant less paperwork, but maybe it meant more, and no one was willing to take the chance just yet. Better the devil you know.

Tom unfroze from shock when Shirley hugged him once more. "What just happened?" he shook.

"We did it! We won—sort of!" Anna chirped, flying in circles around him.

"You got your wish," said Shirley. "You get to remember again, one more time."

Tom thought of home. His old home. His parents. His old life. Another chance to win the heart of Lily White. And it all seemed so quaint, one last life in the 21st century, a relatively comfortable existence, but only just the one after so many in a row... He hugged Shirley hard and tried to embrace Anna but it was awkward as she was the size of a mockingbird and he didn't want to hurt her.

"We must celebrate!" he said, also realising that now was an opportune moment to get the answers to life's big questions, but Anna said his punishment commenced immediately, so Tom's eyes darted between both of them, trying to take in every detail like he was going blind. The last thing he decided to see was Shirley's face.

Tom

He awoke in a single bedroom apartment, in *his* bed. Outside, he heard the dim sound of traffic on 23rd street, the tapping of morning feet marching solemnly to work. He sat up in bed and took in the room. The same room he had been living in when he died the first time. How long had it been since that first time? Or had it been any time at all?

Oh. Shit. Was it all just a dream?

The search for his laptop was immediate. He flipped it open and went hunting for Hitler. No results. He breathed a sigh of relief, and flinched when the alarm on his phone began its irritating call to arms. Time to go to work, apparently.

He wandered around the apartment looking at every little piece of clutter that filled his modest abode. He'd dreamed about this place for so long. Memories so faint he'd almost given them up. He opened the fridge and recoiled at the half-eaten barbeque chicken he had still been snacking on at the time of his death. Wasteful, but it had to go. He made cereal to calm the growing voice of possibilities flying through his head. There was the job he hated but needed. Perhaps he could exploit his knowledge of the world to gain riches in this life? But it turned out all the knowledge he'd accumulated in all those past lives had only amounted to slightly better morals than before. Here he was again; everything changed and nothing changed at all.

He called his parents, both already on their way to work. For each call, the sound of their voice crushed his chest, and he required considerable self-restraint to not break down sobbing. What was the matter? They'd both asked. Nothing, he'd replied. Just wanted to hear your voice. His mum went on about Thanksgiving plans. His dad told him he'd call back after work, when he had a little more time on his hands. Both sounded like good ideas to Tom. And so there he was again, sitting in peace, at home. His home.

He was late for work.

***

The office was almost exactly the same as he remembered it, though the walls were painted purple instead of orange. Was this the only change his travels through history had wrought: a minor divergence in interior office decor?

His co-workers treated him like it was a Tuesday, because it was. He relaxed in his chair for a good ten minutes, listening to the tapping of keyboards, each finger like an ant bringing nutrients to the Queen and Colony. He laughed out loud. This was ridiculous. What was he doing wasting his time in this place? He stood and turned to Janet, seated on the other side of the divider.

"Is Lily in today?"

"Yeah, she's here. I saw her earlier."

"Wonderful."

Tom made his way gleefully across the office maze to Lily's desk, tucked around the corner. She was as beautiful as the last time he saw her, though something had changed, even if he couldn't quite put a finger on it.

Tom sat down beside Lily in a spare chair next to her desk. Lily jumped when she noticed Tom's stupid face. "Jesus Christ, you scared me."

He couldn't wait any longer. This was everything he had wanted. Another chance. He knew a simple way, a brash way, but it was the most straightforward and honest.

"After work I want to sit down with you in a diner, just the diner, nothing more, and I'll give you half of what I have in my bank account, which is admittedly not much... All you have to do is listen to my story, and let me describe to you the last 320 years of my life."

Clearly very uncomfortable, Lily rolled her chair back. "Uh, Tom, you're making me very uncomfortable..."

Tom rolled away from Lily on his chair. "Sorry, I've miscalculated a little here, but I've been through a lot—not that this is your concern—but I've got a story I think I need to tell you."

Lily's eyes darted around the room. Vicky peered over the divider and asked if everything was OK? This wasn't going so swell, but Tom persisted, determined to say the things he'd been holding onto for a very long time. "There's a diner, Bensons on forty-third street. Do you know it?"

Lily nodded, the rest of her rigid in her chair.

"I will be there after work, 6.00pm. All I want is one meeting, though it may take a few hours. If you prefer I write you a letter or an email, I'll do that, but it's not my first choice."

It was at this stage that Vicky decided enough was enough. "Tom, you're being exceptionally creepy right now."

"And I accept that." He stood. "Lily, up to you."

Those within earshot stopped their work and peered over the dividers. Tom wished Vicky all the best and said the same to Lily. As he walked away, the sound of Lily's voice stopped him. "Did you say you lived 320 years?"

***

Tom waited for four hours at the diner before the 6.00pm time he'd told Lily he'd be there. In that time he was visited by Rudiger, now a riot squad horse. The cop he was assigned said they had ten minutes. Tom only needed five. They caught up like old friends from opposing sports teams; that one had suffocated, strangled and exploded the other was treated as more matter-of-fact than carrying any sense of bad blood.

"Still serving justice, I see."

This feels much more peaceful. Less killing. More writing of tickets.

"What became of Sal?"

I bumped into one of his former CARROTA. Deborah. The band broke up after hunting all the war criminals from the alternate Second World War. Wasn't the same, apparently. Sal's taking a break as a tree again. Time for introspection.

"It will be good for him," Tom agreed. "What about Shirley and Anna?"

Rudiger snorted loudly then took a casual shit on the sidewalk. *Haven't heard anything about them. If I do, I'll pass it on.*

"Thank you, Rudiger. For everything."

Rudiger nodded. *Just don't save any more dictators. Or litter.*

"Of course."

Barely 24 hours in his old body, Tom was already the lucky owner of a whole collection of missed calls and voice messages from work, asking where he'd gone and what exactly he'd done to Lily. But these were second fiddle to *The New York Times* and all the other papers cluttering his table at the diner. He'd been seeing what he missed and what had changed. Not much, it seemed.

A voice broke the peace. "Doing a bit of light reading?"

Tom flinched. He turned to see Lily. She was in active wear, perhaps to afford her full mobility in the event she needed to run for her life.

"You're late," he smiled.

Lily sat. Pursed her lips. "What were you doing with that horse?"

"Old enemy who became a friend."

"I brought mace," she disclosed.

"You can keep it trained at my eyes, if it makes you feel any better. Want a coffee before we begin?"

"Payment first."

Tom laughed. "You know, before that bus hit me and all this nonsense began, I remembered having sweet fuck-all in my account. Luckily for you, a Bollywood actress sent money to an old account I never used..."

This is when something clicked in Lily White and her shoulders relaxed. She knew she came here for a reason. "The Bollywood actress who lost her mind on a visit to the Dalai Lama..."

"You heard about that?"

"It was international news."

"Well, there's more where that came from..."

Tom began the story. He told her about Sal, about his poor attempts at vegetarianism, what it was like to fly and then to be a slave, but most of all, he told her about Shirley. Lily corroborated events of history where necessary, intrigued by Tom's claim that he knew the great rock icon Napoleon. And then, once it was done, once his entire history had been spoken to her, all Lily said was, "Shirley."

"Huh?"

"Shirley you can't be serious?" She smiled, and then she slapped him.

Everyone else, the few left at this late hour in the diner, awoke from their midnight stasis and bobbed their heads up like inquisitive meerkats, but Lily did not take her eyes off Tom, nor did she release her smile. "Sometimes a thing needs to be said so simply, just to slap you in the face how painfully obvious it is."

Tom laughed when he finally saw what she meant, what the universe had been saying all along. But it wasn't so simple, he said. "She already has a soulmate. I was too late."

"If what you say is true, which, as crazy as it sounds, may very well be, then I'd say you'd be a fool not to tell her, at least one of these lives."

This got Tom thinking, scheming, bargaining. "Perhaps we could share her, take turns, Anna and I—would that be weird? I'd get to be with Shirley this life because it's my last..." he trailed off. A grin broke on Tom's stupid face. "Thank you, Lily."

"You're welcome, Tom."

He left Lily with a bill for five coffees and an envelope containing thirty thousand dollars. He left in a hurry, because he had a plane, a train, a car to catch in every and any direction, to find Shirley, wherever and whatever she was. Tell her at least once why all those lives were worth dying for. This was a promise, the only promise left he needed to fulfil. And because he was in such a rush, he didn't see the M101 bus, this time coming the other way.

Lying there, dying, again, all he could do was laugh. They'd made him promise not to sing the chant ever again. He didn't know what punishment awaited if he broke that promise, but he felt confident assuming the worst.

So this was it.

Probable eternity as a chicken, or forget Shirley and everything that happened, forever?

Hold on in hope that the universe saw his second chance and decide he was due another, or let go?

Tom laughed madly at the night sky, as Lily and other pedestrians tried in vain to save him. A promise was a promise, but which promise was he to keep?

About the Author

Aden Simpson grew up in Sydney, Australia. He completed a degree in Commerce but then thought:
"Nuts to that, I want to be a successful writer."
He is still working on the "successful" part.

Acknowledgements

I owe my parents every success I have ever had. They are simply the best and I knew I'd won the lottery with them. Mum, I love you. Dad, I miss you every day. My partner, Jess Perkins has backed me 107.8% of the way. My first editor Dave Myrcott is a brilliant fixer of words and sentences and the things that look like this: ";". He also writes his own beautiful prose and will show y'all one day. My second editor, Abigail Nathan from Bothersome Words, did an amazing, eye-opening copyedit and I highly recommend her services. First readers are critical, and I would especially like to thank Craig Tuck for his notes. And Lucas Storrs too. If you need help with making a website and having a beer, Drew Nixon is your man. I could not have created the book cover without the help and advice of Bea Barthelson, Daz Woolley, Paul Breen and Lee Mawdsley. And to all my friends that let me chew their ear off about talking animals and not killing Hitler, thank you for making this journey a little less lonesome.

www.ingramcontent.com/pod-product-compliance
Lightning Source LLC
Chambersburg PA
CBHW021647110726
47902CB00007B/1859